LaCour's Destiny

LaCour's Destiny

By
Robert Downs

Oak Tree Press Hanford, CA

Oak Tree Press
Publishers Since 1998

For information, address Oak Tree Press, 1820 W. Lacey Boulevard, Suite 220,
Hanford, CA 93230.

Oak Tree Press books may be purchased for educational, business, or sales
promotional purposes. Contact Publisher for quantity discounts.

First Edition, August 2015

ISBN 978-1-61009-189-3
LCCN 2015940455

For Jen,
the search ended with you

ACKNOWLEDGEMENTS

There's a never-ending cast of characters who made my third novel possible: I'd like to thank Oak Tree Press for giving Sam and me a shot; my mom, who always fills my life with encouragement and praise and never ceases to be my greatest cheerleader; my dad, who singlehandedly talks me up all over Fairmont to anyone who will listen and calls in a favor or two when he can; Jen, who helped me get in touch with my feminine side and took the proverbial hatchet to my rough draft; my extended family for flooding Amazon with orders and helping me out any way they can (I love all of you!); all the folks who read my unpolished writing; my 2013 West Virginia Writer's Workshop classmates who encouraged me to continue on with my scientific experiment; all my readers who give me faith and encouragement every day; and all the folks I've met who provided a source of inspiration. And I'd like to thank God, who always makes the impossible possible. Any errors in judgment have, and always will be, my own.

CHAPTER ONE

I dress for success, in conservative suits—gray, charcoal, black, violet, navy blue, hunter green, and maroon—either skirts or slacks, with my long hair in a chignon, out of the way of my intense blue eyes. By nature, I look younger than I really am; however, the suits add age to my youthful face, cherubic grin, and dimples. My blouse and pants were pressed, and I'd spent a half-hour on my hair, while my date probably spent significantly less time in the bathroom. Men can get away with that sort of lackadaisical attitude; women often can't.

Aaron Nevers, my date, wore a three piece, navy blue suit with a red and blue striped tie, an Oxford shirt, white, and black shoes polished to a fine shine. With his dark hair slicked back from his face, he could have passed for a B-list actor in a low budget movie. He had a single dimple on his left cheek, and his eyes twinkled every time he smiled. Even though I'm not particularly impressed by cars, he drove a 2009 Nissan 370Z, or so he told me, and he picked me up at my door, waiting with a single yellow rose in his left hand, as he grasped my right hand in his, kissing the top of my knuckles. As far as first

1

dates went, we had reached a level I had previously considered unattainable. But I had no idea where we would go from here, since we were in uncharted waters, and all I saw was blue.

The date started off pleasant enough with some mild conversation, a few questions, a few stares, and a few shots from my water glass. Aaron assumed the appropriate amount of interest, nodding at most of the appropriate places. He was different than my other dates, more attentive, less into himself, more focused on my face than my chest, a lack of challenge in his eyes, and so far he had kept his elbows off the table. He had his shoulders leaned forward enough to let me know he was interested, but not so far forward that he crowded my space. My personal space bubble extends further than most, and I gave him an extra point for sitting across from me. Right now, he was in the win column, and he didn't even know it. But I'd known dates that had started off promising: The one who tried to grab my breasts as he slid to the floor after having stumbled into the wait staff, after having downed one too many Bloody Marys, was at the top of my list of disasters. But I was supposed to focus on the positive, however hard that might turn out to be.

My challenge was to make it through the night without emptying my water glass, food flying, or obscene remarks uttered by the opposite party—the most recent of which happened to resort to obscenities. We were seated in a nice restaurant with a muted ambiance, waiters in pressed white shirts, candles, and live music coming from two guys and one guitar, the vocals a somewhat soothing melody of which I wasn't familiar. The restaurant, however, wasn't the problem: It was my date. Instead of sitting across from me, he was now seated to my right. After having made some lame excuse about needing to use the restroom, he commandeered the chair that was most likely to invade my personal space—and on two occasions, he moved his chair closer to mine, inches away from my left knee, while I inched away in the opposite direction; he stuck his arm around my shoulder, before I gently removed it and leaned in the other direction; he held a Sam Adams in his right hand when he wasn't navigating the circumference of the carpet; I didn't touch alcohol; and his smile had a hint of evilness that he attempted to disguise with play-fulness. But I remained open to the possibility that this might still turn out well even if my instincts had heightened to the occasion. With my personal space bubble shrinking, I wasn't too keen on the end result. The end result could very well lead to disaster: The worst offense involved a police officer and a previous date being dragged away in handcuffs. I took a deep breath and pictured my living room and me in it with no one else around. This seemed to help, although it wasn't quite enough. I preferred to be the one in control of the touching, not the other way around, and certainly not on a first date.

I ordered a small filet mignon, while he ordered a larger version; both came with garlic mashed potatoes and green beans mixed with almonds and cashews. The conversation drifted from jobs to amusing antidotes to previous vacation experiences, and when we reached a pregnant pause, I didn't rush to fill in the gap. My date liked to rock back and forth in his chair when emphasizing a point. I waited for him to break the force field of gravity and end up sprawled on the floor: It didn't happen.

The music men took a break—maybe even a siesta, or that might have been my own wishful thinking—and I stared at this rather amusing gentleman out of the corner of my eye, who had a rather annoying habit of smoothing out his tie every four minutes. Not that I was counting.

"Do you play?" he asked. He nodded his head in the direction of where the band had been.

"I've always enjoyed live music, but I could never hold a tune." I told myself I had an awesome voice when I sang in the shower. I resembled both Beyonce and Christina Aguilera.

"I played in a band once. We were known more for playing loud than being any good. Our best gig was our spring formal, and the only reason we even managed that was the first four bands canceled in a matter of days. The school was desperate, and we were probably even more desperate than they were."

I sipped from my water glass, nodded, and excused myself. As far as he was concerned, I planned to powder my nose. I checked my hair, slowed my breathing—the whole touching and personal space issue—and stared at myself in the mirror for a moment longer than I should have. I'd once had an anxiety attack in the middle of a restaurant, while my date had a piece of lobster between his jaws. After that horrific experience, most of which had to do with the lobster poking out of his teeth, I was determined not to let it happen again.

When I returned to my seat, I found my food waiting for me. Aaron had his hands in his lap. Before I could sit down, he stood up, waited for me to sit down, and then resumed his seat at the table.

When I picked up my fork, he picked up his and held it poised over his plate, as he waited for me to make the first move. I did, and he followed my lead. The size of our bites differed, and the amount of water I consumed to his beer differed, although not much else did.

He said, "I'm told you enjoy sports."

My sister never ceased to fill in a few extraneous details. "I've been known to follow them on occasion."

The air filled with modesty, as my date's nose filled with curiosity. He dropped his fork: It made a soft clatter. Hushed conversations ensued around us, although I tried not to pick up on the actual words. When I wasn't careful, my curiosity got the better of me. Listening was an art form; talking was a skill I still hadn't quite perfected.

"Who do you like?"

"The Steelers."

He almost choked on his piece of steak. He hacked twice, and then he swallowed three sips of beer, each one larger than the one before it. He blinked, his eyes flitting away from my face, the pupils slightly larger than normal.

"Your favorite player?"

"Troy Polamalu," I said. My voice filled with more than a hint of emotion, as I pictured the Samoan darting through tacklers, his long dark hair whipping in the wind.

"Pittsburgh doesn't have cheerleaders," he said.

His concern for trivial matters that had no reflection on the game itself surprised me. I chewed in silence, savoring each bit of steak, before washing it down with additional sips of water. Once, I probably even closed my eyes in delight. Charboiled, the best steakhouse in Hampton, VA, on Settlers Landing Road, has a reservation system reserved for those with careful planning in mind. Often two weeks' notice is required, so Aaron had already reached a level of optimism most of my other dates had not. And he exuded a certain amount of confidence that I found both intriguing and disconcerting at the same time. The whole touching thing notwithstanding.

"You aren't a Redskins' fan, are you?"

"I've always been partial to the Eagles," he said.

Unsure exactly how to respond, I chose to refrain from it altogether. I stabbed a piece of steak that had captured my attention and pretended to look amused.

He quizzed me on my football knowledge, and I accepted the challenge. Most of the questions were answered without hesitation, although he did manage to stump me on a couple of occasions. Growing up, my dad had wanted boys. Fate had laughed at his request, and he ended up with two girls, only one of whom even came close to sharing his passion for football. I'd been to one game at Three Rivers Stadium when the Steelers played the Raiders. I couldn't remember the outcome, but I did recall that it was one of the best days of my life—my dad and I cheering on our beloved Steelers, the roar of the stadium, the promise of a successful outcome hinged on every play— despite the cold weather and the promise of snow in the air. After that experience, I had never been the same, and my fate was forever entwined with Pittsburgh. Although we had more good seasons than bad, we lost a disheartening Super Bowl to the Cowboys when Neil O'Donnell showed a certain lack of judgment on more than one occasion. The loss stuck with me much longer than it should have.

"You were never a cheerleader, were you?"

I shook my head. "What gave me away?"

"Your reaction to my cheerleading comment."

"I don't have anything against the activity," I said. "But I'm not the type of person to paint my face with false enthusiasm and have men leering at me rather than watching the game." Big breasts were a foreign concept to me, and I'd had more than one date comment on my lack of enthusiasm. Besides, I wouldn't take my eyes off the field long enough to do even one cheer-worthy act.

I finished my steak several minutes after him; I decided to forego dessert; he didn't; he placed his hands on the edge of the table; I placed mine in my lap; he leaned forward in his chair; I leaned back in mine; my shoulders remained in that perfect posture position.

When dessert came, he offered me a spoon. I politely declined. While he finished up and paid the check, I excused myself once more.

He asked, "Are you sure your nose needs the additional powder?"

"Probably not. But it doesn't hurt to check."

Everything was in the same place as it was before. I checked my hair in the mirror, dabbed pale lipstick on my bottom lip, and readjusted my blouse and one errant bra strap.

Aaron helped me into my jacket, right before we met the cool night air head on. I shivered as the wind gusted around me. As I feared, he'd saved his most interesting comment for last, and it happened less than five minutes into our walk with his hand lightly brushing my own. The date had gone well enough, or so I had thought.

"Since you're an accountant," he said, "would you like for me to perform an internal audit?"

I opened my mouth, but no sound came out. I stopped in the middle of the sidewalk, as Aaron took a couple more steps before he realized the procession had ceased. I stood in the middle of oncoming traffic, my loose lips opened in protest, the wind whistling through my ears, the ticking time bomb ready to explode upon impact, and a look in Aaron's eyes that I rather wish I hadn't seen.

A minute later—and what felt more like ten—I found my voice. "You know I'm not that type of accountant, right?"

"Does that mean you're not interested?"

CHAPTER TWO

Up until his rather dramatic and a bit overzealous reveal, I had begun to wonder what our second date might entail (should I decide to forgive him for his earlier shortcomings): a moonlit walk on the beach, with a bottle of wine, a picnic basket, and a plaid blanket; a horse drawn carriage ride through Waterline Park, with a view of the stars; reading poetry by candlelight; or taking a swing dance lesson together, before we practiced on our own. My romantic fantasies crashed with more force than a fifteen foot wave against the sand, or a boat capsizing in the middle of the ocean, underneath those same stars.

Aaron had tried to redeem himself—with a smile and a stutter and a halfhearted apology and a devious wink—and failed miserably in his effort, before he pressed his lips firmly together and then shuffled around the corner with his head low.

As I waited for the cab—this particular company was programmed into my memory after more than one failed first date—my foot tapped the sidewalk, my heel striking the curb. The tapping released a bout of pent-up energy that had captured me like a wave, and nearly threatened to cause my bout of luck to lose course. My eyes darted around me, but there was no one nearby to witness my nervous energy. I glanced at my watch, before my hand flicked to my purse, retrieved my cell phone, peeked at the screen, and then placed it back in the confines from which it came.

I glanced in various storefront windows, staring at large screen TVs, digital cameras, liquor, gold rings with large diamonds and gold rings with small ones, slinky dresses, and a silver cappuccino machine that was nearly as tall as I was. Marching up and down the street, I developed a renewed sense of purpose. I passed elderly couples and young couples with intertwined fingers, women pushing strollers, and a rather large man who was glued to his BlackBerry to the point that he nearly stepped out in the middle of traffic before a horn honk jarred him back to reality. I navigated the sidewalk with relative ease, weaving my way in and out of couples, those holding hands being the most difficult to avoid in my march.

Nearly twenty minutes later, the cab pulled up in front of me, and then I ducked inside. I gave the cabbie my address, and then I inched down in the backseat, my head low enough that it was hidden by the seat in front of me. Feeling the rest of my adrenaline ease out of my body, I yanked my cell phone out of my small black purse, dialed a pre-programmed number, and waited an arbitrary amount of time for the connection on the other end of the line. I peeked out the window, my eyes searching for some sense of purpose, and was fascinated by what seemed like a random collection of buildings to my right.

"I'm going to strangle you the next time I see you," I said.

Felicia Dabler, my older sister, lived in Williamsburg, VA with her husband, two small children, and a dog named Elmer. Despite my penchant to do so, I had never actually referred to him as Fudd. Before I heard her reply, screaming filled the background, most likely by the smaller of the two kids. She was small of size, but big in spirit.

"Was it really that good?" she asked. "That's even better than I'd hoped for. You threatened to shoot me the last time, so I believe we're making progress. After the next couple of dates, you'll drop down to just wanting to slap me around."

Elmer howled, and I cringed, jerking the phone away from my ear, as the cabbie's eyes flicked to the rearview mirror. Before I realized what I was doing, I gave a slight smile in response: His expression remained impassive.

I breathed deeply once before I continued. "Do you think this is funny? I just had to sit for an hour and a half and listen to this guy pretend to be interested in every last word coming out of my mouth—"

"That's not so bad," she said.

Bad failed to encompass the scope of my problem. Catastrophic might have been a better response to the end of the date. On second thought, I'd been on dates that turned out much worse, but it was the first time a first date had ever propositioned me while we stood on the sidewalk. I considered myself lucky that no one had managed to overhear his end of the bargain. With YouTube, Facebook, and various other social media, it was only a matter of time before one of my dates made its way to the Internet, immortalized for all the world to see.

I had to take another deep breath to alleviate this particular onslaught. "When his only real intention was getting me into the nearest bed and ripping my clothes off." I analyzed the date closer than I probably should have given its proximity. The slicked back hair should have been a dead giveaway, his finely pressed suit with the small red stain near the collar should have been my second clue, and his ability to hang on every word out of my mouth should have opened door number three. Three prominent signs and I had missed them all. Either I was losing my analytical skills, or I had tossed all my skills and notions out the window. With a little more time, I might have to reevaluate this whole dating thing altogether.

Radio noise filled the background, soothing the fire burning inside of me. On the other end, Elmer's howling had given way to barking. Based on his level of aggressiveness, I'd say another dog, squirrel, rabbit, or some other small creature had captured his undivided attention. Felicia had decided to wait me out.

I placed a hand over my eyes. "This one better not be a stalker. If he is, I'm giving him your address."

"He's too put together for stalking," Felicia said. "You have a very low opinion of the opposite sex."

I also had a propensity for entertaining first dates, a form of entertaining that I hoped never repeated itself. "I have my reasons." I'd been stalked twice last year. This year had warranted a handful of first dates, but no repeat performers, and so far, no stalkers. But it was still too early to tell. The thought crossed my mind that I might eventually run out of men in Virginia. I'd never lived anywhere else, but I decided I'd consider the problem when and if I needed a viable solution.

Of the two stalkers, I considered the flasher to be the most troublesome. He followed me around for three weeks, and for two of those weeks he hid in the bushes, jumping out at random times of the day or night, wearing only a trench coat. Once he probably resorted to flashing me, but my brain attempted to block out the memory. And so far I had succeeded.

"Maybe you should lower your standards," she said.

That was my sister's solution to all of my problems, but I had high expectations for a reason. I didn't want to settle for whatever happened to drop in my lap, and I certainly didn't plan on settling for any of her prize picks. Her setup track record left much to be desired. But my dating escapades did make for rather amusing journal entries, most of which received rather prominent placement.

"You're hopeless."

"Make sure you don't lose the faith," Felicia said.

"Oh, I have plenty of faith, but no real explanation for why it lingers." Actually I did know: I was a romantic at heart. I read enough books to believe in the fairy tale, and I didn't want to settle for a version that was far removed from my fantasy. I also had a penchant for romantic comedies, most of which filled my TV screen and kept me entertained for hours at a time.

As if on cue, the baby and the dog entered round two. I pulled the phone away from my ear, waiting for the circus to enter sleepy time, or start a series of hiccups. While I waited for my sister to defuse the situation, I stared along East Pembroke Avenue, watching cars maneuver as though they were in the middle of a high speed chase, my mind and thoughts on some distant island far removed from what my current situation was, as the cabbie cruised along at just over the speed limit. The abrupt lane changes without a blinker were certainly the most compelling.

"Are you going to be all right?" she asked.

"I'm fine. The sound of the engine defuses every ugly situation, or if I ever enter a true state of depression, I'm sure my driver can find a concrete barrier—"

His eyes flicked to the rearview mirror again. This time I shrugged instead of giving him another smile.

"I know you're not serious, but could you keep the suicide jokes to a minimum? I don't want to visit you in a morgue, even if it's an imaginary one."

"I'll be fine," I said. "And I'll be home soon. As long as I don't have a stalker waiting outside my front door, with a knife in one hand and a bouquet of roses in the other, I'll have the best evening imaginable." I hadn't had a rose-bearing stalker before, but I didn't think it was all that farfetched based on previous experiences.

My cabbie hung a left on King Street, keeping a steady pace in the process.

"There's always tomorrow night."

"I don't have a date tomorrow night."

"You never know," she said. "You might want to keep your calendar open just in case. It's Saturday night."

I sighed, the sound reverberating in the small space. "And I'm booked solid."

"You're lying."

I was, but I decided to withhold the details of my social calendar. I didn't need two bad dates in a row, otherwise I might have to enter a convent and change my name to Frances. And I didn't want an unexpected visitor knocking on my door. I'd probably greet him with a metal baseball bat and my fluffy violet robe. My quick reflexes might lead to an unconscious male, and I wasn't ready to explain the circumstances surrounding the snafu to the authorities, especially since I hadn't received so much as a speeding ticket in my twelve years behind the wheel of a car. As for my favorite lounging outfit, the right clothes made a statement; the wrong ones created a series of nightmares strung together by cable ties. Based on my dating history, I didn't want to give off the wrong impression. Hair, on the other hand, needed just the right amount of attention, or it strayed in every direction at the first whiff of humidity. And I couldn't have that.

"Well, if you think you might change your mind..."

"I won't," I said. My cabbie pulled in front of my apartment complex away from any overhanging vegetation, most of which led to birds, which led to unappreciated deposits on the hood of my vehicle; I handed over the fee plus tip, slammed the door, and rushed for the stairs, before I was cornered by the little weasel below that never seemed to take no for an answer, and always managed to pop his head out of his door when I was most vulnerable, although still rather unlikely to comply with his asinine requests. As far as he knew, I had my hair done more in the past two months than most women had it done in two years. Short men weren't a problem for me; short, overzealous, unattractive men were.

"It's important to stick to your guns."

I slammed my door. "It's the only thing I have going for me," I said. "And even that isn't a guarantee anymore." I did have moments where I questioned myself, along with my path in life. I, however, never questioned my motivation, which sometimes centered on an unhealthy dose of optimism, or where it came from. It remained as firmly in place as the silver ring on my right hand.

"There are no guarantees, sis. Flexibility might lead to new opportunities."

"I've learned a lot of things," I said. "I went to college, remember? And no matter how far I could bend over, I never managed to impress the right man." I still didn't have the man, but I did still have the flexibility. I plopped down on the sofa, the soft cushions rising up to meet me.

"You don't have to throw it back in my face." She meant college. While my sister had sought a college degree, her husband had sought her even harder, and she chose his happiness, kids, and a house with a two-car garage over her own, supporting him before, during, and after dentistry school, until his practice supported all of them.

"So what are your plans for the rest of the evening?" she asked.

I flipped on the TV for background noise, turning down the volume as I did so. "Why do you care?"

"I'm just making pleasant conversation," Felicia said.

I eyed my television set, but it didn't talk back to me. "You can keep it to yourself."

"By next week, you'll love me all over again."

"I love you now," I said. "I'm just not very happy with you." *Or my date for that matter, but I didn't have to worry about seeing him again.*

I'd avoided the weasel, closed my blinds, and with my cell phone in one hand, I started shucking clothes with the other, spraying my slacks, socks, and blouse all over my bed. The ritual helped put my mind at ease, as a sense of calmness came over me.

"That's understandable," she said.

I told her goodbye, and then I pushed the red end button. I pulled on my fluffy violet robe, grabbed a bag of baby carrots from the refrigerator, and then shoved *Notting Hill* into my DVD player. At least in the movies they always managed to get it right.

CHAPTER THREE

Night slipped into day, and I slipped back into my regular routine. I'd been called to work on a Saturday. Not the first Saturday where I gave up my personal life for my work one. Not working certainly had its advantages over working, but a tendency to daydream coupled with my cyclical schedule often meant that I'd spent more than a few Saturdays at my desk as opposed to in the theatre or with my nose pressed to a rather suspenseful novel, or glued to the latest blockbuster to hit the small screen. Most Saturday mornings I woke up to yin yoga. This Saturday was no different: I just had to deal with the abbreviated version. I rolled out my blue mat in front of the television, stretched, conducted a handful of warm-up poses, and then ended with the dragon, seal, and saddle pose. I condensed what was usually an hour long workout into a half-hour.

Even though I could have dressed down, I chose a violet suit and a cream colored blouse with my hair in a chignon. I added a touch of makeup and a hint of pale lipstick before I closed my front door, and then started my electric blue Corolla with a sun roof and six-disc CD changer, of which five of the six slots were currently occupied with

Sarah McLachlan albums. Various artists captured my attention at different moments in my life: Katy Perry, Kelly Clarkson, Carrie Underwood, Saving Jane, and of course, Sarah McLachlan. I had other artists I listened to, but these were my top five and captured the majority of my moods.

The yoga helped. I focused on my current project, which I had been working on for the past week. I'd formulated the majority of the details, and I only had a few pieces of the puzzle left to go before I handed in my report and moved on to the next major venture. I hadn't planned to work this morning, but I couldn't say no to my boss either. Cooper Strut, a man who could have passed for an aging rock star, called me as I had a cup of green tea in one hand, and the latest issue of *Cosmopolitan* in the other. He told me he needed a small favor, which usually involved me working when I wasn't supposed to. This time was no different. He needed results immediately, and I probably needed to have my head examined for succumbing to his request. Other than a few secretaries, I was in a male-dominated office, and I needed to keep up appearances for appearance's sake, which meant I had to work twice as hard as my male counterparts who spent just as much time gossiping as some of their female contemporaries, in order to further my career.

After our phone conversation, I downed the rest of my cup, and then filled a silver mug with a black lid for traveling purposes. On my way out the door, I stuffed a handful of Jolly Ranchers in my pocket. If I ran out, I always kept spares in my trunk for emergency purposes, restocking at Costco when I began to run low. I'd been forced to raid my stash on more than one occasion, but my multipurpose bag was still more than half full. I had swapped it out about three months ago, since my Jolly Rancher habit never seemed to waver even as our economic situation changed.

I took the stairs to the third floor, unlocked my office in the middle of the hall (just past the bisection point of the floor), and the only one with a glass door (probably some prank of which I had been made unaware). Without glancing in either direction, I closed the door and flipped on my overhead light. Minimal lighting covered the floor with only one or two offices currently occupied. My office, one of the smaller on the floor, had two filing cabinets (for previous projects stored in numerical order), a single guest chair, maroon, shag carpet (about which I had sent more than one memo), and no personal effects of any kind.

As to my current project, I had gone over our books twice already, and Cooper still wasn't satisfied. He didn't see where the drop in income could have come from based on our steadily increasing sales. Each time I had gone through our books with a rather large magnifying glass I'd noticed a number of write-offs that we'd taken that would have decreased net income now, but would have prepared us for steadily increasing income in the future. Since we weren't a public company, didn't have any shareholders to answer to, and Porter Reede, CEO of Wired Consulting, ensured all employees were well-compensated, and that we each had a personal stake in the company, I didn't see why I needed to make a third pass over the books with an even more microscopic view on our profits and losses. But I rolled my black ergonomic chair behind my rather large desk, popped a grape Jolly Rancher in my mouth, set my tea just out of reach, booted up my computer, and resumed my meticulous search through the company's massive mound of electronic paperwork (most of which was contained in spreadsheets, Access, and Microsoft Project). Over the next couple of hours, I reviewed invoices, monthly statements (of which I'd produced many of the reports myself), internal company documents, memos from Cooper and Porter, as well as outgoing and incoming electronic transfers. As before, I didn't find a single irregularity. I chewed through a few Jolly Ranchers, and I drank most of my tea, stopped for the occasional bathroom break, walked over a limited part of the third floor to stretch my legs, observe my surroundings, and clear my head, and otherwise avoided as many people as I could (based on a minimum number of overhead lights that wasn't hard to do).

Wired Consulting started out as an IT consulting firm, specializing in ways to help corporations expand to the Internet, use social media effectively and efficiently, streamline email and inboxes, and create online databases for storage and backup retrieval purposes. But as our clients grew in size and our number of referrals took an exponential climb, we expanded into management consulting, specializing in all aspects of business management, effectiveness, and efficiency. Our client base extends in either direction from Virginia and covers nearly 60 percent of the Eastern Seaboard with our revenues and profits increasing at a fairly constant rate.

Unlike our company, I wasn't in the best of financial positions. I'd gotten in debt in the past, running up a massive credit card debt (free credit, mixed with free souvenirs, mixed with the consumption of one too many alcoholic beverages, along with an itchy shopping finger had led to one too many extraneous purchases) that I was slowly paying off, several years after the initial spending spree that had taken place in and just after college. And I still had some outstanding student loans, most of which were being pared down on a fairly regular basis. Even though I managed a partial tuition scholarship, I'd chosen a private institution for reasons I still couldn't quite fathom, although it had sounded like a good idea at the time. Those two debts coupled with my spending habits meant that I pretty much lived paycheck to paycheck (my financial cushion was only one or two tissues deep). I hadn't graced the unemployment line, but I didn't put it past myself either. I lived on the edge, and I showed no signs of backing off. Clinging to the edge of the cliff by my fingernails was my idea of financial responsibility.

After supplying the various inputs to our accounting program, I checked my figures, and ended up with the same result. I sipped the rest of my tea, and then I popped a watermelon Jolly Rancher in my mouth, savoring the taste, as I stared at my computer screen, and the myriad of numbers that winked back at me. I stood up, stretched, did a full circle of my office, and then sat back down and organized the massive pile of papers on my desk that had piled up over the past week. Without the phone ringing, my boss coming through my door at the most inopportune of moments, or the latest round of gossip making it to my part of the hallway (most of which I tried to avoid), I had more than enough time to focus on the odds and ends that I happened to be rather good at neglecting.

My office withheld a view of the ocean (looking out at a sea of green and concrete and graffiti instead), although I heard it was rather nice this time of year, but a bit on the cold side. I didn't even consider going near the water unless the outside temperature was seventy-eight degrees or higher, and right now we were well below that weather-wise, and we showed no signs of improvement.

I rediscovered the water cooler at the other end of the hallway, deciding I should fill my body with something else besides green tea and Jolly Ranchers, and I rediscovered a coworker in the process.

"Have you seen Dana?" she asked.

We'd already exchanged names on a previous occasion. Mine was Samantha LaCour. But I answered to Sam.

I stepped to the side to let her go first. "Does she usually work Saturdays?"

"She's been gone for almost a week."

I filled my mug with water: I'd already rinsed it out twice in the bathroom. "I didn't realize she was missing," I said. "I'm usually the last one to know." I also made a habit out of not prying into other people's lives. I couldn't always say the same of my coworkers. One of their favorite games (and this involved both male and female) was to find out who I happened to be dating at the moment. More often than not the air was filled with disappointment.

Norma said, "You should come out and visit more often."

"Have you seen the pile of paperwork on my desk?" I shifted my weight to my left foot. "Besides, what are you doing here?"

"It's quiet on the weekend," she said.

"I'm sure it's quiet at six in the morning," I said, "but there's no way I'm getting up that early to come to work."

Norma Beemer nodded her head, and then she hung a right at the water cooler, heading back to her office, where the gossip mill remained in full force. I'd known gay men that were less of a gossip than she was. On the other hand, I probably didn't know enough people to make a valid assessment. Over the years, though, I had managed to increase my reach, and I made more of an effort when the situation warranted it.

Returning to my office with my previous project out of the way, I delved into a report Cooper had asked me to produce, and thus the reason for his call at eight o'clock this morning. He wanted a history of every payment we received from Grate Marketing, one of our largest accounts and our first client, and a firm that always managed to find itself in the middle of some sort of scandal. The latest happened to be CEO Victor Uglow caught with two call girls, one of whom serviced him at the time of the snapshot. He had been on his deck, next to his pool shaped like a horseshoe, sunbathing in the buff, which he did rather frequently, and the picture was shot with a telephoto lens by an amateur photographer who remained nameless, although he did receive $5,000 for the photo, selling it to *Peepers Magazine*. Not knowing if the firm would survive yet another scandal, I had been called in to assess the situation from a financial standpoint to include the number and frequency of the payments we received from Grate Marketing.

Like my previous task, the one before me seemed rather daunting, especially since I was expected to cover a three-year timeframe, and it would require reviewing various memos between our two companies, electronic transfers, and invoices. My boss wasn't a patient man. He'd found out about the task last night (based on the publication of the photo that day), and he wanted the report in his hand as soon as possible (meaning Monday afternoon). It didn't bode well for my personal life, but I would manage to get myself out of another rather awkward date. Based on my recent track record, my dating history wasn't exactly moving in an upward trend. I had managed to avoid talking to my sister today, and I didn't plan to wait by the phone, since some of her threats never reached the execution level.

Grate Marketing had managed to compile a number of idiosyncrasies over its sixteen years of existence, and it was known more for being in the headlines than remaining out of them. If this was what a company had to do to market its brand, I wasn't interested, but there were any number of people who were. The Hampton Roads area, a popular tourist destination in Virginia, was not exactly known on the international circuit, yet Grate Marketing had a reputation on this coast as well as the west. A strategy focused solely on the latest headlines worked for Britney Spears, Paris Hilton, and Kim Kardashian, and apparently it worked for corporations as well, as long as the CEO had enough antacid tablets to deal with the subsequent backlash. Since many of the scandals involved Victor himself, I assumed he had more than enough tablets for the job. I, on the other hand, had neither the stomach nor the capacity for so much disorder.

When I perused the records of Grate Marketing, I found a bit of useful information, although it was completely unrelated to my current project: Several payments were made to Dana Wilson, a marketing department secretary, without any ties whatsoever to Grate Marketing based on what I'd been able to dig up in the accounting records. Being of the curious sort, and as far as I was concerned, not entirely unjustified, I decided to do some further digging on Dana. Maybe her disappearance was more than just pure coincidence.

CHAPTER FOUR

The movie theatre, an AMC 24, was reasonably quiet, or at least my particular movie was. One of only twenty-two people in the theatre, I had my choice of seats. I chose a seat about midway off to the right hand side, out of the way of the majority of patrons, with most individuals having chosen the middle or the left side. Neither Aaron nor the weasel happened to make an appearance, but it was a rather close call for about ten seconds, until the picture became a bit clearer. The movie, one of those rom-coms with beautiful actresses and perfect pectorals, made me briefly regret my Junior Mint splurge. The film didn't leave a lasting impression, and neither did the patrons, but it did give me time to process what happened to Dana. The outlook was neither promising nor encouraging, but I needed additional inputs for my paper trail, and I had run out of data.

A mid-range department store chain, however, provided the lock picking kit—the opportunity I needed to gather additional inputs re-mained behind closed doors—and I splurged on the purchase thanks to American Express. I also had Visa and Mastercard, one of which happened to be maxed out. Barnes & Noble surged with activity, while Coliseum Mall did not. I tried on three bras at Victoria's Secret, none of which allowed me to look like the cover models at the front of the store, so I remained unimpressed. I did a few extra laps around the circumference of the mall to help the Junior Mints out of my system.

I'd reached my current course of action—the breaking and entering solution—after a brief run-in with Frankie Kensington, during which she told me to get lost in no uncertain terms, and a pile of what might be useful papers caught my attention as I removed myself from the rather offensive situation. I'd also hit a research hitch in that I had started to gather a few details about Dana Wilson, but I needed additional data to complete the economic picture.

I'd sipped more than my share of water, stalked around my office space, paced in a circle before I turned it into a square, pondered hacking into the computer, while leaving behind a digital footprint, and briefly considered removing myself from the situation altogether, and just letting the course of events take over. But I needed balance in my world. As for Frankie, her attitude proved rather unusual in her lack of concern for her secretary; I completed Cooper's latest task with plenty of daylight left to spare; and I needed an outlet for my overactive brain.

The thought of a surveillance monitor capturing my face caused a mild panic attack: my heart rate increased, my right hand shook for about two minutes, a headache occurred, and mild abdominal cramps entered my world. But I pushed through the pain and the nausea—thus the trip to the mall—and decided to usurp my fear with what I hoped was knowledge and equality.

As I left the mall, many of the panic attack symptoms resumed with renewed force, but I cranked up the radio, sang along to the music, and lost myself in the utility of driving. With each flip of the turn signal, my power grew, until confidence and strength and mild shaking took over.

~ ~ ~

I waited until the parking lot was deserted before I reentered the building. I glanced around, feeling as though I was in the middle of a bad horror movie and about to end up with an ax in my neck. Blue and green tile covered the floor in a somewhat haphazard manner, with slightly more green than blue tiles, while the lights above had been set to dim. There were two elevators, but I chose the stairs, making my way to the fourth floor.

Other than my feet slapping the stairs, echoing louder than the beating of my heart, silence filled the air, and I tasted the faintest hint of chocolate and mint in the back of my mouth.

As for Dana's office, I'd chosen this particular time, because my fellow coworkers, including Norma Beemer had gone home, and the cleaning crew wouldn't come through until tomorrow morning. Dana's door was at the end of the hallway. She was the pass through for Frankie Kensington: I'd heard she wasn't a particularly stringent gatekeeper. But she did keep out the occasional tormented soul, who may or may not have flirted with her at one time or another, while she may or may not have responded in kind. She was an attractive woman with high cheekbones, a penchant for skirts, and a loud laugh. The laugh I noticed more frequently than her cheekbones or skirts.

Cameras were placed on the various floors, although not inside the offices, and I decided I could explain away my rather unusual behavior if the question ever came up. Our equipment was state of the art, and we had a lot of information; however, the average layman couldn't decipher our intentions without a head for business. Although not intentionally, I'd made more than one date's eyes roll back in his head when I mentioned profits, losses, annual reports, and monthly statements. I didn't end up with a second date.

I stood outside Dana's door for a moment, unsure if I really should go through with what I was about to do. I had the distinct feeling, although it may not have been warranted, that once I started there was no turning back. I'd never broken the law before, other than two speeding violations, and for which I had been let off with two warnings. Once I started a project, I saw it through all the way to the end, sometimes to Cooper's dismay. My life as I had known it was about to change: I was about to cross an invisible line, and once I stepped on the other side, I couldn't immediately jump back across the threshold, remove all traces of the line, and pretend that everything was as it was before. I took a deep breath and let it out even more slowly.

My hand shook slightly as I removed a pack from around my waist, placed it on the ground, and selected my tools of the trade. I chose two picks from more than a dozen, placed them in the lock, and twisted. Nothing happened. I repeated the process thirteen more times with the same picks, ending up with the same exact result. I selected two more, and then I repeated the process. I turned the picks in various directions, wiped sweat off my brow, set them down, and selected two more. I willed my hands to stop shaking. Had I been a whistler, this would have been an opportune moment to carry a tune.

The overhead lights flickered above me, and my heart had increased to a rather rapid rate. Sweat had begun to form on my hands, the condensation covering my palms. I smoothed out my skirt, clearing my hands in the process. I paced the floor, shook my hands in the air to remove the cramp in my left hand—my index finger throbbing harder than the rest of my fingers—grabbed water from the cooler down the hall, and then returned to the scene of the crime. As the picks failed, I set them to the side. I had six to the right in the used pile, and more than six left inside the leather carrying case that folded up about as well as a wallet if only a good bit larger. I selected two more picks, focused even more intently on the task at hand, said a silent prayer in my head, and then twisted the two tools. I heard a click, as the lock tumbled free, and as air escaped from my lungs, I murmured a thank you to no one in particular. I hadn't realized until that moment that I had been holding my breath in silent anticipation of my next attempt. I also realized that if I was going to improve my breaking and entering skills, I would need sufficient practice, most of which could be conducted with my iPod and the proper melody. I packed up my picks, putting them back in their leather pouch, and stepped through the open door. I'd been in this office several times before, but never at night and never alone.

The air felt heavier inside the door than it did on the other side.

I flipped the switch bathing the room in fluorescent light. The light clicked overhead as it warmed up. Dana's office was slightly larger than mine with three leather chairs, an oak desk, two large filing cabinets, three pictures, two plaques, and a dog themed calendar on the wall nearest the door. The thought of rifling through someone's desk while said person was not around did cross my mind. Before I talked myself out of the task, I shoved the thought aside. I needed to discover why she was not around. Nothing more. If she had been on leave, Norma Beemer would have known in an instant, and she wouldn't have posed the question as curiously as she had. Norma, a meddler of the highest order, made it a point to know every piece of office gossip, followed the schedules of every individual more closely than they themselves did, and would not have made such a grave error on Dana's whereabouts for the past week. Her mind trapped various pieces of information almost as well as my own, only her meddling had reached a much higher level. With her head tilted at just the right angle, she offered both an authoritative and inquisitive side, neither of which suited her complexion.

I searched Dana's desk methodically, starting with the disorganization that had become her desktop. Since she was a reasonably neat individual, I could only assume Frankie Kensington, who wasn't nearly as neat herself, had started depositing various papers on Dana's desk, and the migration overrun had been exhibited in full force.

Papers were placed at various angles on various portions of the desk with both rhyme and reason curiously thrown out the window with more white than wood currently staring back at me. None of the angles were perpendicular to each other, and a few papers had even migrated as far as the floor, two of which had been flipped over in the process.

I started on the left hand corner near her computer—the cleanest side—and I worked my way to the right, setting aside various papers as I went into the bottom right hand corner where I had cleared space for any unusual finds. When I was finished, I had a small stack of papers comprised of memos and electronic transfers. Next, I searched each desk drawer, finding notepads in one drawer; pens, pencils, highlighters, staples, paperclips, Scotch tape, and scissors in another. It wasn't until the last two drawers that I hit the jackpot. The two drawers contained Dana's personal files. Both drawers were locked, and it wasn't until I fumbled around underneath her desk that I found the key. I grabbed the pile of papers and made copies at the copy machine down the hall, before I returned the stack and messed up her desk once again, putting the papers back as close as possible to their original locations. I flipped off the light and bolted the door on my way out.

Upon my return to civilization, I saw no unusual activity, no unusual individuals with rather large knives or swords, and no former employees that had managed to hold a grudge. A full moon was overhead, blazing in full force, and my stomach had started making rumblings of its own. It was time to move on.

CHAPTER FIVE

I perused Dana's file over a bowl of steel cut oatmeal (breakfast of champions) from Panera Bread with my cup of tea just out of reach. It had been a restless night filled with memos and bank accounts and desk paper disorder and a mouse that had somehow managed to infiltrate the entire nightmare with a nervous twitch and a pair of beady eyes. The eyes proved to be the most troubling aspect, little black dots that caused my eyes to pop open in the middle of the night, and I probably would have uttered a scream if I had any air left in my lungs. Instead, I flopped back on top of my bed and punched my pillow for good measure.

Aside from the evil mouse, what I found disturbed me: Dana had memos between herself and Victor Uglow CEO of Grate Marketing discussing her fee for services rendered. In the documentation I possessed, I couldn't find out what those services were, but they had taken place on at least two occasions, according to the papers I had in my custody. Both dalliances occurred in public places: local restaurants with a fondness for discreteness, the meals involving wine and dessert. In the past six months, she had received four payments of varying amounts with the highest being fifteen thousand and the lowest at seven thousand dollars. Whatever services she had provided covered a timeframe around the first payment, and these services could have continued until her disappearance, or still may have been ongoing, despite her change in scenery. The scene less promising than I might have first suspected, but I followed the money trail, since it never lied, and it never asked for child support.

In his last memo, Victor mentioned that she might want to take some time off, but he didn't say why or for what purpose. The payments had been made directly from Grate Marketing's accounts, not the personal accounts of its rather shallow CEO (who preferred his trysts at low rate motels, if I believed the previous scandal). The memos had started right around the time Dana began seeking employment elsewhere, according to pages from her personal calendar that I had found among her pile of papers, most of which lacked even basic organization. But I didn't see any job offers among her stack. Either I may not have looked hard enough, or she may have kept those particular papers elsewhere, since seeking out other employment was considered a felony at Wired Consulting and at least one person had suffered the threat of termination from placing his talents on the open market (Facebook wasn't always your best friend). He had asked for forgiveness and was forgiven, but the damage had already been done, and he was fired less than a year later under slightly suspect circumstances. The year prior he had been the company's top performer in discovering new business, and he was well on his way to repeat the feat before his termination had been complete.

Garrett Everest had filed an unlawful termination suit, which was thrown out of court by a judge who happened to be very good friends with Porter Reede. Garrett relocated to Richmond before he found employment. If grudges were demons, his might have been accompanied by two or three. His temper angled nicely with his syrupy demeanor (he once tossed an office chair at a plate glass window), and he and Dana had an office liaison that was caught by a hidden security camera (before it was discreetly erased two days later). And he still traveled to Hampton twice a month on business, stopping at Wired Consulting before being forcibly removed from the building. As a person of interest, he was certainly on my list.

What I couldn't explain was Dana's undocumented leave of absence. I needed more paperwork to include Grate Marketing files from Victor's desk. And I needed it now to complete the picture, my own amateur lock picking skills notwithstanding. The lock picking tune-up wasn't necessarily a necessity, but I did consider it rather mandatory.

Kelly Clarkson's sophomore album *Breakaway* pulsated in my head. I had my iPod tucked into my pocket, ear buds jammed in my ears, and I sang along to the first song on the album entitled "Breakaway" as I methodically practiced on my bathroom door. Each time the lock clicked back into place I started over, and each time I appeared faster than before. But I hadn't made as much progress as I would have liked, the tools proved just a bit too tricky for my inept fingers. I had started with Sarah McLachlan, and I moved on to Kelly Clarkson. I'd lost track of how long I'd been attacking my bathroom door, but I'd gotten to the point where I'd made enough progress, so I moved on to picking the lock blindfolded, deciphering the tools based on touch alone, feeling the differences among them, the idiosyncrasies that determined how slowly or how quickly I could pick a lock, and sensing the tumblers shift beneath my slightly more capable fingers. I removed the blindfold after the fourth song, after I'd managed a reasonable amount of success. Success was measured in increments, and I stared at a chasm as wide as the Grand Canyon.

I graduated to the front door where the deadbolt proved even trickier. The song "Gone" played on my iPod, as I struggled with the deadbolt, which required more finesse than the bathroom door. I made it all the way through *Breakaway*, before I started in on *My December*, but it wasn't until the second song on that album "One Minute" that I had a major breakthrough. The lock clicked with authority, and I nodded my head in triumph. My ear buds, however, remained silent throughout the whole endeavor. As I practiced my petty theft attempts, I polished off two cups of green tea and a glass of water. I also filled my head with more than enough lyrics to add to my off-key performances and various solo acts in the shower. Both my drain and mirror might just proceed with a standing ovation the next time I broke out in song. Despite my success on the front door, I kept at it, knowing my fingers needed to be nimble, and that I might not have plenty of time to be merry in my progress. The thought of male breath on my neck caused me to shiver involuntarily. When I reached the song "Haunted," I packed up my tools and declared the practice a success. But I kept my curtsying and bowing to myself.

Although I wasn't sure I could execute in the same manner of my systematic practicing, I was determined to give it my best effort.

I had been wearing black jeans, dark running shoes, and a black hooded sweatshirt over a gray t-shirt. I had my hair pulled back in a ponytail, and I had a touch of makeup with the slightest hint of eye shadow. I kept the outfit and the makeup, closed my front door, and raced down the steps toward my car. It started on the second try, instead of the first, and I turned up an eighties rock station, as I backed out of the communal parking lot, where my eyes had thankfully not witnessed any communal activities, heading towards my fate at Grate Marketing.

Traffic proved lighter than usual for a Sunday afternoon, as I took I-64 East through the Hampton Roads Bridge-Tunnel to Norfolk before I picked up I-264 taking the Independence Boulevard exit toward the Pembroke area. I merged right on Independence, and then I turned right on Columbus finding parking in a public garage. I wrapped my tool belt around my waist, covered it with my sweatshirt, and yanked my hood over my head before I walked five blocks, the wind whipping at my face, and the slight chill in the air turning my cheeks cool to the touch.

The walk eased the stiffness in my knees; the sidewalk proved white, wide, and even; and California Pizza Kitchen had a line out the door.

The front door proved more intrusive than I expected, but I hummed a melody as I set to work. The sidewalk behind me was empty, the noises that surrounded me had more to do with engines than people, and the lock took more than three minutes. The clock in my head ticked in a rather furious manner, as all my efforts felt for naught. I closed the glass door behind me, locking it, as I surveyed the empty lobby. A two-guard station was set before me with both chairs empty, security cameras panned overhead at various intervals, less than a few seconds apart in coverage, and blue paint covered the walls. The painted tile represented ocean waves: I hoped for a calm sea, but I was prepared for rough waters.

Two elevator doors beckoned me, both directly behind the guard station; dark leather sofas were off to the right, a matching set, between the station and the glass doors. The rest of the lobby was empty, including the walls, and there was no stairway access to either the right or the left. It too was located near the elevator doors. Soft lights embedded in the ceiling, resembling the stars in the sky, guided my way.

Since my hooded figure was already on display for the cameras, although I had done as much as I could to conceal it, I chose the elevator on the right, and punched the button for the eighth floor, one below the top level. I stepped off the elevator to a series of glass doors: I chose the ones straight ahead. This lock proved easier to pick than the front door, as it only took ninety seconds. I closed the door softly behind me, walked around the twin receptionist desk, and came face-to-face with solid wood doors that were probably at least one hundred years old and had been refinished recently with nickel-plated handles. This lock proved the most extensive of all: I had to pick two locks, each one taking more than two minutes. I shook out my hands, opened the door, and noticed the large bay window in front of me with smaller windows on either side of the largest one.

Solid wooden objects, most of which were carved out of oak or pine and depicted voluptuous nude women, filled the office and a bulletproof glass case filled with firsts: debut albums from bands I'd never heard of, first edition novels in mint condition, and first edition collectible Hot Wheels miniatures. The carpet proved thick enough to bury the soles of my shoes, and it would have taken me more than twenty paces to get from one side of the room to the other.

I glanced at the ceiling, and noticed more of the recessed overhead lighting, as well as three security cameras, all of which were blinking red. If I thought I could get away with it, I might have even managed a smile.

Although I wasn't sure what the blinking meant, I did know I hadn't won the lottery or a million dollars or the Publishers Clearing House Sweepstakes. I jogged behind the desk, crouching behind a monstrosity that could have easily hidden three of me and still had more than a foot leftover. My heart tickled my rib cage; my mind leapt from one thought to the next; and the air around me turned heavy. My heart beat faster than if I had just finished my third mile.

I lifted my head from behind the desk, noticing three security monitors off to my right, as my eyes peeked above desk level. The three monitors concentrated on the front door to the outside world, the lobby area, and the receptionist zone right outside the twin oak trees. The one that depicted a view of the front glass doors showed two men in white uniforms, possibly building security, with solemn expressions on their faces. Neither of the mouths moved as the two gentlemen stepped inside. I dropped my head below the desk and started counting, wondering how long it would take them to find me. I hadn't worked on a cover story: My teeth were too straight and my complexion too clear for me to claim vagrant status. When I reached sixty, not my favorite number, I peered over the desk again and stared at the monitors for several seconds: All of them were blank. I breathed out, completely unaware that I had been holding my breath. I stood up, stretched my legs, and made it as far as halfway between the massive desk and the large wooden doors before I heard a pair of voices in the reception area.

I hurried behind the desk, occupying the space where the chair had been, stuffing myself tighter than a tuna fish sandwich.

One of the doors banged open.

"You see, you've got nothing to worry about," a male voice said. "I told you it was a false alarm."

"The boss isn't going to like it," the other said.

"It's not the first time there's been a glitch in the system."

I didn't move a muscle as the two men circled the room, coming as close as two feet away from my hiding spot, my breathing so constricted I thought I might pop a blood vessel, before two sets of footsteps retreated, and the door slammed shut. I swallowed the Jolly Rancher that had been sitting near the back of my throat, coughing repeatedly until my passageway cleared.

I waited a full minute after the door closed before I eased the chair back and resumed a standing position. I left the wooden nude statues and bulletproof glass alone; instead, I meticulously searched through the files on Victor's desk. His desk proved more organized than Dana's. I discovered several files, along with a number of papers of potential interest that I copied at the machine in the receptionist's area, before I placed them back on his desk in their proper order.

Taking the elevator to the bottom, I passed the security desk, checked that the door locked when I closed it, and stepped outside once more, never realizing that I had set off the alarm for the second time.

CHAPTER SIX

The drive home proved somewhat more eventful. Several seagulls hovered near The Hampton Roads Bridge-Tunnel, as I stayed in the right lane as often and for as long as possible. The radio station I tuned to belted out classic rock. A black Mercedes cut me off on the Hampton side, and a silver Lexus gunned his engine. The man in my rearview mirror had gray hair on the top of his head and a gray mustache above his lips. His hands moved in an exasperated gesture. I withheld my impulse to wave; instead, I glanced down, turned the radio station up a notch, and hummed a few bars of "Stairway to Heaven" under my breath.

Traffic on Mercury Boulevard proved considerably heavy, and the Coliseum Mall parking lot was more than three-quarters full, an unusual occurrence. I pulled into the Starbucks located within walking distance of my apartment and grabbed a green tea to go. To tide me over, I popped an apple Jolly Rancher in my mouth. I savored the taste while it lasted and grabbed my cup from the barista with a slight nod of my head. Cup in hand I meandered my way through the tables, the talking and animated conversations, the man in the corner who tried to look interested but not interested at the same time, past the small line that had formed at the front door, with more than a few teenagers evening out the numbers, and out into the slightly chilly weather where the wind had turned the coldness up a notch.

Back at my apartment and with no further incidents with the wea-sel—maybe he was on holiday—I spread my papers out on my living room floor, since this was where the majority of my space congre-gated. My green tea sat on my table within easy enough reach. I di-vided the pile up: memos to the top right, internal company docu-ments to the top left, balance sheets and income statements to the bottom right, and electronic transfers to the bottom left. I spent the better part of two hours reading through each document, highlight-ing important pieces of knowledge with a blue highlighter as I went. According to the memos, Dana had provided marketing services to Grate Marketing on four different occasions, and each time her fee increased slightly, her rate more than tripling at the rate of inflation. No less of an authority than Victor Uglow himself had signed off on the services, and the documents gave no indication anyone else had even seen them. The electronic transfers matched what I already had. When I reviewed the balance sheets and income statements I noticed an increase to the shareholder's equity line that wasn't consistent with the company's recent profits: It proved smaller than I expected. That meant money had gone elsewhere, and I needed to find out where it went.

The internal documents told me Victor had decreased his position in the firm recently, and this proved inconsistent with the steady profit sharing he had taken over the years. In fact, the spike hap-pened around the time he and Dana had begun their partnership. What I needed to know was if Dana had a marketing degree and where Victor's money had gone, since I didn't have access to his per-sonal accounts, and I knew just who to call.

We exchanged pleasantries, his voice at an octave consistent with my own. I heard fast and furious typing in the background, his hands beating at the keys like a scorned lover.

"Could you slow down for just a minute?" I asked. "This is important."

He typed for perhaps another minute, and then the typing stopped.

"How can I help you?" He delivered the line with more than a hint of sarcasm. Similar to what I remembered from McDonald's cashiers, or maybe that was my own jaded view.

"I need to find out if Dana Wilson has a marketing degree."

"Who's that?"

"A colleague of mine," I said. I'd already planned to give away as few details as possible. He wasn't just an expert in gossip: He was an expert in Internet gossip.

"You can't just ask her?"

"She's missing." I decided not to add that I had broken into her office, grabbed a handful of documents, and that my image had been plastered on camera. The questions would probably start tomorrow, if not sooner.

"And you're trying to find her?"

"Exactly." I picked a document off the top of the pile, reviewing it as we spoke.

"And how does the marketing degree come into play?" he asked.

"I'd rather not go into all the details." I already needed to prepare for the inquisition. Possibly my own funeral. Maybe I could ask Don to send carnations.

"Why are you involved?"

"My curiosity has gotten the best of me." It had been known to happen on occasion: I followed the threads when they presented themselves. The best ones led to multiple explanations and didn't involve my slightly overbearing boss, who may, or may not, have taken a weeklong anger management in the past. Even though it was over a year ago, he was still stuck in the denial stage.

"You're not doing something illegal, are you?"

"Possibly," I said.

The pause lingered for more than a minute. Typing resumed in the background at warp speed. I shuffled a few papers on the floor, rearranging the piles in chronological order.

"So who's the man in your life?" he asked.

While we never discussed his relationships, since I had no desire to hear about his four-way chats with supposed female underwear models, he had no problem bringing up mine. "What makes you think there's a man?"

"Sweetie, there's always a man with you. The problem is you can't get him to stick around for long. Maybe you should hit him right between the eyes with one of your roundhouse kicks, or you could just throw a lasso around his neck."

The lasso incident had only happened once, and it was by sheer accident. Nothing more. In fact, I hadn't even been drunk at the time. It had been a party challenge, although in hindsight beer pong would have taken longer but might have actually caused me fewer headaches. There was a date involved with lasso guy, and it didn't go well.

"I'd rather not have him incapacitated," I said.

"It's always an option. When you get desperate, you might want to consider it. Or maybe you prefer not to discover true love, so you discover all the wrong men in the world. It's your own form of a dating handicap."

Don Stader, while an expert in World of Warcraft, wasn't necessarily an expert in love. Due to the horror stories I'd told him, he wouldn't go on a blind date, even if he thought there was a chance Claudia Schiffer would sit down on the other side of the table and stare at him with longing affection. And if by some stroke of genius he was face-to-face with her, his tongue would swim around in circles, instead of forming actual words.

"So what am I supposed to do with your requested information?" he asked.

"Why don't you fax it to me?"

"You don't have a fax machine," Don said. And then he hung up before I could offer a word of protest.

I reviewed the papers again, just in case I had missed a vital piece of information the first time, working in a methodical manner. Definitely not counterclockwise. The second review turned up nothing else of substance.

I grabbed a yogurt out of the fridge along with a banana and fresh raspberries. I stabbed a piece of banana, shoved it in my mouth, and then my phone rang.

"You missed a great opportunity," Felicia said.

I stared at the half-eaten yogurt in front of me and decided I was in the middle of a blissful situation. "What are you talking about?" Her threat of a date popped into my mind. "I didn't think you were serious."

"You should have answered my call."

"I was a little preoccupied." I decided to leave out the breaking and entering part, since she sang louder than Elmer and the baby when she was under pressure. When we were kids, she once pointed her finger so fast in my direction that I thought it might fall off.

"What were you doing?"

"Checking into a missing person at the office," I said.

"Since when did you become a detective?"

"I'm expanding my role within the firm." But my pay would remain the same. I decided to work on living within a budget, and I was nearly there. My prior obligations, though, made the living a little tighter than I would have liked. If impulse buying had been a college business course, I might have avoided a mountain of debt before graduation.

"Don't let your curiosity get the best of you."

"It's kind of hard not to," I said. "Better women than me have tried and failed."

Elmer howled in the background. The baby cried, and then the dog whined louder. My sister emanated soothing tones, and then bliss resumed in the background. I polished off the remainder of my yogurt and fruit.

"You shouldn't get in over your head. You can't afford to bail yourself out of jail."

I didn't know how I would pull off being in two places at once. I had never been a magician's assistant let alone a magician. "I won't," I said. "It's sort of tied to a project I'm working on. Maybe I'll even give my boss a slight discount."

"Don't get yourself shot."

"I don't think you have to worry about that." I didn't own a gun, and none of my friends did either. I'd heard one too many hunting accident stories, as well as a few random shooting fiascos. Before I'd even met Colt or Smith & Wesson, I decided we wouldn't get along.

"I'll always worry about you," Felicia said.

I said goodbye before the situation proved even worse for me.

~ ~ ~

Two hours later, I showed up five minutes before the designated time, a punctual habit that my best friend Cadence Surrender didn't possess. I chose the largest rocking chair on the patio. My feet just barely touched the ground. I chose not to rock for fear of falling out of the chair. A slight breeze tickled my face. The jacket wrapped around my shoulders kept me warm.

Cadence and I had been best friends for nearly as long as I could remember. We'd had a falling out more than five years ago (not because of her lack of punctuality), but we circumvented the damage with three phone calls and the relationship survived.

Cracker Barrel and its country store atmosphere intrigued me—some of the candy wasn't available anywhere else—while Cadence enjoyed the southern style comfort food. She arrived ten minutes after I did, and in less than two minutes we were seated. Prompt service at a conveniently low price. That would have made a good t-shirt.

She stared at me across the table, her grin nearly as wide as her face. "When's the last time you and I did this?"

"Two months and eight days," I said. I picked up the menu, even though I had already chosen my order ahead of time.

Cadence shook her head, closed her menu, and dropped it on the table. "You have a memory like a steel trap."

"I do when it comes to numbers." I'd been known to memorize a string of numbers twenty-five digits long without putting forth much of an effort.

"You always had more intelligence than you knew what to do

with," she said.

"You say that like it's a bad thing." I happened to be somewhat fond of my intelligence.

She waved her hand in a somewhat dramatic fashion. Our waiter thinking he had been summoned dodged two other waiters carrying trays, took our drink and dinner orders in militaristic fashion, and nodded his head politely before he darted away. He couldn't have been older than nineteen. "But your taste in men lacks a certain amount of pizzazz."

"You've set me up with some interesting ones," I said.

The hostess had placed us at a wooden table where Cadence and I were the center of attention. She enjoyed it more than I did. Around us most of the tables were accounted for, with only five tables currently empty. The "Jump All But One" Game was off to my left: I hadn't touched it other than to move it. I practiced on my own and conducted myself rather admirably, but never when Cadence was on the other side of the table. She commanded a bit more attention than I would have liked, and I received several more stares than I was used to in the process.

"It wasn't on purpose, I assure you."

"You sure do come up with a lot of assurances," I said. "And how many of them are you willing to place bets on?"

"Not too many, I hope." When it came to the ponies, Cadence had a bit of a gambling problem. Sports, however, she managed to avoid altogether.

I had trouble with her distinction. "You've quit?"

"For the time being."

"You don't think it will stick?" I asked.

She had a problem making anything stick, including relationships. "Has it ever stuck before?"

"You don't trust yourself?"

"I know I have my limitations."

I knew I had some as well, but I didn't always know what they were. "I could help you."

"You're always willing to help everybody," she said.

Our meal came and went; the check came and went; I paid, waving my hand at a meager protest from Cadence; we said goodbye (the hug lingering for an extra second); and both of us promised to meet again sooner the next time. But our good intentions didn't always match up with reality.

CHAPTER SEVEN

I'd already downed one cup of green tea, and I had my second one in front of me. A pocket full of Jolly Ranchers provided a sugar boost when I needed it. The stack of paperwork hadn't moved since Saturday, and I had a few new emails positioned at the top of my inbox, most of them from my boss who managed to come in a good hour earlier than I did, and liked to start each day by delegating at least seven tasks. I decided to avoid reading his emails until I finished more than half of my second cup of tea. Each email proved even more urgent than the last (based on the subject line) with the one at the very top of my inbox accentuated with a red exclamation point. I turned my gaze away from my monitor to the stack of organized papers on my desk, the piles in the same position I had arranged them, each pile exactly the same height.

I managed to dream about a crime induced life the night before. The dream ended with me in jail, a five-year sentence hanging over my head, and my lawyer laughing hysterically at me from the other side of the glass partition. I'd been told I might only serve three years, assuming I could stay out of trouble. Since trouble managed to get me behind bars in the first place, I wasn't quite sure how I could reduce my sentence. But I nodded to the cop with a gold stud in her right ear, the top of her ear clipped at an unusual angle from her left, her fingers already showing the first signs of arthritis, her arms slightly larger than the rest of her body. She was several inches taller than me and quite a bit heavier than I was, and she shoved me with such force that I tripped once I reached the middle of my cell, slammed my knee against the bottom bunk, and pitched myself face forward into my cellmate's chest. Before I could offer a heartfelt apology, I woke up with a start.

The buzz of the intercom removed me from my reverie. Cooper Strut summoned me to his office in an ostentatious manner, as his voice rose with each passing word. I would have cringed, if I thought it would've done me any good.

His office was directly above my own (I could hear his thought process with each stomp of his foot and each circular turn), his well-used office furniture had a red tint, his walls held only two plaques and one picture (a beach landscape scene), and his navy blue three-piece suit had creases sharp enough to pierce skin. His eyes were filled with intensity, and his hair was slicked back with unusual force.

Cooper motioned for me to remain standing. "You mind telling me what you were doing at the office on Saturday evening?"

"I was working on your project," I said.

He kept a neutral expression. "You missed out on the middle part of the day."

"I decided to take a break." I left out the part about needing an empty building. I decided to keep Barnes & Noble and the romantic comedy a secret as well.

"What did you do?"

"I'm not billing you for the extra hours," I said.

He nodded. "That's good because I didn't approve any overtime. But that's not my only concern." He waited; I waited even longer. "You were also in Dana's office. But you didn't try to hide that part either."

"I executed a strategic part of my plan."

He asked, "How did you get in?"

I shifted my feet on his plush carpeting. "The door was unlocked."

He drummed his hands on his desk, and then he leaned back in his chair. The creases in his forehead narrowed slightly. "Why?"

"Maybe the cleaning crew left it unlocked."

"The cleaning crew doesn't come until Sunday morning."

I bit my lower lip. "Oh."

"Is that all you have to say for yourself?"

"I needed a few more documents," I said, "most of which happened to be located in Dana's office. I sort of planned it out ahead of time. I didn't want to leave my accounting work to chance, and I wanted to give you the best product possible."

"And this is all related to your project on Grate Marketing?"

I nodded. I decided not to add that the link was thin at best and probably nonexistent at worst. I was rather glad I looked the part; otherwise, I might have had this conversation at the Hampton Police Department before I ended up in a cell with a woman twice my size who liked to snort Cheerios through her nose.

"You mind telling me what else is going on?" Cooper asked.

"I'd really rather not."

"Do you plan on putting in more unusual hours?"

"I might work a few late nights," I said.

His fingers drummed on his desk, and then he sucked in his right cheek. The narrowness between his eyes remained narrow. Through the pause I could hear the quiet pulsating in the room, which might have been my heart, or it might have been Cooper's nostrils.

He rubbed his forehead. "Do you enjoy giving me a headache?"

I shook my head.

He dismissed me with a wave of his hand.

I returned to my office, melted into my chair, and wiped my forehead with my left hand. I spent the rest of the morning typing up my report on Grate Marketing. I triple checked my spelling and grammar (Cooper must have been a grammarian in his former life), highlighted my findings on a separate coversheet, and then walked the report to Cooper's office. He was on the phone—I waited for him to finish—before I handed him the report and was once again dismissed from his office.

I didn't have another project pending, so I made a phone call instead. Don answered on the second ring, but I only had half of his attention. I exchanged pleasantries with him while he typed, his fingers moving in rapid fashion. More than once I heard a small grunt that coincided with a keystroke. When the typing had reached a dull roar, I jumped into attack mode. "So what did you find out?"

"Dana Wilson doesn't have a marketing degree. She's twenty-four credits shy of a degree in communications. She dropped out of college three weeks into her senior year."

"And she never bothered to finish it?" I asked. "Why?"

"It might have something to do with an abortion she had less than a month later."

"Who's the father?"

He paused. "I'd have to dig deeper to find that information."

"Could you?" I asked.

"Possibly." He paused. "What are you going to do for me in return?"

"Remain your one and only true friend. I'm better equipped to handle the job than most of your online counterparts."

"That doesn't pay my rent," Don said.

"True," I said. "But it does buy you true happiness."

"I never believed in the fairytale. You, on the other hand, have more than a few needs that probably need to be met."

I thanked him profusely and hung up before he changed his mind.

With detectives still on my brain, I punched in the number for the Hampton Police Department. Officer Ben Xander answered the phone; I told him my name and the reason for my inquiry. "Are you actively investigating her disappearance?" I asked.

"No one has filed a missing persons report."

"Oh. Maybe her family just hasn't gotten around to it yet."

"How long has she been missing?" he asked.

"A week."

It was his turn to pause before he filled the silence. "How do you know Dana?"

"I'm her colleague," I said. "I only learned about her disappearance on Saturday from a fellow coworker. Because her disappearance
was tied to a project I worked on, I did a little digging of my own. I've
discovered an interesting link between Grate Marketing and her."

"You don't remember me, do you?"

"Should I?"

"High school. You were class of oh-three, right?"

"Maybe." I hoped he didn't have my vital statistics staring back at
him on his PC. Damn DMV.

"Maybe I was class of oh-two. You were one of the quiet ones, sat
in the back of the room, might have been Algebra II, and thought no
one paid any attention to you. You had a personal space barrier that
must have been a mile wide."

"How do you know all that?"

"I'm a cop, remember? It's my job to notice people."

"But you weren't a cop in high school."

"True. But I was in training. Always knew I wanted to be one. I
just had to put in the time until I could get my diploma." He paused.
"Maybe we should meet. You could fill me in on all of your weird-
ness. You do get a lunch break, don't you?"

I told him I did. He told me to meet him at The Coconut Café in
half an hour. Before I could stage a protest, he was already gone.

~ ~ ~

Ben was smaller than I expected, only a few inches taller than I
was. He stood up when I approached. Narrow waist, thick shoulders,
curly brown hair, large calves, large hands, and a slightly crooked
front tooth. His hand enveloped my own—after trying unsuccessfully
for a hug—his handshake firm, his grin forced. I motioned for him to
sit down. And then I wrung out my hand underneath the table, before shifting in my seat.

"Have you ever been here before?" he asked.

He didn't bring up my no-touching policy. "Once," I said.

"But you didn't come back?" I told him about my bad date that had gotten worse, the bowl of soup that had ended up in my date's lap, and how I had nearly flattened my competition in the middle of a crowd, a woman with bug eyes, a tight-lipped smile, too much makeup, and only half of a dye job.

"You mean he went home with someone else?"

I nodded. "An ex-girlfriend that just happened to be sitting three tables over. Her voice was taller than she was."

"Was that before or after you tossed the soup in his lap?"

"That was near the end of our date when the ex-girlfriend let her presence be known. He didn't do a very good job of hiding his intentions." I didn't feel it was necessary to add the part about the three-some.

He cracked a wider grin. "Maybe you need to work on your taste in men."

I nodded. And then I shifted my weight to the other cheek. The wooden chair was nearly implanted in my lower back, and my head had started a dull throb, probably from a lack of oxygen to the brain, based on the flashback to the date that had gone awry.

He stared at me with more than a hint of amusement, as he waited for me to breathe again, or possibly blink. I couldn't remember doing either, but then I did have good reflexes. At least that's what my self-defense instructor had told me, right after I kicked him in the balls by accident, after which he had emitted a small yelp and fallen to his knees, surrounded by a series of female hands, most of which appeared to want to do more than console him.

I emitted a small squeak; Ben raised his eyebrows. Then, he leaned back in his chair, crossed his arms over his chest, and waited for me to blink. I did.

When our waiter came, I ordered a soup that featured squash, carrots, and coconut; Ben ordered the chicken noodle with just a hint of coconut.

With regard to Dana, I gave him a rough outline, and as he asked questions, I filled in the details, and ended with a summation of my observations.

"What exactly do you think you're doing?" he asked.

I shrugged, took a sip of water, and stared at a crack in the table. Probably from a fist that had slammed down too hard, a verbal exchange that had gotten more than slightly out of hand. Over time, the crack had spread. Now it was several inches long, a giant crevice that had appeared at the center of my world, and I had no idea how to proceed. I was out of my area of expertise. My left hand shook under the table, another reflexive gesture, and I willed it to stop.

"I don't like it when my life is out of order. Dana's disappearance has left me with a clouded view of the world. What if something's happened to her?"

He held up a hand. "I think you're getting ahead of yourself."

"I'm not," I said. "I've asked around. She's just gone, and I have the paperwork to back it up. I can show you—"

"Which you obtained through illegal means."

"I'm not looking to build a case. I just want to know what happened to my colleague."

"So you can get your life back in balance?" Ben asked.

"How did—?"

"This is what I do for a living. Besides, you were always more than a little out of sorts. You always sat in the back of the room, tried to keep a desk on either side of you empty, and nearly fainted more than once when the teacher called on you, even though you knew the answer and were completely engaged the whole time."

"Are you a stalker?"

"No, I just pay attention," he said. "And you've always been a bit of an oddball."

I stared at the crack again. It might have been laughing at me, I wasn't sure. But at least my hand had stopped shaking. I opened my mouth to speak but nothing came out.

"But you're good with details."

I looked at my hands. "And you don't have an active interest in the investigation?"

"What investigation?" he said. "No one's even reported her missing. For all we know, she could be on vacation."

"But she's not."

"Because you've snooped around and you pay attention. Admit it, you didn't even know who I was when you called."

"Well, I—"

He shook his head. "You're a terrible liar."

"What should I do?"

"Drop it," he said. "But we both know you won't." I nodded. "You need to at least be careful. Just because you have a clearer picture now than you did before doesn't mean you have all the details yet." He paused. "What do you do?"

"I'm an accountant."

Ben nodded his head. He didn't look surprised at all. Maybe a little curious. Nothing else.

Our food came. He talked as he ate; I focused more on eating than talking. I listened to his thoughts on Dana's disappearance, and then he flashed back to his high school days. He was popular and a jock and no good at math. He told me he'd help me, off the record, since this wasn't a formal investigation, and I believed him. I said, "What should I do?"

"Continue to keep your eyes and ears open. And don't do anything stupid. And if you don't stop wringing your hands under the table, I'm going to handcuff you to your chair."

I looked up, eyes wide.

He looked at me and laughed. "Some things never change, Blondie. Especially not you."

CHAPTER EIGHT

Doing what I do best, I dug into Dana's financial background. What I found disturbed me as much as her connection, however slim it may have been, to Grate Marketing. To put it simply, her outputs exceeded her inputs. For the past year, she spent money faster than she made it. She'd depleted her savings account, not that there had been much to begin with; her 401k wouldn't have lasted her a year under normal circumstances, and these weren't normal times; she had four credit cards, two of which were maxed out; and she had no real assets to speak of. She leased a black BMW, rented the same apartment for the past two years, spoke French proficiently (she had lived in the country when she was eight, but hadn't been back since); and she had a 50-inch LCD TV which caused her second credit card to reach its limit. If it hadn't been for the cash infusion, she probably would have maxed out her other two cards, one of which was a store card with a twenty-two percent rate. Jerry Duncan, her boyfriend up until a month ago, lived in a similar fashion, only he had a little more money to play with when times proved tough. His savings account balance was a little higher, and none of his three cards were maxed out, although he'd significantly increased his intake recently and couldn't sustain the trend for long. Maybe he had high hopes for a cash infusion.

While I didn't have a corporate reputation to uphold or tweak, or a particular lifestyle to maintain, I couldn't treat life as though it were a seedy romance, and all I needed to do was find enough sexual exploits to cater to a boy band. But I did need to keep myself out of trouble more often than I found it. Often, this was a wish filled with more than just a little hope, without much substance to back up the whole process. My life found the abnormal all too familiar, with a heavy emphasis focused on what might have been. My mind, however, needed nothing short of a miracle to find its true bearing.

What I didn't yet know was the extent of Victor Uglow's chicanery, if any was to be found, and Dana Wilson's exploits, aside from her financial endeavors and unusual ties to Grate Marketing. If there was a stronger link, I hadn't found it yet, so I decided to keep digging. The not so genuine often outlived the genuine. But I did know Victor looked out for his company's best interests, he had a soft spot for women, and an even larger one for loose women. Dana fell on one side, and she might have fallen on the other as well. Reality had collided with the dream world, and the collision had aroused more than just my curiosity. Dana had marks on her hands, but I didn't know how deep the marks went. Numbers, while extremely useful, could only tell me so much. I'd need to dig even deeper and faster to find the truth, and I had to do it on my own time, otherwise I'd arouse the suspicions of my current boss, who had a penchant for emails and results and not much else. Her past intrigued me, but it didn't offer me everything I needed.

Where I stood on the third floor, overlooking a blooming flower garden, mostly white with patches of pink and blue and purple, that should have shown the first signs of decay, since I had never seen them attended to or watered with any sense of regularity, I listened to the sounds of space, the slightest echoes that reverberated throughout the interior, the clicking of heels and a hint of formal chatter that filled the air, watched a small crowd thread through the maze of the cavernous monstrosity I worked at throughout the week, the people moving like tractor beams with only one destination in mind, smelled cleaner, mainly lemon, and compounding money, and hoped my small stature and choice of outfits would go unnoticed. Invisible had a certain ring of familiarity to it. I'd managed the same throughout high school, or at least I thought I had, until I ended up with Ben Xander sitting across from me with more than just confidence reeking through his pores.

The faintest whiff of vanilla drifted from the floors below, and I was caught off guard by the attractive and pleasant scent. Either perfume, or a flower, I wasn't sure which. I breathed in and out twice, gathered a bit more courage knowing that I would need it, and then sought out Frankie Kensington, vice president of marketing, otherwise known as Dana's boss. I didn't have a specific plan in mind, or even an appointment, but I did have questions, and I hoped for the best. If I had believed in luck, I might have crossed my fingers.

Despite Frankie's stature within Wired Consulting, her office was sparsely furnished, her view was on the verge of being nonexistent, and her sofa was made of fake leather. A few plaques covered the right wall, as well as the back one, consisting of her shaking hands with some semi-famous people, many of whom I was only vaguely familiar with. I did see undergrad, as well as graduate diplomas, but there was no doctorate, so I wasn't as impressed as I could have been. Had she bothered to smile, or even look up at me, I might have given her more leeway. But she hid behind her desk with her arms folded in her lap, the glare of the monitor reflected in her glasses, closing herself off to the world around her. Her hair was short with flecks of gray that she didn't bother to cover up; her makeup was minimal; and her lipstick was a moderate shade of pink.

I stood, after I had knocked tentatively, shifting on the balls of my feet, since I hadn't been offered a seat on the sofa, and since the fake leather might disrupt the lines of my hunter green suit. Her eyes had flicked to my own, before returning to the screen. She shifted papers around, and then played the hunt and peck method with her keyboard, and what sounded like no more than two fingers typing away.

When I noticed there was no gatekeeper outside, I had taken a chance that she might see me, even without the appointment.

Her secretary had called in sick today, or so she'd told me, and based on the information I received from Norma, had been previously indisposed for the past week. Of what, where, or why, I still didn't know. But I planned to find out. My mind, through no real effort of my own, drifted back to the flower garden, with the white lilies, many of which were in full bloom, while others were mere buds, just waiting for the opportunity to burst to life. Much like the life I hoped to lead. My reality, however, lacked a certain amount of comfort and interest; my hands remained loosely at my sides, as my eyes flicked around the room. Not really focusing anywhere in particular. It was more a nervous habit than my own curiosity.

When her attention turned toward me, motioning me inside with one hand, while she continued to type with the other, I shifted my focus to Frankie.

She spread her hands. "Are you here for the secretarial position?"

I shook my head, and then I started to open my mouth.

She held up her hand. "I have an interview in less than fifteen minutes. You'd better make this fast."

I adjusted my suit jacket. "Maybe we should talk about Dana."

"What's there to talk about?" she asked. "I have a hole that needs to be filled, while Dana is off doing whatever it is that she's doing." She'd stopped typing, so she waved both hands in the air. "I can't wait for her to return." She paused. "Who are you exactly?"

"A concerned colleague," I said. "I work on the third floor."

"And what do you do?"

"I'm a forensic accountant."

"And what are you here for exactly?" she asked.

"To find Dana."

"She's not lost. She's just gone, and I have no idea when she'll be back." She started to dismiss me with her hand.

"Wait," I said. "What can you tell me about her?"

"Are you doing some sort of school project?"

I shook my head.

Frankie asked, "I'm not going to get rid of you that easily, am I?"

Since no response appeared to be necessary, I didn't offer one.

"She's a good employee," she said. "A bit tardy at times, but nothing that can't be fixed with a bit more discipline. She has a strong sense of opinion, a warped sense of reality, and she placed her faith on thankless dreams."

"What made her good?" I said.

"She was well-organized, dedicated, and had a strong sense of herself. While I could push around some of my previous secretaries, I couldn't mold her the way I wanted to. She had her own motivations and intentions."

Her emphasis of the word previous intrigued me. She'd gone through four secretaries in four years: I'd checked. "So you and her had a few disagreements?"

Frankie nodded. "On an almost daily basis. She was a rather adept sparring opponent, and I'm sorry to see her go."

The interesting choice of phrase didn't escape me. "But I'm not sure she left voluntarily. Do you even know where she is?"

She shoved her chair back, stood up, and then glared at me. "Of course, she did. I'm sure she got a better job offer, and she couldn't wait to get out from underneath my grasp. Now, I'm stuck without a suitable replacement, her desk is piled high with papers, and human resources tells me it'll be another two weeks before we can hire a permanent replacement. What am I supposed to do in the meantime?"

"But she's only been gone a week," I said. The focus on her intrigued me even more. And she hadn't even bothered to ask the purpose of my inquiry. I made a notation on my notepad.

"I'm shorthanded as it is," she said. "Do you have any idea of the workload in marketing? Our biggest account needs our undivided attention, and I'm forced to answer the phone." Without even knowing the ins and outs of her department, I knew she meant Grate Marketing.

"You don't know where she is?"

"If I did, that would certainly make my job easier. All I'd need to do was call her back to work and hope she didn't take off again. She's been calling in daily before I arrive at work, and she doesn't answer her cell phone when I call her back."

"You mean she's done this before?"

Frankie nodded, and then she rested her hands behind her head.

I asked, "Did you approve her leave?"

"That would have been convenient, wouldn't it? But, sadly, no, I wasn't privy to that sort of information. As for her leave, it didn't come across my desk."

I made another note. "You and she must have had an interesting relationship."

"That's a bit of an understatement."

My suit was understated; I, however, was not. In the interest of avoiding a verbal backlash, I decided not to point out that the world didn't revolve around her or me. Cruelty, complications, and contradictions filled the world I knew, and I hadn't yet found the key to unlock the truth. "But what about her?" I asked.

"You're concerned, I understand. But she'll turn up sooner or later. I'm sure she's just fine." She held up her hand and made a forward motion. "Now, if you'll excuse me, my interview is here. If you'd like to speak with me again, you can make an appointment like everyone else."

As I left Ms. Kensington's office, I couldn't help but feel my world was more than a little bit off. Frankie didn't seem as concerned as she should have; already filling Dana's void, if even only temporary, and as Dana's boss, she should have approved her leave, or at least had more insight into her whereabouts. She had admitted to disagreeing with Dana on multiple occasions, the clash of strong wills appeared to be a battle of epic proportions, if I had been reading her tone of voice right. She was efficient in our conversation and her dismissal of me, her eyes boring into my own on more than one occasion, studying me and extracting what she needed. Both her movements and comments appeared calculated, giving away nothing more than what was required. At least nothing that I couldn't have found out through the gossip and rumor mill, her appointment even showing up a minute early, which didn't seem like a coincidence to me.

Frankie wasn't as dumb as I would have hoped, not that I would have expected less from a corporate vice president. And I hadn't learned enough information to make myself dangerous. But I would soon enough, or I'd keep digging, even if it meant using my hands. Before I returned to my office, I paid another visit to the terrace overlooking the flower garden: It reminded me of hope as much as my own life did. This time, I didn't smell even the faintest hint of vanilla.

~ ~ ~

When I returned to my office, I discovered a Post-it note on my desk. Cooper wanted an in-depth look at the financials of the marketing department. No mention of the previous reports that I had given him, nor any thoughts on how I might improve my future reports. But I didn't have any red ink stains bleeding across my desk either. He also wanted to present the Grate Marketing analysis to his fellow executives; therefore, he needed a longer summary, and he needed it by tomorrow afternoon. The note was choppy, the handwriting even choppier, as urgency practically exuded from the little pink tablet. Even though I needed to work, my thoughts drifted to a woman I barely knew, who had left for some undetermined reason, and who probably wouldn't come back anytime soon, or if she did, I'd end up being one of the last ones to hear about it, especially since her boss and I weren't exactly on the friendliest of terms.

Until I determined why Dana left, and the urgency she might have felt as she walked out the door the last time, I decided I'd have a hard time determining where she might have gone. She could have stayed home, left the city, or even left the state. Victor had national name recognition, but I still wasn't sure she had left because of him. It could have been the matter of a simple illness, or it could have been something much more serious: a problem that a doctor's note simply wouldn't fix.

Her expensive taste might have been courtesy of Jerry Duncan, although her massive output had continued even after her relationship with Jerry ended. She paid the minimum on her two maxed out credit cards, and based on her spending and related income, it didn't appear that figure would increase anytime soon. In fact, the decline appeared steeper, as though the edge of the cliff was close at hand, and at any moment, her fingernails might give way.

I was relatively new to the concept of juggling two careers, especially since I had nothing more than my own curiosity to sustain me through the second one. The two blended together about as well as pistachios and marshmallows. Even if I kept the two separate, I'd worry about one career spilling over into the next, and the boundaries that popped up between the two. I'd already had to introduce them, and it would take more than a simple handshake to put the two on speaking terms. A financial trigger might set me free, or it might blow up in my face.

I had researched Dana, but I hadn't looked into her family. That would come later, assuming I managed to keep the job.

CHAPTER NINE

The first blow lashed out at me inches away from my face. My right hand moved instinctively to block it; I followed it up with a left hand jab. I struck out with my right foot inches away from my attacker's knee; he backed off accordingly a slight grin encompassing his face. He performed an elaborate combination of blows, all of which struck my stomach, and all of which offered less damage than they could have. I backed up until I was nearly at the wall, as the cushioned padding nudged the underside of my bare feet. My hands balled into fists; the world around me blurred; and through the mirror I observed spectators as well as my opposition. Stepping into his next blow, I hit him with a solid uppercut, loosening my fist as I had been taught to do. He struck the mat, and then he hopped to his feet grinning as wide as a mile. I bowed low, and he followed suit.

"Have you been practicing?" Dave Griffin asked. He was a self-defense instructor with white teeth and dark skin, and I'd heard he ironed his t-shirts.

"Only in my mind," I said.

The rest of the class clapped its approval, forming a circle around us, before another individual entered the inner sanctum.

After the sparring where pads were worn and contact proved to be minimal, Dave led the class in breathing exercises, a series of kicks and punches that would fell even the largest trees, and some final stretches to keep our muscles loose and cramp free. I wiped sweat from my brow with a towel, guzzled water from a Nalgene bottle I had brought for the occasion, and nearly stumbled into Ben Xander.

"Have I seen you here before?" he asked.

"I come most Mondays and Wednesdays. How about you?"

He sucked in air and water with equal vehemence. "I like a good challenge, and this proves a better workout than a stationary bag that weighs less than you do."

"So you don't come religiously?"

"I choose my workouts carefully."

The rest of the class funneled out around us. Dave slapped me on the shoulder on his way out the door, offering a few words of encouragement. His smile just happened to be one of his best features, and he appeared to use it without a second thought. One woman in a pink leotard was left in the studio, stretching near one of the mirrors, and massaging her right thigh in between leg bends. I chose my outfits a bit more carefully than she did.

When pink leotard woman left, Ben asked me about the case. I told him I had spoken with Dana's boss, Frankie Kensington.

"What did you find out?" he asked.

"Most likely, she's lying, or she's hiding information. What I don't yet know is why, or whom she's protecting. But I plan to keep at it until I find out."

I polished off the rest of my water, and then I popped a watermelon Jolly Rancher in my mouth. When I offered Ben one, he declined.

"Do you have dinner plans?"

I told him I didn't. He mentioned an Italian restaurant that wasn't Olive Garden, so I was intrigued. Since this wasn't a date, just business and more catching up, I showered, applied a minimal amount of mascara and makeup, tried on three different outfits I didn't like before I found one that I did, drove my car, and met him at Luigi's, where he was just inside the doorway and more than two minutes early. I half-smiled and shook his hand, this time I didn't even flinch.

He peered at me as if I smelled funny—I'd have to remember to visit the powder room at the earliest opportunity—or maybe in my haste to rush out the door my outfit didn't match, or I'd forgotten my purse or cell phone or I had a pen stuck in my hair. The half-smile disappeared immediately, and I rocked back on my heels.

"Are you always this self-conscious?" he asked.

"It's a family trait," I said. "I hear it's inherited."

"You fidgeted in class, too." He paused. "Bet you didn't think I noticed."

I assumed he referred to high school, which made it even worse. "I didn't think you'd remember." And, of course, he ended up making me even more fidgety, to the point that I would have been better off downing a Red Bull and two espressos where I could have achieved the same result, albeit much more quickly. If that was his aim, then he jumped over the bar rather nicely, and he was looking at a perfect ten from all three judges.

Before he could offer a smart reply, the host signaled us. She offered Ben a smile and a frown and a nod for me. Not that it mattered, but other women did offer up habits of which I was unaccustomed to: These often focused on a man and offered up hair pulling and clawing to entertain the masses.

The table was near the back but not as close to the back as I would have preferred—all the way was just about right—and, of course, there were other couples seated around us, most of whom were engaged in animated exchanges and conversations, none of which I could hear, though, without seeming a bit too obvious.

I covered my face with my menu to peruse it more easily and to give myself the opportunity to regroup. Ben made a comment, of which I heard about half, and I grunted in reply, with the added sense of femininity.

I sensed the brief lull in the conversation suited me more than it suited Ben, but he kept his menu up in sport-like fashion. The silence proved soothing. After what I assumed was the appropriate amount of time, but probably only two minutes, I placed my menu on the table, and then folded my hands on top of it. Only a few seconds later Ben followed my lead.

"You know, you give weird a whole new meaning."

"Funny," I said, "that was never brought up in my report cards or parent teacher conferences."

"But you're not helpless."

I asked, "Do you always offer psychoanalysis to members of the opposite sex?"

I scooted my chair back and stood up. Ben, on the other hand, remained seated.

"Are you leaving me?"

I showed the first inkling of a smile before I placed it back in my purse. "I need to use the powder room. I think my nose could use a little more rouge."

"Is that some sort of code?" he asked.

"If you want it to be—"

"And if the waiter comes—"

"I'll have a small antipasto salad to start followed by the mushroom stuffed ravioli. Lucky for you one of quirks isn't indecisiveness." Before he could talk me into dessert, I disappeared, placing one foot in front of the other like I'd been taught in school.

In the bathroom, I smoothed down the front of my pink blouse, checked to ensure no errant pens had navigated to my hair, poked through my purse to ensure all was in place, rinsed my hands off in the sink, and then tossed the proffered paper towel from the dispenser into the wastepaper basket.

When I returned to the table, after circumnavigating a room much larger than my apartment, with enough nooks and crannies and side roads to cause even the best laid plans to go astray, the candle acknowledged my presence before Ben did. It had enough wick to go for at least a day at its current rate. The candle, not Ben. As for Ben, his eyes hinted at more than just a casual observance, although I had no idea what to do with this particular piece of information.

"What else have you got for me?" he asked.

"A string of payments to Dana via Grate Marketing." I provided him with the rest of the exoskeleton to help complete the picture.

"Victor Uglow has eccentric tastes."

"What's that supposed to mean?" I asked.

"Well, if he executed a dilly with his dally, it wouldn't be the first time. He hasn't met a woman he didn't like. You better not let him take a look at you, Blondie."

"What's that supposed to mean? I thought he didn't have a type."

"True, but you do have breasts and a vagina, so that makes you fair game."

At least two couples stared at us. If I were in a waving mood, I might have offered one. Instead, I stared at the linen tablecloth as I planned my next move. While I gave his comment a minute to digest, our waiter arrived with an antipasto salad for me and a bowl of soup for Ben.

I took a wild stab in the dark at my antipasto salad and at Ben. "And how does your girlfriend feel about your particular take on our gender?"

Half of a smirk escaped his mouth. "She takes it all in stride."

I shook my head. "I bet she does."

I didn't tell him, or my ravioli, about my series of unfortunate events, otherwise known as a string of bad first dates. But I did offer him further details about my job, and he managed to pretend like he was interested, even though most of it went over his head. He even nodded his head at the appropriate times. And when dinner was over, he insisted on picking up the tab, even though I offered to pay my share.

A handshake outside ended the evening.

~ ~ ~

Life was filled with misguided relationships: those that worked, and those that didn't. Most of my friendships fell in the former category, and most of my dates fell in the latter category. My hopes often fell somewhere in between; my dreams, however, were mired by the unusual and the inconsequential.

I stared at my monitor, and it stared back at me. I'd completed half of the marketing report, and I started to develop the first signs of a headache. I scooted my chair away from my desk, stood up, and fixed my eyes at a point on the other side of the glass doors. When my head cleared, I sat back down, rubbed my forehead, and punched more numbers into my algorithm. The equation spotted accounting irregularities, and so far I had found none. That didn't mean I wouldn't keep trying. I'd already reviewed the records from the previous two years. Since Cooper's Post-it didn't specify a time period, I decided to continue looking until I found something significant, or until my headache rendered me useless. The battle raged on with no real end in sight.

Before I could wave the white flag, my phone rang.

"Are you still curious about the father?" Don Stader asked.

I switched the receiver to my left ear. "Absolutely."

"What do you know about Tommy Buchs?"

I'd dated a man with the same name. He had a temper, and he'd threatened me with bodily harm on our last date. He hadn't stalked me, so he didn't rank as highly on the list as some of the other less scrupulous men I'd dated. He told me that one day he'd get even with me. I waited with grave uncertainty for that day to come, but it never came to pass.

"He's the father?" I asked.

"You bet. Does that mean I win some sort of award?"

"Definitely." I sipped from my mug of green tea.

"And that means I'm off the hook for the rest of the evening?"

I waited for a beat, but he said nothing more. "Do you have a date?"

There was an elongated pause on the other end of the line.

"Care to tell me about it?" I asked.

"I'd rather not," he said.

Before I could increase the intensity level of my questions, and actually extract useful information, he hung up.

When I looked up from my desk, a man in a blue uniform stared at me; the smirk was optional and had been included with the package. *How long had he been standing there?* I had no idea. His hair had been lost in the rinse cycle, one of his bottom teeth was chipped (possibly a fight that had gone very wrong, or a playground accident in his youth), and he had an earring in his left ear. He was a small man with a rather large presence. The name on his blue shirt said Buchs, and he told me his first name was Tommy. His right hand rested on his gun, while his left hand rested on his hip.

"Are you Sam LaCour?" Tommy asked.

I didn't smile. "How can I help you, officer?"

"You don't remember me, do you?"

I did remember him. He had an evil temper to go with his chipped tooth and cocksure attitude. He'd made an idle threat that I'd never forgotten, and the look he'd given me at the time told me he wasn't joking. He had more hair and a bit more weight at the time, but his attitude had remained surprisingly consistent.

"What are you doing exactly?"

I adjusted a pile of paperwork that didn't need adjusting. "Do you mean right this moment, or with regard to Dana's disappearance?"

He leaned on the door, the frame remained in place. "How about both?"

My eyes flicked away from my monitor. "I'm analyzing our company's financials. You're welcome to have a look, but I'm not sure you'd understand all the numbers. As for Dana, I'm actively looking into her whereabouts when I have a few inactive moments."

He shook his head. "You're overstepping your bounds, little lady."

"So the department is pursuing the matter?"

He caressed his weapon. "Where did you hear differently?"

"I'm not at liberty to say."

"It's okay," he said. "I know you've been talking with Ben."

"Our paths have managed to cross a few times." A lunch, a dinner, and a self-defense class came to mind. For someone on the outside looking in, it might have even appeared as though we were dating. His girlfriend, however, might not have approved of the situation.

"That's not all I've heard."

"Are you jealous?" I asked.

"Not hardly." He took a step forward. He still had a long way to go to reach my desk, but he managed to make a bit of progress.

"But all the same you do seem rather interested," I said.

"Only as it relates to your involvement with my department."

"Since when did it become your department?"

"It's certainly not yours," Tommy said. "You don't have a badge or a license. And you don't carry a weapon, unless you have a firearm stuffed in your handbag."

"But I am privy to information your department would have a hard time gathering. Since the police have reached a certain level of bureaucracy exceeded only by third world countries without access to the Internet, I might offer a breath of fresh air."

He grunted. His hand hadn't moved from the door. "Do you like your job?"

I stood up, my spine as rigid as a steel bar. "Are you threatening me?"

"I wouldn't dream of it," Tommy said. "I'm merely making informed suggestions."

I breathed deeply and assessed his threat. Realizing that his temper hadn't changed, nor had mine, I resumed my presence in my chair. Yoga and deep breathing exercises, not self-defense classes, helped me keep my emotions from spiraling out of control.

"What can you tell me about Dana Wilson's disappearance?"

"You have a lot of nerve, don't you? You're the one that's supposed to be talking to me, not the other way around. How did you even get involved in this incident in the first place?"

"One of my colleagues told me about Dana's absence for most of the past week." I conveniently left her name out of the discussion. "When I looked into another matter for our firm, our paths crossed again, at least on paper anyway. So I did more digging, and I discovered some irregularities." My presence wasn't a coincidence either. And I was willing to bet, neither was the presence of Tommy Buchs. He had been a bull who liked to show his horns before, and it appeared age had only increased the size of his rack. With a licensed firearm in his possession, along with a set of gleaming handcuffs, I could only imagine the extent of his damage.

"Such as?"

"She was being paid by Grate Marketing."

"So?" he said.

"Technically she still works for us, so why are payments being funneled into her checking account off the books and off our records? If we make the assumption she works for Grate, why doesn't she have a marketing degree? And if she hasn't started working for Grate, why has the firm paid her four times in varying amounts for unexplained services? Once could be considered an accounting error; four times happens to be an entirely different matter."

Tommy nodded. "You need to drop this. No good can come out of what you're doing. This isn't an active case or an active investigation, and as far as we know, she's disappeared for reasons that we aren't privy to. You're causing yourself a massive headache that will only turn into a migraine."

I shook my head.

"Is that a no 'I won't cause myself a headache' or a no 'I'm not dropping the investigation?' "

"The latter."

He hitched his pants up a little higher. "You know, we could always bring you in."

"And charge me with what?"

"Obstruction of justice," he said.

"Technically, and to use your words, this isn't an active investigation."

"You're still stepping on my toes." He took another step closer.

"By digging into the numbers and talking with witnesses? Numbers are what I do for a living. As for the witnesses, well, those came up over the course of conducting normal business."

"Now you're speaking to witnesses?"

"I haven't harmed anyone," I said. For that matter, I hadn't even come close. But the possibility did still exist.

"What else have you been doing?"

I didn't mention my two bouts of breaking and entering, or my discussion with Cooper Strut. I didn't need a reason to be hauled to the police station, and I didn't want to drag my imaginary attorney into the mix. What I did want to do, though, was continue on my present course of action and hope I caught a break.

He scratched behind his left ear. "You'll have a heck of a time finding her. It's not easy finding someone that doesn't want to be found. Your manhunt might be short a few men."

Before I could conjure up an adequate reply, he'd already left my office, and presumably the building. He certainly did know how to use an exit line effectively.

~ ~ ~

Jerry Duncan drove a yellow pickup truck, with a chrome bumper, chrome wheels, and an NRA sticker in the back window. His house had steel bars on the windows—probably a safe bet from the looks of the neighborhood—a missing shutter, vinyl siding, and a steel front door that must have been a foot thick from the looks of it.

The man who opened the door had one hand in his pocket, and the other scratched the back of his head, his brown hair was close cropped, he had a gap between his front teeth that some women might find attractive—I was not one of them—while a shotgun rested next to the door, just within his reach and well out of mine. What I needed were longer arms or quicker reflexes, just in case he had any bright ideas.

"Are you Jerry Duncan?"

"Who wants to know?"

"I'm Sam LaCour," I said. "I'd like to ask you some questions about Dana Wilson."

"So you're a cop?"

"No."

"A private investigator?"

"Not exactly," I said. "I'm a concerned colleague."

He tipped his head back and laughed. "How did you find me?"

"You're not that hard to find."

He contemplated that while he scratched his chin. His eyes, however, didn't flick toward the shotgun. "You know that Dana and I
broke up, right?"

"I do," I said. "She ended the relationship. You still have feelings
for her, though."

"What?"

"It's in your tone of voice," I said. "There's a sense of longing. Besides, it wasn't all that long ago, was it?" He nodded. "So it was a
relatively safe bet that you might still carry a torch for her. Even if
the flame is flickering out."

"But you wanted to speak to me anyway?"

"You dated her for two years," I said. "You probably know her as
well as anyone."

"But you don't."

"You're right," I said. "But I'm learning. And I hoped you might be
willing to fill in a few of the details. It would make finding her a bit
easier."

"How quick are you?"

"Quick enough."

"You know why we broke up?"

"I have a good idea."

"You mind sharing it with me?" he said. "Because she still hasn't
given me an answer. She just walked away, and she never even bothered to look back." His eyes turned hard before the softness returned
again. His left hand moved to his shirt front where he scratched his
chest absently. He gazed out into the distance before he focused his
attention on me again.

His tone of voice told me everything I needed to know—he still
had feelings for her; he didn't know what to do with that information; and in the process, it tore at his insides like a jalapeño pepper.
He had hostile down to a science, and he still hadn't bothered to
move the shotgun. I was on the outside looking in, and if he started
firing, I was ill-equipped for the task at hand. A few self-defense
classes wouldn't help me against a loaded weapon. I, however, had
learned how to defend myself against a knife wielding opponent at

least twice my size. Given my stature, it wasn't hard to find someone up for the assignment.

"What do you know?" I asked.

"That she had a relationship with her boss."

"Frankie Kensington?"

"Not that one. Her other boss: Porter Reede. The head honcho."

"And the relationship is still ongoing?"

"When she walked out the door, I didn't bother to ask her. Maybe I should have; maybe it would have given me peace of mind, or at the very least, a quick peek inside her head."

"When exactly did she walk out?"

He peered up at the sky. "A little over a week ago."

"So right around the time she went missing?"

"If you say so," Jerry said.

"You didn't know she was missing?"

He shook his head.

CHAPTER TEN

I had more than one potential liar on my hands, but what I didn't know was why. Although I had no hard facts, and I dealt in mostly suspicions, Frankie Kensington had spoken confidently and with authority about her friendship with Dana, but behind the scenes I had seen the actress hard at work. Her thoughts were formed rapidly and the tale had a certain amount of believability, but it was just that: A tale told to appease my curious nature and send me off on a hunt in the woods without a shotgun. If she was good friends with Dana Wilson, she would have known more about her disappearance, and she wouldn't have been trying to pawn her off on another department behind her back. Her track record told me that secretaries didn't last, and her actions had certainly spoken louder than her words.

On the other hand, Jerry Duncan had been both saddened and shocked by Dana's rather abrupt breakup, and he harbored emotions he wasn't quite ready to deal with. The breakup came suddenly and without warning, at least from his perspective, and his feelings ran deeper than he ever would have admitted to me upon our initial meeting. While he may not have known about her disappearance, he had been trying to track her down, possibly to get the last word in, before she removed himself from his life forever. He looked sleep deprived, with dark circles under his eyes, and it wouldn't have surprised me to learn he'd driven by her house in the middle of the night hoping to catch one last glimpse of her.

Tommy Buchs had pumped me for information, as he was more interested in taking than giving, and he had been bluffing from the minute he stroked his gun. According to Ben Xander, the Hampton PD hadn't even been aware of Dana's disappearance, until I had raised the red flag and spoken with him one-on-one. There was no case, and it had not subsequently fallen on Tommy's desk, although some legwork from Ben might eventually change the circumstances, and now Tommy wanted to take credit for my work, start a case from the middle of the race, and discover all the pieces of the puzzle, all while holding a cup of coffee in one hand and his gun in the other. What I didn't know was how closely Ben and Tommy worked together, since Ben had never mentioned him before, but for all I knew, the two could have been partners, or at the least close colleagues, despite the sharp differences in personality, most of which had sheared off on Tommy's spiked edges.

Through no real fault of mine, Dana's disappearance had taken on a life of its own, and I needed to keep track of all the subsequent players, most of whom appeared to be dancing while I stood still and tried to orient my feet. More than likely, I'd need something larger than a notepad and paper, and I'd need to use more than just my math skills.

I eased to a stop at the red light, pulled down the visor, flipped open the mirror, and inspected my appearance. My eyes, I'd been told, were striking blue; my cheeks had a slight natural red color; my hair was dirty blonde with a slight natural curl; despite having braces, I had one tooth on the bottom that sat at an unnatural angle; and my shoulders were a bit larger than I would have liked, although I'd received several comments to the contrary. The sun beat through the windshield like a bad acid trip, and my right hand had stopped shaking some time ago from my previous encounters with Tommy and Jerry, although neither one had been the least bit threatening. Most of my previous confrontations popped out of my head at unnatural angles.

"Girl Next Door" a song by Saving Jane emitted through my speakers and into my consciousness. As the light turned green, I continued to hum along to the lyrics, picking up I-64 East, and when the opportunity presented itself, I went south on I-664 utilizing the Monitor-Merrimac Bridge-Tunnel to take me to Chesapeake. Under most circumstances, the traffic is lighter through the MMBT as opposed to the Hampton Roads Bridge-Tunnel, or HRBT, but on this particular day a fender-bender had occurred in the recent past (luckily it was outside of the tunnel and off to the side), and it proved just interesting enough to cause the traffic ahead of me to slow down and document the occasion in their minds and possibly on Facebook or Twitter. I, however, chose to ignore the spectacle altogether, even though I passed right next to it in the right hand lane. Before I reached the other side of the tunnel, I managed to make it through "Who's Cryin' Now," as my humming decreased in intensity.

I pulled into the driveway of my parents' double-decker house, which didn't provide me with many fond memories. I'd grown up in Newport News, but my dad talked my mother into moving to Chesapeake after I graduated from college, and he decided he needed another career change. My mom went along for the ride, thinking he was just entering another phase in his life, but the move, and the house, stuck. His new career, however, proved to be short-lived; luckily for him he found another job on the rebound where he was presently still employed. The porch swing had been added by my mother, while my dad preferred the indoors most days. He had a knack for computers, and all other things electronic, that I hadn't inherited from him, but I did inherit his love of numbers.

My mom, a small woman even by my standards, answered the door in cream colored pants and a sky blue blouse that accented her eyes. "You're not in trouble, are you?" she asked.

I opened my arms, wrapped them around her, and gave her a brief hug. She took this to mean that I was, as her head tilted upward toward my eyes, a questioning look on her face.

"I'm fine, mom. Why do you always assume the worst? I work with numbers all day for a stable firm in a stable industry. It's not like I have to wear a flak vest to work or walk around toting a gun and a Taser."

"I'm your mother," she said. "I was given the right to worry when I gave birth. My need has only increased with your age and lack of suitable male partners."

She produced a can of pepper spray from her pocket. "Here," she said, "I want you to have this."

"Why?"

"You never know when you might need it."

"You haven't been speaking to the police, have you?"

She crossed her hands in front of her. "Are you in trouble with the law?"

"No," I said, "but I have been looking into a missing person at work."

She always had a sixth sense when it came to me and danger. Luckily, I didn't see any lurking around the corner; otherwise I could have sprayed it with my new self-defense device. I ran my hands over the can, which was about the size of a small flashlight.

"Where did you get it?" I asked.

She narrowed her eyes. "From a police officer."

"You didn't take it from him, did you?"

She rolled her eyes. "Of course not."

"How does it work?"

"All you have to do is press this button," she said. "But it's currently in the locked position. You can tell because this part is red." She pointed to a small square.

I held the bottle up to my face, staring at the small nozzle, and pressed the button. A cloud of mist formed in front of me, and I coughed. My eyes felt like two individual fireballs that had been scrubbed with jalapeño peppers. Tears formed, my eyes shut involuntarily, and I began to cough more rapidly. I danced on the porch, bumping into what was most likely the brick wall at least twice.

"Don't cough," she said. "You'll get it in your mouth. And that's even worse than having it in your eyes."

Her hands waved through my tears, and she stepped back about five feet.

"I need some water."

"You don't want water," she said. "It won't fix the effects."

"Then what do I need?"

"First, you need to get away from the mist; otherwise you'll just make it worse." She shoved me inside and slammed the door. "A solution of milk and water should do the trick."

My mom dragged me down the hallway, plopped me next to the sink, and grabbed the milk from the refrigerator. She poured a small shot glass full of half-milk and half-water and handed it to me. My eyes appeared to have their own heartbeats, and the tears flowed much more easily. I tilted my head back, dumped half the shot glass into my left eye, and then I repeated the same process for my right one.

When the tears had decreased to once every ten seconds or so, and I stopped seeing red everywhere I looked, I glared at my mother.

"Oops," she said. "I guess you proved me wrong. Well, at least now you know what happens when you spray yourself. I went through the same motions with the officer."

My mom and I made our way to the sitting room where two small dark leather sofas kept us company. An antique grandfather clock was at the far end of the room, and there was a single bookcase on the adjacent wall filled with various history books from the Civil War forward. One of the sofas enveloped me, and the other one enveloped my mother.

"How did you know I'm mixed up in just more than my regular work?" I asked.

"I'm your mother. It's my job to know these things, and to see you're given whatever assistance you need along the way. How was your date?"

"He's not going to make the cut. He propositioned me as we were leaving."

"And the other possibility?" she asked.

"That never panned out. I was previously indisposed, and I missed that particular transaction altogether."

She leaned forward, her outstretched hand nearly touching my knee. "You could always find your own version of Jonah. At the rate you're going, your sister is the only one who will be making contributions in the grandkid arena."

I gently pushed her hand away, glaring at her through the last remnants of my tears. "Maybe I'm not as lucky as Felicia."

"Or maybe you're not as interested in settling down," she said. "But you do lead a more interesting life than she does."

"Mom, I deal with spreadsheets all day."

"Apparently that's not all you've been dealing with. Do you ever stop to consider that you don't need to create order from disorder?"

"It's a part of who I am," I said. "I can't just change my genetic makeup."

"I suppose I have your father to thank for that particular gene."

My eyes shifted to the window. "Where is dad?"

"He's working."

I stared at my mother. "On a Tuesday evening?"

"Don't even get me started on your father. I'm sure you got your stubbornness from him as well. He could be outnumbered three-to-one, with his opponents more than twice his size, and he'd keep swinging until the end, even if he didn't have a baseball bat or a glove handy."

I just smiled. No matter how old she got, my mother never seemed to lose her ability to overanalyze any situation and show a lack of disappointment with the results. High standards remained very much a part of the LaCour household, and while my mother never admitted it outright, I could sense her hesitation with my chosen profession. I didn't bother to give her any specific details on my new hobby—and she didn't ask—as this would only add to her current state of distress. As for the majority of my dates, they never would have made it onto the porch, let alone through the front door. Even without a gun handy, my dad would have taken it upon himself to rearrange a few faces, if the boys didn't live up to his standards. Perfectionists to the end. My sister had fallen just outside the fence, while I had fallen directly in the middle of it, and I smacked every board on my way to the ground.

~ ~ ~

Traffic was light on my drive back toward Hampton as the Monitor-Merrimac Bridge-Tunnel lit my way home. Carrie Underwood provided the musical inspiration, even though I didn't hum along to the lyrics from her second album. The apple Jolly Rancher, however, did provide me a certain amount of comfort. The concoction of water and milk didn't make its way to my suit jacket; the tears and blinking had subsided long ago. My mother's worrying stuck with me, but I couldn't change her or myself. My eyes felt raw and overused, as though I had just recovered from a bout of serious grieving over the end of a two-year relationship. Since none of my relationships to date had ever made it that far, I could only speculate as to how I might feel.

I grabbed a sandwich for the road, and it rested on the seat beside me, along with my purse which contained the can of pepper spray. I also had a bottle of water resting in one of the cup holders, and a handful of CDs shoved into the glove compartment.

I pulled into a parking space next to the building—the rest of the lot was empty—and I used my key to unlock the front door to Wired Consulting. The lobby hadn't changed from the last time I entered the building unannounced. No guards or dark shadows awaited me, although I could easily explain away the additional workload with my gung-ho attitude. Should I meet the other side of Cooper's desk again, I had a few different excuses prepared, and depending on the direction of the meeting, I would choose my alibi wisely. One of these days I might even prove adept at thinking on my feet in front of a one-man firing squad.

I had the set of lock picks wrapped around my waist, as I took the stairs to the fourth floor. Outside of Dana's office, I glanced in either direction—the hall was filled with eerie silence—before I picked the lock on the second try. I stepped into her office, and closed the door behind me before I flipped on the light. The hum of the overhead light as it sprang to life provided its own sort of acoustics.

Walking toward her desk, I noticed the computer was no longer there, and that all the paperwork had been removed from her desk. I opened the various drawers, checked underneath the wooden space, and even turned over her chair. But all traces of Dana Wilson had disappeared before my eyes. She might as well have never worked at the firm.

I flipped off the light, closed the door, made a left, and took the stairs to the floor below. I unlocked my office door, flipped on the light, and perched myself behind my desk. I booted up my computer and went to work.

Concentrating hard at my desk, I didn't hear the footsteps. But I did hear the pounding at my door and the click of a weapon. "What the—?"

My head jerked up and a pop entered the space between us, as my neck screamed in silent protest, and the gun was pointed directly at my head. I swallowed hard, and said what I hoped were my last rights, although I was a little new to that particular experience. Those stupid self-defense classes didn't provide a solution to disarming a murderer more than ten feet away with a chair that had an unnatural squeak. Besides, it's not like I could fly across my desk and disarm my opponent. Although the thought, even if it was a fleeting one, did hold a certain appeal.

My eyes shifted upward, hoping I could look my attacker between the irises before I met my maker. "Ben?"

"What are you doing here this late?" he asked.

"Working," I said. "Are you trying to cause me heart palpitations?"

He stared at me for more than a moment. "We went over disarming an opponent in self-defense class."

I glared back at him. "Not from across the room."

"Maybe you're a little rusty."

"I don't think so." I paused. "Aren't you supposed to say police before you shoot someone right between the eyes?"

"I did."

I shook my head. "I distinctly recall a 'What the—' before my fingers stopped slapping the keyboard and my eyes traveled north. Besides, what's this all about anyway? Are you trying to get rid of a few bodies?"

He rubbed his eyes and then placed his gun back in its holster. "You tripped a silent alarm."

"And you're the savior?"

"This particular time," Ben said. "Next time, you might not be so lucky. There's no one else here, right?"

I shook my head. "Next time, I'll be a bit smarter."

What I discovered over the next two hours neither surprised nor shocked me. At least not the way Ben had done. Porter Reede had made similar payments to Dana, although his payment frequency had increased from four to five, but the overall amount and the individual payments were for smaller amounts than those from Victor Uglow. Based on what Jerry Duncan told me, assuming he had told me the truth, I guessed it had something to do with her relationship to Porter. At this point, I began to think of blackmail, because she did have an abortion in her past, and for all I knew, she might have had more than one.

As for Tommy Buchs, he had a history of violence, with two suspects filing complaints against him. Neither made it to court, so he had never formally been convicted, but the documentation remained just the same. Dana had also filed a complaint against him, claiming he abused her, but that charge had quietly gone away as well. He had two cars and a leased apartment to his name, but no liquid assets— stocks, bonds, CDs, or money market accounts. He did have a checking account where the balance fluctuated between $1,000 and $2,000. The last suspect had filed his complaint eight months ago, so he had discovered the path to redemption, gone below the radar, or had gotten cleverer in his abusive tactics. Based on what I'd experienced firsthand, I would have leaned toward the latter.

What proved most disconcerting, though, was he hadn't disclosed his prior relationship with Dana, and he appeared to be actively involved in tracking her down. I didn't know his exact motivation, but I started to develop a reasonable hypothesis.

CHAPTER ELEVEN

Jerry Duncan and Dana Wilson incorporated much of this hypothesis. Through a peek at her phone records, I learned she'd called the cops on him twice in the midst of their two-year relationship. No charges were ever filed, but there was a record of the two calls, and her initial statements, which she halted when it came time for more serious action. It was either abuse, or she had a severe mental disability that I wasn't aware of, and which happened to lack any documentation whatsoever. I'd heard abusers were real charmers: They fed their victims lies about how they would never do it again, or they'd changed, or they had sought help, had spoken to a psychiatrist, or dark spirits had overcome their bodies, only to turn around and do it again when the opportunity, or the trigger, presented itself. More than likely, the worst of them didn't feel guilty about it and probably didn't feed their victims lies about seeking help, and they sought out women who didn't realize they deserved better.

Dana met Jerry through a mutual friend, and sparks had flown immediately. The relationship moved at warp speed, and in less than two months, she had moved in with him, albeit in a different residence, where he had previously cohabited with another woman. When his relationship with Dana became serious, he had shown the other woman—Jessie Trager—the door. To say the romance with Jessie had been a whirlwind was an understatement. In less than a month, the two had moved in together—he had moved in with her— and six months later there had been talk of marriage. A ring was never produced, and then along came Dana. Jessie had threatened Jerry more than once over the phone, to the point that he had considered a restraining order, but he never followed through. Dana had to have known of Jerry's previous relationship, unless she had managed to become completely oblivious to the world around her, but I couldn't ask her how she really felt about it. Either she liked trouble, or once she discovered she was in the middle of it, she had no idea how to get out of it.

Her life moved at a breakneck pace; that given a few years, it would be hard to keep up. She had disappeared over a week ago, and she had not bothered to call Wired Consulting once (in direct opposition to what Frankie had previously told me). In the time she had been gone, her computer along with all of her records had managed to disappear, and I had no authority to figure out who had staged the disappearing act. Even though the cover-up was internal, that didn't mean her disappearance was. The suspect list had just grown longer, and I wasn't at the point where I could start eliminating people.

Flirting with disaster didn't require much effort: All it required was a willingness to get ahead and a loose sense of morals. With all that had come before and all that was to come after, I didn't know just how far a ticket to paradise would take me, but I planned to enjoy the ride. Intermission might prove rather costly, or it might allow me to reach a few definitive conclusions.

Tommy, Jerry, and Porter proved a rather interesting love rectangle, with the three relationships not divided evenly. Jerry and Porter were the most recent, with Tommy more than likely a distant memory, except for his penchant for stalking. Dana, however, had been oblivious to his tendencies for a period of their relationship. I, however, wasn't nearly as nice, or as forgiving, and I showed him the door before he decided to spar with me. I knew I could go the distance, but I also knew it wasn't an even match. Yoga wouldn't have helped me in the situation, and neither would my self-defense class, unless I could flip him over my head, poke out his eyes, or spray him with my can of pepper spray. It had survived its first battle with flying colors.

Porter, on the other hand, might as well have been made of wax paper. Wired Consulting managed to have no negative press, despite his willingness to expand his enterprise. Opulence often met resistance, but in his case he had been spared all negative publicity. As far as mysteries went, it rivaled the latest Janet Evanovich novel, minus the blown-up vehicles and bad guys on the run. I made a note, and then I moved on. On the other hand, Porter used his charms to perfection, and personal arrogance seemed a rather frequent calling card. He had sparred with Victor Uglow on more than one occasion, but as far I knew no actual punches had been thrown. Yet, the media had not picked up on the story, and if I hadn't seen it near the marina on my lunch break, I wouldn't have believed it.

The encounter took place on the docks where their boats were stowed diagonally across from each other. Victor rocked the docks—and Porter's boat in the process—dropped anchor with a bit too much authority, and then proceeded to walk away as if nothing had happened. Porter called him a name not worth repeating, and the two men stood eye-to-chin on the dock, with Porter being nearly a head taller than Victor. It didn't help the matter that Victor had a girl on each arm—one drunk and the other not—with the drunk one calling Porter a preppy SOB. Porter had reached out his hand to the drunk in the bikini, and Victor slapped it away, right before he tossed his fist in Porter's direction. Porter's face turned red, and then purple, although it wasn't due to a lack of oxygen. But before he flattened Victor to the wooden dock, and then stomped him into oblivion, he walked away as the drunken blonde cackled.

Although I couldn't yet confirm the rumor, I'd heard Porter walked out of more than one board meeting, leaving the rest of the directors to jump out of the sixth story window, if they so desired, and without even a glance behind him. He'd also lit into more than one negligent manager who managed to show more inclination for Internet surfing, music playing, or daydreaming tendencies in the middle of one of his notorious longwinded monologues. Although I hadn't known anyone to jump, or fight back when the abuse entered the full-on realm, I had known one or two people who considered the possibility for a short period of time, before rationality once more entered their world. I, however, always managed to entertain the thought of an irrational moment or two, not that I would ever follow through with my dreams, but it certainly helped make the cause more enjoyable.

~ ~ ~

A stack of papers greeted me at the door the next morning. Only the top sheet was visible—I noticed it was my last report—and it was covered in red ink. Every third line was crossed out, and comments were inserted in the margins, as well as the top and bottom of the sheet. I flipped through the rest of the pages, until I found a big red X crossed through the next to last page. I tossed the report on my desk, placed my cup of tea beside it, and then performed a few yoga stretches to clear my head.

Despite my ability to follow the rules, Cooper changed roads repeatedly and possibly time zones as well. But he did manage to stay on the same planet, although I feared it was a distant one. Jupiter came to mind repeatedly, although I had no idea of the travel time, and I didn't have a spacecraft or rocket handy. No matter how much time I spent on a report, and no matter how many times I pulled out *The Elements of Style*—I had two copies, one in my desk drawer and one at my apartment—I always managed to fail the rules of writing in Cooper's eyes. Aside from Cooper, I'd often been praised for my work, and I'd even been nominated for three bonuses, two of which I ended up seeing in my paychecks, and one of which was probably still on layaway. If it ever came my way, I decided I'd use it to pay down my student loans. Or I could always obtain a motorcycle that I might never ride to impress a boyfriend that I currently didn't have—

the helmet, however, wasn't optional, and the bike would always remain too large.

I rubbed the last remnants of sleep from my eyes, sipped my tea,
and booted up my computer. Before I could enter my password, a
soft knock entered the room. Knocks I was used to, soft ones, though,
were a new concept for me. My visitor entered before I could utter a
word.

"I heard you've been busy," he said.

I wondered if he viewed the security tapes from the previous evening. Another knock followed, but this one was across the hall. "I
have a hard time sitting still," I said. I offered him a chair, and he
took it before I could change my mind.

"You might want to watch where you point your toes," Ben Xander
said.

I typed in my password, hit enter, and watched my monitor come
to life. "Are you saying I might have them pointed in the wrong direction?"

"Do you even know what you're doing?" he asked.

I sipped my tea. "Not exactly," I said. "I make it up as I go along."
I didn't need to add that I wasn't a full-fledged detective nor did I
bother to point out the time. But it didn't sound as though my name
was at the top of his most wanted list.

His gaze flitted around the room before landing squarely back in
my direction. "Your office is a bit on the tiny side."

I glared at him. "It suits me."

He leaned backwards, and his facial expression remained in the
neutral position. "You might want to work on your approach. If
you're looking for enemies, I can hand over a few without you putting
in the extra effort."

"What are you talking about?" I asked. My mind focused on the
right cross I had failed to land Monday evening. I didn't enjoy losing,
even though my instructor had struck the mat. If I had been just a
split-second faster, I could have touched more than air.

"Your chat with Tommy Buchs," Ben said. "There's a history, isn't
there?"

"A bit of one." The details remained more firm than hazy, and his grin had haunted my dreams a time or two. If I hadn't already been involved in self-defense classes, I would have started just so I could protect myself. He was one mean mother after a few cocktails, and not the fruity ones.

"He doesn't like you."

"Is it that obvious?" I asked. I hoped he wasn't on a first-name basis with Tommy. Even worse, maybe they were former partners, or possibly current associates. The thought caused my right hand to twitch involuntarily.

"I wish it weren't."

"Why do you care? Are you writing a biography?"

He shrugged right before he leaned his arm over my other chair. "I'm curious." He rolled his shoulders in a backwards motion before he resumed the leaning.

"I want answers and order, and I'd like to solve this chaotic mess, or at least wrap my hands around the Houdini act. I wouldn't want to see an epidemic break out."

His eyes flicked around the room again. "Are you working on it?"

I shuffled the papers, moving the ones in red to the top of the stack. Of the twenty page report, I had five pages I was able to move to the bottom. "Probably not as much as I should be." I preferred hand-to-hand combat in these situations, but Ben wasn't exactly my size. And I wasn't prepared for a spirited confrontation.

Ben leaned back in his chair a little farther. "I'm not either."

"Are you checking up on me?"

He shrugged. "After your snafu, I thought it might be prudent to make an appearance. You're about as subtle as gonorrhea."

I stood up, smoothed my skirt, walked around my desk, touching the edge as I made my way to his chair, and then stopped about a foot away from him, pulled my hand back, and then stopped. I took a deep yoga breath, harnessed my chi, and then exhaled slowly, my exhale loud enough for Ben to hear.

"What the hell do you think you're doing?"

I said, "I'd like to ask you the same thing."

"Help," he said. "It's a four letter word. You might even find it use-ful once in a while. You can't treat a missing person like a math prob-lem."

I'd walked back to my chair and sat down. "I find math very relax-ing. This case, not so much."

Ben said, "Then there's a good chance you're making progress, or at least your car isn't stalled on the side of the highway waiting for a tow."

How did he know about my car? Well, it hadn't stalled yet, but it certainly seemed headed in that direction. Or maybe it was time for another tune-up. I tried listening to my car, but most of the time it didn't talk, or my frequency wasn't tuned properly. I shuffled a few papers on my desk, tried to look important, and probably failed mis-erably at the task.

"So are you making progress?" Ben asked.

"It's not moving as quickly as I'd like. Dana's still missing, and I still have way too many suspects. I thought you might be Cooper."

"Who?"

"My boss," I said. "He's probably going to call me in his office be-fore long—"

"Good luck."

"That's all you have to say to me?"

"You're lucky I didn't shoot you when I had the chance," he said. "It might have saved me a lot of trouble."

"Does your girlfriend find you this endearing?"

"Most of the time she probably doesn't, but she's real good at hid-ing her emotions."

"I bet—"

"Do you always show more passion than sense?"

"It's a LaCour family trait. I inherited it from my father who in-herited it from his father."

He crossed his arms over his chest and inched back a bit further in his chair. "What did you find out?"

I rearranged my pile of papers, adding a few more to the stack and shuffling the remainder. "Dana's computer has disappeared, along with the rest of the files off her desk."

"How many times have you broken into her office?" he asked.

"Twice. But I don't plan to do it again. Although I might have to venture across the street—"

Ben held up his hand. "I don't want to know. You should work on keeping the law breaking to a minimum. How many laws are you aiming for?"

"As few as possible," I said. "Dana also had more than one abortion." Maybe she couldn't always get it right the first time either.

"Maybe she has trouble staying with one man."

"It's probably more than trouble," I said. It could probably be construed as a sickness. I'd heard the epidemic had been going around a bit, but I tended to steer clear of the action. "But trouble is always a good place to start." I just needed to ensure I stayed out of it for the foreseeable future, unless I wanted to end up on the most wanted list. If my picture wasn't plastered all over the company's homepage by noon, then I was probably safe. If it was, then I might want to consider changing my look. I'd varied it very little since college.

"What about Jerry?" he asked.

"He hasn't seen her in a week."

"And Porter?"

"I haven't asked him yet," I said. "I can't exactly talk to the CEO of my company without creating at least a few waves. Even I'm not crazy enough to drop anchor in my own vessel."

CHAPTER TWELVE

A German bank account popped up on my screen. A well-funded German bank account. One that had probably seen its share of moveable funds for years and funded rather efficiently and expeditiously. Why not Switzerland or the Cayman Islands? I have no idea, but this particular account took me longer to find, because I wasn't looking at Germany. I had focused my attention elsewhere, for obvious reasons, and I was pleasantly surprised by this result. My Internet bots had come through for me from a program provided by Don Stader that I had obtained through less than legal means.

If I had thought about it a bit more carefully, I might not have loaded said program onto my work computer, but I had scanned *Fun Bots* with my antivirus software, and after reviewing the red inked paperwork that had grazed my desk like a fatted calf, I needed a breather. And Ben wasn't entirely helpful either. I mean, he meant well, or at least I thought he did, but he still had some issues to work through, present company excluded of course.

My research, however, had taken me across the board and across the plains, and I was probably raking up more frequent flyer miles than George Clooney's character in *Up in the Air*, which just happened to be one of my favorite movies, sentimental value included. It went well with my purple robe and popcorn.

~ ~ ~

The aging rock star look had returned with a vengeance. This time the three-piece suit was gray; his hair might as well have been slicked back with oil; his arms were crossed and tucked underneath his armpits; and he rocked back and forth, the motion antagonizing rather than calming the collective gasp contained within the room. He stared up at me with a slight smirk on his face, and the walls followed suit, containing the beast within.

Cooper Strut had a wraparound microphone on top of his head, the mike twisted up toward the heavens. Berber carpet thicker than a cement block stood beneath my feet. With my fingers, I combed a strand of hair above my right ear, a reflex action I couldn't seem to replace. I stood at attention with my back straight and my head held high, staring back at him even though my mind implored me to look away.

He stared back at me; neither his eyes nor his head removed themselves from the equation. He shuffled a stack of papers on his desk that had started out perfectly even.

"Once wasn't enough for you," he said. "You mind explaining to me why your image is on the security cameras again."

I used my index finger to poke at my left thumb, and then my eyes flicked at a spot above his head. "Maybe the camera recycled its image."

He tucked his hands underneath his chin. "And you honestly expect me to believe that?"

I shrugged. "It sounded better in my head." If the carpet were involved, it probably would have laughed at me.

"You wore a different suit," he said.

"I thought we had black and white cameras." At least that's what we'd been told. But then lies and half-truths blossomed like wildflowers around this place. If placed in the middle of the atrium, the lilies wouldn't have a chance.

"The pattern on your suit was different. If you're going to come up with a story, you might want to make it more believable next time. Now what was the purpose of your visit?"

I stared at the carpet again. If nothing else, it was good practice for the unemployment line, where I was probably headed sooner rather than later. "I needed to practice my lock picking skills," I said. "I failed valiantly the first time around. But as you'll notice—if you watched the tape—my time improved significantly the second time around. However, I do know how to take criticism."

Cooper rubbed his forehead, and then shook his head. "Maybe you should consider letting Dana go. It could be hazardous to your health."

Breakfast reappeared at the back of my throat: I swallowed it back down. "Do you want to get rid of me?" I asked.

"I happen to be very pleased—"

I smiled sweetly, executing another well-placed swallow in the process. "Then what's the issue?" I shuffled on the balls of my feet, since I'd been standing this whole time.

"Maybe she vanished for a reason. Has your *side job* led you to any definitive conclusions, or are you just wasting the company's time?"

I didn't have an easy answer to his question: Maybe that was the point. I shifted my weight from my right foot to my left; my right hand jerked before I brought it back under control; and my eyes never left his desk. I noticed he'd placed additional emphasis on side job, which, in turn, caused a slight increase in my shifting.

I didn't have as much money saved up as I would have liked, and I didn't have any prospects lined up, should I find myself at the front of the unemployment line with my right hand thrust out in front of me and my eyes cast in a downward position, as the harsh overhead lights beat against my scalp. The lights, most likely, reflecting off the floor, and possibly burning my retinas in the process.

I asked, "Do you think someone in the company was involved with her?"

He shook his head and frowned. "Why would you even ask the question?"

"She wasn't exactly known for her discretion within the office. And based on recent events, it'd be hard to rule out such a scenario."

"Do you have any proof of this?"

I shook my head. "But I do find it convenient that she might have had a relationship with someone, either inside or outside the office, and now she's gone missing. Who's normally the primary suspect when the wife is murdered?"

Cooper shrugged. "I have no idea."

"The husband."

"But she wasn't married."

He failed to see my point, or he played the dense card on purpose. It's not like I was a detective either, and there was only so much questioning I could do before the security guards with sunglasses started hovering around my desk, providing me with banker's boxes and a one-hour time limit to pack up my crap. So I waited out my sentence and hoped Cooper blinked first.

"Do you think she was let go?" he asked.

"I'm not sure what to think," I said. "I can't even seem to get a straight story out of her boss. The gossip mill has provided me with an additional thread or two."

He tapped a stack of papers against his desk. "Maybe there's no story to be found."

"Or maybe there's a cover-up."

"Are you prepared to lose your job over this?"

The unemployment image grew in importance, with harsh lights and unhelpful souls blocking my entrance to the pearly gates, as my mind filled in the rest of the blanks. "I like my job very much."

"Why don't we keep it that way?" Cooper said.

I shoved my way back to my office before my head ended up on the chopping block. I didn't like the way Dana's existence had been brushed under the carpet. I wasn't sure how many friends she had to start with, but she might not have that many left. Despite the suspect nature of her character and her disappearance, she deserved more than an index finger flick to the head. I'd never graced an unemployment line with my presence, and I didn't want to start now.

I took the stairs, my heels clicking and echoing in the enclosed space, and I took deep breaths as I counted steps. When I stopped at the water cooler, I bumped into Norma Beemer.

"You should come with me," she said.

"Why?" I asked. The hesitation in my voice was more than evident, and her reaction was more than consistent with my response.

Her gray hair flopped in her face, and she shoved it aside. "You and I need to talk. Meet me in the employee break room."

The employee break room consisted of two tables and seven chairs. One of the tables tilted at a slight angle, while the other one managed to remain level. There used to be eight chairs, but the eighth one had gone missing sometime over the last year, and no one managed to locate its hiding spot. The Coke machine managed to eat every other quarter; the coffeepot needed to be replaced; the glass door had a crack larger than a handprint; and the pale blue tile had hairline fractures. Each time I walked in it caused my right eyelid to twitch for approximately two seconds.

"I heard you're looking into Dana's disappearance."

"You certainly started the initiative," I said.

"Do you trust me?"

"I hardly even know you. And I didn't know Dana all that well either." Although Dana was a distant cousin on my mother's side, a part of my mom's family that she preferred to forget even existed. And I happened to be rather adept at missing more office functions than I attended, keeping my social presence to a minimum. I hadn't bothered to major in office gossip either. Aside from my current situation, I avoided more problems than I found myself in the middle of.

"You've run into more than a few dead ends, haven't you?"

The employee break room was the only room in Porter Reede's complex where cameras were left out of the equation. It certainly put me at ease, aside from the reflexive twitch, and I gained more than a bit of confidence along the way. The glass door offered the opportunity for spying, but the chance we would be overheard was minimal at best. The break room contained a lot of secrets, or at least I hoped it did.

I nodded.

"And you haven't wondered why that is?" she asked.

"I've had plenty of time to concern myself with Dana," I said. "Despite my math abilities, I still can't make any of it add up. Maybe I'm playing with bad data. And through an old acquaintance, I've learned that erroneous tangents often occur in these situations."

"Or maybe your competition is one step ahead of you. I heard Dana's office has been cleaned out, but then I'm sure you already knew that."

"Just how much do you know?" I asked. I definitely needed to get out more. I huddled in my office like I was riding out a hurricane or tornado, and I only emerged for scheduled meetings, conferences, and bathroom breaks.

"My path didn't usually cross with hers, but I have ears all over this building. Did you discover her abortions?"

I folded my hands on top of the table. "I know she had more than one."

"One of her boyfriends just happened to be a cop." Norma leaned across the table, practically shaking its foundation. "Don't you find that a little convenient?"

"I find the whole situation rather convenient," I said, "but not very convenient from Dana's perspective. What do you suggest I do?"

"I'd take a look at all parties involved, if I were you, and I'd also examine those who weren't all that close to Dana either. I'd suggest you consider everyone a suspect...if you do really want to learn the truth."

~ ~ ~

Frankie guided me into her office by my lapel, her other hand resting on my shoulder, squeezing with just a bit more effort than I would have liked. She pointed to a chair as though it might eat me alive, should she command it to do so. Her glasses were perched on her nose, about midway, and her nails dug into my shoulders. Her office appeared less used than most and more masculine than feminine.

"Why did you hassle Cooper?" she asked. "Do you want to take your rightful place in the unemployment line? Or are you just entertaining offers?"

"Dana disappeared," I said. "I've taken more than a few wrong turns, and I hoped I might discover a few of the right ones." My hands rested on the arms of the leather chair, as opposed to my lap, and I sat forward, just in case the black leather decided to eat me alive. I wanted to ask her why she was so concerned, but I held my tongue. If I kept at it, I might even learn why, or at least be able to make a few assumptions. My eyes were cast in a downward fashion, which seemed like a more than appropriate response, given what I had just previously experienced in Cooper's office.

"Maybe you should commence the information dispensing stage. If we wanted to press charges, we'd be within our right to do so."

I hadn't discovered her legal knowledge before, but maybe I hadn't been looking hard enough. Or maybe it was never hers to begin with. "If I had any information to dispense, you'd be the first to know it. Have you had any luck hiring a new secretary? I noticed the empty desk."

She asked, "Are you looking for gainful employment?"

"No," I said, "I just have a genuine interest in people. With the current economy, either the salary isn't right, or it might be the job."

Frankie nodded. The papers on her desk readjusted themselves, and then she leaned back in her chair, staring at a point just above my head. It was where a plaque should have been located but wasn't.

"You've been looking for her for a few days now."

Her statement wasn't in the form of a question, so I assumed I wasn't supposed to answer. My right hand itched. I popped a blue raspberry Jolly Rancher in my mouth, and I offered her one as well—she didn't take it.

Her office had a cluttered feel to it, despite the lack of clutter. A cloud of competition hung in the air like the American flag. My mind drifted back to the pile of papers on my desk, probably increasing in both size and difficulty. Red ink remained a familiar friend in my life. My pen, however, remained in my pocket, and my mouth remained in a neutral position, clinging to a hope I couldn't ignore. The hard candy helped keep me otherwise occupied, while I waited for her to continue.

Frankie asked, "You occasionally do find answers, don't you?"

"So I've been told. I often go where the math takes me, or in whichever direction the facts point me. As for Dana, I'm making it up as I go along. I'm sure I'll be able to document the process sometime in the near future. Stories, like rats in a sewer, never age well."

"What details do you feel my story lacks?"

"I'm not sure yet," I said. "But I don't think truth is at the top of this organization's to do list. As for useful information, my access has come up a bit short. If I hadn't bumped into an overzealous employee, I probably wouldn't have any idea about Dana's current whereabouts. And I still don't know the extent of the problem. Do you know why she had a business relationship with Grate Marketing?"

Frankie stared at me for a long moment before she shook her head. Her lack of a quick decision left me wondering why. I didn't consider it a particularly hard question.

"What about her current boost in income?" I asked.

"For what?"

I kept my eyes trained on the floor. The carpet appeared rather lovely, except for a small tear about a foot away from me. "I can only speculate, but I'm led to believe it's for services rendered."

"What kind of services?" she asked.

"My point exactly."

"Are you a detective, or an accountant?"

"Why can't I be both?" I asked.

Frankie tucked a strand of gray hair behind her left ear. She turned her chair at a slight angle away from me. Then she stood up, paced on her side of the desk, looked out the window long enough for me to begin to worry that our conversation might be through, and I might have a stack of boxes awaiting my imminent return. Before I decided to make a rather expeditious exit, she sat back down and turned toward me. Her smile turned devilishly close to wicked.

"What do you hope to prove?"

"I'm not here to prove anything," I said. "I just want to know what happened to my colleague. She deserves more than us pretending that she didn't even exist."

CHAPTER THIRTEEN

The room smiled back at me when I entered, and no boxes awaited me. My screensaver flashed in the background: a generic one with the company's logo that had been implanted on all the desktops. My mug of tea had reached room temperature, and my overhead light greeted me with a soft, quick blink. A whirring sound emitted from my desktop, a new feature that it had picked up in the last week or two, and that I had called the helpdesk twice on, both times a solution was rendered that proved to be only a temporary fix.

After I typed in my username and password, and after I scooted the red marked papers aside, I dug into Dana's background again, once again focusing on the money trail, since numbers never lied, and people sometimes did. After an hour or so of digging through the information online—another program I had obtained through Don through less than righteous means—I discovered she had lost everything at one point, but suddenly she was well again, and within only a few months of the previous loss. Her empty bank accounts suddenly had a generous cash infusion and the massive credit card debt had disappeared as well. This was around the time she had dropped out of college and when student loans offered the strongest sense of catastrophe, and there wasn't a job prospect in sight. I shivered at the thought, placed both hands firmly on the desk and scooted away.

Sipping my lukewarm tea, I pondered the current situation. Dana had a history with money, and not the good kind either, and she had a string of boyfriends, most of whom proved to have a less than scrupulous nature. Her taste in men hovered at the wrong extreme, along with her financial endeavors and spending sprees; she'd had more than one abortion; she hadn't risen higher than a secretary, even though she had shown evidence of wanting to work her way up the chain; her family was considered an outcast as far as my family was concerned; and she had taken money on the side from Victor Uglow, a character with a less than scrupulous nature as well. I didn't like it, and there wasn't much I could do about it, except continue to move in a forward motion.

Returning to my bleeding papers, I knocked out Cooper's changes in a couple of hours, along with anticipating another round of changes that might come my way, and upon completion, I set the stack aside, as a brief smile entered the equation.

~ ~ ~

After the workday, I'd made arrangements to meet with Elena Tearz, Dana's best friend at a tea room that served decent tea, along with a wide variety of finger foods, scones, and scrumptious desserts, or so I'd heard. Depending on the site, online reviews could be helpful, or not so helpful. The Medallion Tea Room had been given four stars by a reputable service, that I had previously used, and I had high hopes that my expectations and reality would meet.

The back right hand corner had been reserved for us: a room I had not entered before. The shades were drawn; the lights and loveseat were antique; the lamp was made of copper and steel; the shade was cream colored; and the accoutrements caused me to step back in time more than a half century. Paintings, also antiques, occupied two of the walls.

My companion awaited my arrival and smiled up at me when I

passed through the beaded curtain. The room smelled of black tea and ancient history, although the carpet remained plush. Linen napkins stood at attention on either side of the table embedded in a teacup that resembled fine china more than the mugs I had stuffed in my cupboard and pulled out when the opportunity presented itself. Inspirational messages occupied the tea service with what I could only assume were mixed results.

With the loveseat presently occupied, I chose the chair with the stiff back and thin arms. I offered my hand, and she clasped it in both of hers, her long, thin fingers draped over mine. The teapot didn't say hello, but then it didn't need to. I reached out to pour her a cup, but she waved me off. The motion passed quickly before my eyes. I filled my own cup and waited her out, staring at her with more than a hint of expectation.

"Do you really want to help Dana?" she asked.

I nodded.

"But you work for Wired Consulting?"

She wanted to see where my allegiances fell, and I couldn't blame her. If my best friend went missing, I had no idea how I would react. Cadence and I had our differences, but I couldn't imagine a world without her. And Cracker Barrel might never be the same again.

"I don't let one world encroach on the other," I said. "Maybe I found out about Dana for a reason; maybe I'm the one that can help bring her back." I didn't add about my relation to her; in fact, I hadn't told anyone. I figured it was safer that way.

"But you didn't even know her—"

I shook my head. "It doesn't matter," I said. "What matters is that I try to help her. Your friend may have swallowed a skunk covered in razorblades."

"Do you even know what you're doing?" She paused. "The police have started a file, as well as an investigation—"

"That has led nowhere," I said. "Tommy may not have Dana's best interests at heart. And, as far as I know, the investigation is not currently active."

"Are you referring to their relationship?"

I nodded. The teapot stared up at me with pleading eyes, and I seriously considered acquiescing to its request. The possibility of hope lingered, as I listened to the voices in the hallway and the room directly across from our own. A man and woman were filled with life, as well as volume, coupled with a hint of sarcasm. Her life resembled that of a hyena, while his was deep and more controlled.

She stared at me over her cup of tea—our server having poured her a cup—long enough for me to realize she had viewed more than just the wall behind me or my suit. Her eyes never left my face for long and had peered behind my defenses. My teacup rattled briefly, but I had the plate beneath it to catch any stray drips. She sat forward, and I leaned as far back as I could in my chair. She searched my face for more than just the hint of makeup.

After several minutes of absolute silence, her lips moved. "How much do you know about Tommy?"

"Tommy and I have a brief history, with strong emphasis on the word brief."

"Dana missed the signs of trouble. Instead of focusing on his many shortcomings, she thought the relationship might work. She ended it abruptly, and he's never forgiven her."

I asked, "What happened?"

She placed the plate with the cup of tea on the table between us. "He has a history of violent tendencies. Her naiveté almost led to hear demise."

"He tried to have her killed?" I asked.

"It's not that simple—"

"Nothing in life ever is," I said.

"While she was with Tommy, she had an abortion. She was young enough and stupid enough to think it might work. But I helped her see the error of her ways. She wasn't ready for a child, and she certainly couldn't handle the responsibility of raising one on her own."

I stared at the teapot between us. "How did the relationship end?"

"She broke it off. That's when Jerry came into her life and created a whole new set of problems." She sipped from her teacup and closed her eyes, in what I could only assume was pure bliss based on the slight smile that had encompassed her face. She left out Jerry, but I understood her concern.

One of Elena's teeth was slightly crooked, while two of her front ones were skewed in the same direction. I could sympathize. I had a tooth I wasn't happy with, and if I ever saved up enough money, I'd have it pulled and capped. I figured I was looking at around eight hundred bucks for the job, money that I currently didn't have.

"You're nothing like Tommy," Elena said. "I'm not sure what you saw in him."

I shrugged. "I have no idea," I said. "He does have a hint of charm, although it's very small and diminishes rapidly. I decided the best strategy was to exit stage left."

"Are you more concerned for her welfare or boosting your own reputation?"

"I have no reputation to boost," I said. "If I can make Tommy look bad, though, that's probably worth a couple of bonus points."

Elena sipped more tea. Her eyes were hard, and her lips were wet. Elena and I had reached a level of understanding about Tommy, even though much had been left unsaid. But if she told me she had sworn off all men, because there weren't any decent ones out there, I'd have probably tipped my seat over and my drink would have assumed a circular flight pattern. Fat chance of that happening—she wore a wedding band on the all-important finger, with a big, fat diamond to match. Her drink was more than half gone; her eyes leaned down instead of up. Her cream colored shirt buttoned up the front; her slacks were one size too big; her shoes had scuff marks on the sides; her hair was straighter than a blade of grass; and her eyes were the color of cinnamon sticks.

"You're filled with surprises," she said, "and you have more self-confidence than I ever possessed. What's your secret?"

"I worry more about numbers than I do relationships."

"You can't trust men," Elena said, "and on occasion, even women let you down. In both cases, they'll lead you astray every time." She paused, her cup near her lips, and took a tentative sip. "Maybe you're right about numbers."

I nodded toward her hand.

"I found the last good one out there," she said. "And if I ever lose him, I'll have to join a monastery and change my last name. Dana, on the other hand, had better ideas when it came to sex, and she wasn't afraid to use her charms to her advantage."

"You mean her relationship with Porter?"

"That's the one," Elena said. "When it came to career advancement, Dana slept her way to the top." She had neither a hint of remorse nor jealousy in her voice.

She excused herself, heading toward the powder room, as I pondered this new development, statistical probabilities about relationships notwithstanding.

Dana's status at Wired Consulting remained in the secretary arena, yet she had at least one source of additional income, and I hadn't ruled out the possibility of others. Despite Frankie's best efforts to prove otherwise, I didn't consider Dana's relationship with Frankie to be particularly healthy. It survived at the toleration level more than it did any other. Dana might not have a strong moral code, but I couldn't fault her for using whatever talents she might have had to her advantage. If I had more body than brains, I might have taken a similar path, but I liked to believe my strong sense of morality would win in the end.

I refilled my cup, and I clutched it in my hand, the heat providing another focus for my already troubled mind. Hearing only snippets of conversation, I withstood the temptation to piece together the rest of the puzzle from my next door neighbors. Instead, I focused on Dana, and my growing obsession with her. She had more problems in her life than I had realized.

"What happened with Jerry?" I asked.

"They had a big fight before she left. After Jerry found out about her relationship with Porter, he started tossing coffee mugs like they were Frisbees—he had a temper hotter than molten lava. And he wasn't a big fan of sharing, not that I could blame him. He had his arms wrapped around her neck before she kicked him in his nether regions. He doubled over in pain, and she bolted for the door. And I haven't heard from her since. That was almost two weeks ago. If she's still out there, she doesn't want to be found."

I nodded. Notes, as well as a few doodles, filled my notepad. I wrote almost as fast as Elena talked, but I was at least two or three words behind. "Why do you say 'if she's still out there'?" I asked. "Are you concerned she might have been killed?"

"She's gotten herself in more trouble than I could have ever hoped for her, and she's not real good at learning from her mistakes. Most of her worst ones she's repeated on more than one occasion. Her interests haven't revolved around change."

I added another note to the pad. "Maybe you're a lot stronger than she is."

"Maybe that's it." She paused. "Or maybe she doesn't know how to say no."

Had I lacked strength, I might have settled for a less strenuous hobby; instead, I developed a backbone, and showed wrong men the door, dragging them out by the shirt collar when necessary. I hadn't needed to resort to using my fists or my feet, but I hadn't entirely ruled out the possibility, should I deem it a necessary requirement of staying alive. If I couldn't execute what I learned in self-defense class, I'd end up in a whole heap of trouble rather quickly.

"You had the urge to tell me something more before," I said, "but you stopped rather than let the words leave your lips."

"How do you know—?"

"I have a talent for reading people," I said.

"But you're not a cop—"

I shook my head. "I prefer to deal with numbers: I'm an accountant."

"The two don't really fit together."

"It's as much a curse as it is a blessing." I didn't need to tell her about my need for balance and order. If given enough time, she could figure it out on her own.

Her teacup remained suspended in midair. She looked at it, and then she looked at me. Her eyes were heavy, hard, and filled with darkness. She sipped from her cup before placing it back on her saucer. "Dana's had more than one abortion."

I nodded gravely, my eyes fixated on a spot on the floor: a flaw in the carpet that no one had noticed. I lost the autofocus on my camera: Dana's picture remained blurry. Dana had a brother—who was an infrequent companion—the details of their falling out remained outside my peripheral vision. Dana was the younger of two children with her brother Oliver three years older than she was. She was originally from Morgantown, WV; she went to Robert Morris University, formerly Robert Morris College; and she'd had two more abortions than I had, with the second one involving a certain CEO of Wired Consulting. He, on the other hand, never learned the details of the mysterious baby, and as far as I knew, she had never used her unplanned pregnancy to exploit his money or his wealth, which went against everything that I had learned about Dana so far. Maybe she was afraid of him, or maybe she didn't want to waste a good opportunity to up the ante. But before she could execute her plan, she turned up missing, and so far, anyway, she still hadn't been found, despite my unique approach to her disappearance. Other than Norma Beemer and Elena Tearz, I might have been the only other person who wanted to see Dana return to Hampton, VA.

~ ~ ~

Cadence Surrender, my best friend since the third grade—ever since she punched me in the nose, and then proceeded to dust off my pants, fix my hair, and two days later beat up the boy who had been the source of our disagreement—viewed a no as only one letter shy of a yes. I, on the other hand, took a more reasonable approach to the concept of right and wrong. While she went through men the way most women disposed of shoes, she was an even more loyal friend than I was, and when necessary, she packed a mean right cross, jabbing better than the average sparring partner. Despite my newfound knowledge of self-defense, I had yet to take her up on her challenge inside the ring. I feared for her life as much as I feared for my own.

Her only weakness was men: Her radar often picked up guys who were only slightly above deadbeat status. And since she often fed me blind dates, the way a crack addict seeks out a pipe, she aided my subpar track record of the opposite sex. I couldn't hold her lack of knowledge against her, since she tried harder than most washing machines. She stopped at my apartment while I was in the process of changing. If she hadn't banged on the door and then raised her voice, I might have left her outside.

I opened the door just wide enough for her to enter before I slammed it rather abruptly, and possibly drawing the attention of my neighbors across the hall.

"I heard you might have a new man in your life," she said.

I slid the top I had been holding in my hand over my head. I'd been told on more than one occasion that it matched my eyes. "Where did you hear that?"

"My ears are more fine-tuned than yours are. You might want to work a little harder at keeping secrets."

She had on Nike jogging pants, a black headband, three-inch heels, and a tube top. She'd thrown a light jacket, with the zipper halfway down, over the tube top.

I asked, "Do you mind telling me where you get your fashion sense?"

She smirked. "I have more sense than you do. Is this new man's name Ben?"

"I think you need to reveal your sources," I said. So I could squelch the gossip mill once and for all.

"I happen to have journalistic integrity."

"You don't even write in a journal." I, however, kept a journal outlining my various dates, as I focused on their shortfalls more than their strengths. If nothing else, it might make for a good comedy routine someday, should I ever get over my stage fright.

"You're not going to hold that against me, are you?"

I shook my head.

"We need to work on your independence," she said. Cadence didn't believe anyone was really independent, and she didn't do a very good job of hiding this. In fact, she couldn't have found restraint in the dictionary, even if I pointed her to the right page. But she did trust me implicitly, and I trusted her, except when it came to her advice on men. And when she tried to tell me I wasn't independent, I tried to tell her nicely that she was full of crap. The smile helped.

Showing more restraint than usual, I bit my tongue and smiled, in that order.

"One of these days, you'll see the error of your ways," she said, "or you'll become the cat lady, and you'll end up short a few good cats."

"I happen to enjoy cats," I said, "but I don't plan on having any of my own." Once one appeared, there was a good chance for two or three, and then it ended up being ridiculous.

"Does this man in your life have a name?"

"Ben Xander," I said. "He's more like a former high school acquaintance that managed to get reacquainted with me rather than a new possibility for my future. Without his help, I'd have no idea what to do about Dana."

"You have to start somewhere," Cadence said. "And for once in your life, you might end up starting at the front of the line, instead of the back."

CHAPTER FOURTEEN

The punch struck me on the nose, pushing cartilage back against my face. The air surrounding me became heavy, and I shook my head to eliminate the dull ringing in my ears. I thrust my hands out, and stepped back from the next ensuing blow. I struck out with my left foot, and felt only dead air, the sense of heaviness hanging between us. I danced to the left, the shin guard sliding down my leg, as my opponent danced to the right. I twisted to the right, and my opponent twisted left. Cheers filled the otherwise quiet background before the silence proved deafening. The mat was blue and heavy beneath my feet. I'd disposed of my shoes, and I wore a pair of loose fitting jogging pants of the Nike variety. Mine were black with a single white stripe down each leg. My top was breathable, loose fitting, and made of a moisture whisking material. It was damp with perspiration. I'd pulled my hair back from my face in a severe ponytail, but several strands had come loose through the various bouts of sparring. I swiped at a strand of hair as well as a bead of sweat above my right eye. The instructor placed two fingers in his mouth and whistled, signaling the end of the match. I held out my hand, and my opponent shook it, shaking his head as he did so.

As I walked off the mat, the heavy air lightened around me.

The wooden bench proved sturdy beneath me; a water bottle soothed my otherwise parched lips. The place next to me was empty, but it didn't remain empty for long.

"Do you always have that fire in your eyes?" he asked.

"Only when I have my sights set on the right prize. Winning certainly isn't everything, but it does prove rather invigorating just the same."

"You have a knack for sparring with men much larger than yourself."

"I don't have much choice in the matter," I said. "Most people are larger than I am. I can either choose to be quick and use my small stature to my advantage, or I can end up face down on the mat."

"That's happened to you before?" Ben Xander asked.

"On more than one occasion," I said. "It's definitely not something I want to repeat, though." I ended up splayed on the mat, and my opponent had placed his hand on the side of my neck to check for a pulse. Heat had rushed to my face, and I vowed never to end up in the same position again. So far, my vow had worked.

"You won't always have a shin guard to protect you."

"A can of pepper spray works as well," I said. I swiped a loose strand of hair out of my eyes, turned my head away from his gaze, and took another long drink of water.

"Are you packing?"

"Only when it's required." My pepper spray hovered in my purse, and my purse was inside my locker, along with a change of clothes.

"How often do you find yourself in precarious situations?"

I'd never kept an exact count, but even as an accountant I'd managed to end up in a situation or two where I wasn't the one holding the largest weapon. "Not very often," I said. "But there's always the chance that I might discover a suitable moment or two in the near future."

He placed his own water bottle to his lips and tilted his head back. He'd sparred with an opponent his size, and he'd landed more blows than the opposition. He also moved quicker than I anticipated. He was almost as quick as I was. Almost.

Ben asked, "You don't go looking for those moments, do you?"

I shook my head. "But I don't plan to shy away from them either." I decided not to focus on my night ventures, when at least half a dozen individuals—most of whom probably didn't understand the art of discretion—could overhear every word out of my mouth. I didn't particularly like the concept of a jail cell with my name on it either. And I'd already had more than one encounter with my overzealous boss.

"Do you have your tool belt handy?"

"I wouldn't know what you're talking about."

"It's only a matter of time before Grate Marketing discovers you," Ben said. "You might want to work on your stealth abilities if you hope to become a career criminal." He smirked for an instant before his face returned to normal.

"I've already had two conversations with my boss Cooper Strut." Even though he might have already discovered them, I spared him the details.

"He sounds like a horse."

"There are probably times when he fulfills his name requirements," I said.

Cooper walked with a slight limp, favoring his right leg. Supposedly, he fell off of a horse when he was seventeen, broke his leg in two places, and had walked with a limp ever since. He had a penchant for telling stories, but I'd heard nothing to contradict his tale.

"Maybe you should work on a new game plan," he said.

"I don't have a particular one in mind." I paused. "What I do have is a set of circumstances that I can't rightly ignore and then continue to live with myself. But I seem to be one of the few folks who want Dana Wilson found. Even Tommy appears to have his own agenda." I'd already had one visit from Officer Buchs, and I wouldn't have been surprised if I had another one in my future. The second one probably held even less promise than the first.

"You can add me to your camp. I've found normal situations

sometimes reach abnormal limits. You might want to prepare yourself for a bit of jetlag."

"Tommy Buchs—"

"—doesn't know how to deal with a certain type of female," he said. "For the moment, that's an asset you possess, but if you're not careful, it could become a liability. Tommy doesn't know how to deal with smart women."

I nodded. Most of the class had dispersed, including our instructor, yet I found Ben's company intriguing and slightly off-putting.

He placed a hand on my shoulder. "You do eat on a regular basis, don't you?"

"What did you have in mind?" I asked.

"Nothing fancy." His eyes flicked off of mine.

"I don't need fancy."

Bub's Bar & Grille had a flashing neon sign of a mostly clothed woman, and there were more motorcycles and pickup trucks than pacemakers splattered across the parking lot, most of which needed either a car wash or a paint job, and in some cases, both. Based on the parking lot alone, the thought of a shower entered my horizon and wouldn't let go. On second thought, two showers might be in order, and I might need to make use of the community garden hose.

"While fancy may have completely left your radar, I didn't mean you could offer up the possibility of hepatitis. If I want to die, it'd be easier to walk in front of a bus."

"Seriously, Blondie, you need to get out more. Bub's has the best bar food in town."

"Well, at least I know where all the road kill ends up."

He tapped my shoulder. "You're such a sweet talker."

Upon entering the bar, I tried not to inhale. But the thought of passing out concerned me more than lung contamination. The cigarettes and cigars assaulted my nostrils worse than an old man who had bathed in a mountain of cheap cologne, and in two minutes I received more leers than walking through a construction site. Trying not to pay too much attention, otherwise I might risk short-circuiting my brain, I decided to implement my stern look and considered impaling any man within a three-table radius who decided to linger too long in my direction. In desperate need of a ball cap, I placed both elbows on the table and bowed my head.

"Are you all right?" Ben asked.

"Claustrophobic moment. It'll pass."

"You really do help redefine the term weird. If I thought you were joking, I'd laugh."

"If you start to laugh, I'll march out of here and take a cab home."

"It's really not that bad."

"Of course," I said, "they're not staring at you."

He shook his head. "You're paranoid. Maybe your brain needs a reboot."

I glared at him, before turning my attention back to the menu. It was thick enough that I could drop it off the third floor of my apartment complex and knock out an unsuspecting resident. The menu was several pages long and over half of those pages were devoted to the art of inebriation, an art of which I had decided it was better not to partake. The food appeared simple and slightly questionable but appeared edible upon initial inspection. A throbbing appeared in both elbows based on the fact that I'd placed my full weight behind my leaning, and I continued to scan the menu, even though I had already decided on a course of action.

"Are you sure it's safe to eat here?" I asked.

"You really don't get out much, do you?"

"Is that a question, or are you making fun of me?"

"Making fun of you is too easy. Maybe I need to find a new line of work." He paused. "If you take deep breaths, you can probably avoid a panic attack."

"It's the smoke," I said. "I think it's singeing my eyebrows. I recently had them waxed."

The table leaned a little to the left, and most of the patrons leaned a little to the right. Bub's was more than half-full with two-thirds of the population of the male persuasion, and half of those either wore cowboy hats or appeared as though a cowboy hat was on the horizon. The tables were a mismatch of colors, and fishing gear peppered the walls, a few of which happened to be photos of men holding fish, one of whom might have been Bub. All it needed was a strobe light and a pole.

A waiter with slicked back hair and possibly missing a tooth presented himself—he resembled a previous date that had not gone well, except he was a bit on the young side, although that could have been fabricated as well. Ben ordered the chicken; I ordered a burger well-done with a side of sweet potato fries. A well-done burger limited the possibility of whatever E. coli might have appeared on the scene and in the kitchen.

When my burger came I devoured it with as much enthusiasm as a chocolate cupcake with sprinkles, and I slaughtered the sweet potato fries.

"Did you skip breakfast...and lunch?" Ben asked.

I shook my head. "I don't like the taste of smoke with my burger."

~ ~ ~

After Ben and I said our goodbyes, a handshake once again sealing the deal, I decided to return to the scene of the crime. In this case, Grate Marketing proved more intriguing than another office visit with my boss, who had more than enough ammunition to show me the front door and the shade-wearing security guards. The front doors proved less intrusive this time, and my fingers danced nimbly through the locks. I managed to select the right picks on my first attempt, and I didn't need nearly as many tries as I had the first time to end up on the other side of the glass doors. Images of dinner, half of which involved smoke inhalation, filled my mind, even as I did my best to concentrate. Knowing my tendency to daydream wasn't one of my better habits, I focused on the mistakes of last time, not wanting to make the same ones. Before I stepped through the threshold, I peered in the glass doors once the lock had slipped cleanly away. The tinted windows blocked most of my view, although squinting helped my eyesight considerably, as I made out a hint of the blackness beyond. My right hand shook with anticipation, and I popped a Jolly Rancher in my mouth to dull my nerves, flavor bursting inside my mouth as clear as a spring rain. Sugar rushed toward my brain; I closed the door swiftly behind me, flipping my hood up as I walked. Security cameras didn't monitor the outside—I didn't know why—but there were plenty of them inside the building, scanning at random intervals, picking up every trace of the dark hood that covered my face, and what I hoped wasn't a clear view of my features. Since I learned the layout last time, I didn't bother to look up, even as I had avoided doing so before, knowing red lights and small, dark lenses watched my every move.

The security desk remained a fraction of what it was during the day—both seats remained empty—and quiet provided my only sense of refuge, as dull clicks followed my right of passage. Still not knowing how I had tripped the silent alarm before, I remained on amber alert, my heart slamming against my chest like a dumbbell being slammed back into place on the rack at the local gym.

Deciding to try something new, I chose the elevator on the left, and once again punched the eighth-floor button. The doors closed swiftly and silently, and an automated voice announced the floors without the slightest hint of an accent. I stared down at the floor, checking out my black shoes against the blue tile. Knowing this elevator was like the other one, I kept my eyes in a downward fashion. Two cameras watched my every move, although I didn't have many moves to watch. The rapid ascent was quicker than I expected, or remembered, but it remained unpleasant at best. More dull clicks filled the small space, none of which came from me.

I picked the lock of the glass doors in front of me in sixty-five seconds, the door shutting and locking behind me. I attacked the large wooden desk with abandon and precision, knowing the trophy case filled with first edition novels, debut albums, and Hot Wheels miniatures wouldn't help me find a missing woman who, at the moment, might as well have been on the moon and taken the last available spacecraft along with her.

The doors of Victor Uglow's desk were all locked. Using a handful of smaller picks, I picked each lock and discovered the contents of his desk one drawer at a time. On the monitor to my right, a red light blinked, and I shoved myself inside the empty hollow, yanking the chair in swiftly behind me. Two minutes later a pair of voices filled the secretary's office outside, and I swallowed hard, trying to avoid lodging the sticky candy down my windpipe. I succeeded. The cherry candy kept me company in an otherwise pristine office filled with a hint of lemon and a strong dose of masculinity. Had I been able to peer over the desk, the hard lines, severe angles, and overabundance of leather would have been my first clues.

The door burst open, and I heard two voices: both male. The men discussed football the way women might discuss old boyfriends or newborns or fashion magazines.

"Do you really think the Steelers can take down the Patriots this year?" the first one asked.

I wanted to stand up and shout yes, possibly hitting my head on the thick wood just inches away from my cranium. I passed on the opportunity.

"The Jets haven't done well recently," the other said, "but I have a feeling they might be due as well. Mark Sanchez manages to make just enough plays when he needs to."

"He doesn't have the playoff mentality exhibited by Big Ben or Tom Brady."

"Don't rule out Joe Flacco either."

"What about Matt Ryan?" the first one asked.

I heard a pregnant pause in the conversation, as I listened intently, the Jolly Rancher jammed up against my cleft palate, my breathing and heart rate both inching forward in short bursts the way a turtle might move across a lost highway.

"You think we're looking at another false alarm?" the first one asked.

"Why not?" the other said. "The system hasn't acted right the past few days."

"You shouldn't leave the Bears out of the equation either."

"Jay Cutler isn't exactly a playoff tested quarterback," the other said. "Besides, he burned down a whole neighborhood on his way out the door in Denver. You don't mess with karma, unless you want to end up in a full body cast on the side of the road waiting on an ambulance in the middle of a snowstorm."

When the enemy lines had abated, I grabbed a handful of files, marched to the photocopier, rapidly scanned the text before copying what appeared to be the more interesting ones, returned the files to their proper location, and then hustled down the stairs. I didn't bother to wait on the elevator.

~ ~ ~

The next morning came earlier than I anticipated. I combed through the files the night before, and with the files I had pulled previously, I started to gather a rather interesting story about Victor Uglow. He had started his business with nothing more than a song and a prayer, and twice he'd avoided bankruptcy, but only narrowly; he had a secretary on his payroll who made twice the going rate; he had a shell corporation in Indonesia that was responsible for a large majority of Grate Marketing's profits; he owned an island off the Mexican coast; and he had three state representatives in his pocket, one of whom had narrowly avoided a political scandal with a suspect intern last year.

He also had my face on video, albeit slightly covered, and he had two goons special-ordered to my office. Neither was much taller than I was. One of the two was quite a bit wider, while the other could have passed for a totem pole. The wider one Preston Konter had pale lips and pale skin, while Oscar Labarge had the darker skin of a lifetime recipient to the tanning bed who didn't want to miss too many opportunities under the artificial light. After introductions—theirs not mine—the conversation plunged downhill faster than an adrenaline junkie on a snowboard, and I wasn't sure how to navigate the rough terrain. I'd only been yelled at by my mother, sister, and a one-date wonder with Tourette's syndrome.

"We have your face on video," Oscar said. "What do you have to say for yourself?"

I nodded gravely and shuffled my mountain of paperwork. "Are you going to press charges?" I asked.

"Victor hasn't decided yet," Preston said. He tried to stand even taller: It didn't work.

I nodded again and shuffled more papers. "Are you sure it's me?"

"What's left to interpret?" Oscar asked.

"I do have a common face," I said, "and I've been told that particular security system has been prone to error. Should I point out its specific flaws?"

"How would you know?"

"I looked it up on the Internet. I have a propensity for research."

"So we've noticed—"

"We'd appreciate it if you didn't break into our complex anymore." Preston hitched up his pants, which didn't happen to be falling down at the moment. "If you want us to get the cops involved, we will, but it's a situation and a nuisance that we'd just as soon avoid."

"Am I exposing your security vulnerabilities?" I probably had more than a few vulnerabilities of my own, since I'd received visits from two sets of prying eyes on each of my visits to Grate Marketing, and I had no idea how I'd been exposed so quickly. I needed to fine-tune my breaking and entering skills, and I could use a better disguise. One that didn't have trouble written on the front and back.

"You really do need some help," I said. "I was just an amateur at this a few days ago." I still was, but I didn't need to make it too obvious.

"Maybe, maybe not," Oscar said. "But now you consider yourself something of an expert. If your hooded façade ends up in the next highlight reel, you'll see how high our connections go."

"I'm smarter than I was just a few days ago—"

Preston stared at me, hard. "What do you want from us?"

"I planned on asking you the same question," I said. "I know you didn't just come here to make idol threats and read me the riot act. I'm sure you have a higher purpose." I opened my hands a few inches and tried an open-ended look with my eyebrows slightly raised and my head held high. The manner and fashion with which I pulled off this gesture might have given me an additional opportunity or two.

"If you like the prospect of jail, maybe you should keep it up."

"How do you even know it was me on camera?" I asked. "You don't have a clear picture, do you?"

"Are you trying to bluff your way out of this?" Preston asked. Of the two, he had a harder time with basic concepts and lacked a reasonable amount of intelligence. But he hitched his pants up when he needed an additional boost to his authority. He'd already done it twice. If I thought it might help, I would have pointed this out.

"I'd like to know what's really going on," I said, "and I have a stack of files that proves somewhat suspicious activity." I paused. "I've even managed to read most of them, and it's not light reading." I tapped the only stack of papers within my immediate vicinity.

"So you're admitting that it was you?"

"I'll admit no such thing," I said. "The files could have just shown up on my desk. I have connections as well, and not just at the local department stores."

"And I'm a Christmas bell just waiting to be rung," Preston said.

"I might be able to track down a large mallet." For emphasis, I took an imaginary swing.

"I heard you carry pepper spray in your purse," Oscar said. "What else have you got in there? It's larger than your garden-variety contraption."

"I'm not at liberty to say," I said. "Besides, how would you know about my canister?"

"We have X-ray machines."

I offered another eyebrow raise. "How do I know you're not bluffing?"

Preston asked, "Would you like me to recite the color of your underwear?"

"No, I most definitely would not." My face flushed bright red, and I gnawed on the Jolly Rancher that had only moments ago been jammed against my right cheek. I sat on the other side of my desk, my view obstructed by a Christmas ham and his remains, the unpleasantness most likely leaking through the gap in my office door. I had a two-headed snake that wouldn't hit the ground with a single squirt of pepper spray. I felt about as free as a caged bird with my ankle strapped to a twig. My right hand developed a slight twitch.

"Are you threatening me?" I asked.

Oscar stared at a spot just above my head. "We're asking you to cease and desist—"

"—all present activity," Preston said.

"Or at least the breaking and entering part." Oscar scratched his head. "Mr. Uglow isn't particularly happy that you've stolen several of his files."

"I only have copies," I said.

"Copies can be just as dangerous if placed in the wrong hands."

"Do you think I'd resort to blackmail?"

"It wouldn't be the first time."

My mind immediately leapt to Dana Wilson, but I didn't know if my mind had made the right leap, only that it seemed like a good one based on the present situation.

"Accountants often don't get mixed up in this much trouble," I said.

"Let's hope it stays that way."

CHAPTER FIFTEEN

"What are you doing here?" the burly cop asked. His blue shirt said Thomas: I didn't know if that was his first name or his last. He towered over me by several inches, with a scar above his right eye, a long neck, and a crew cut. His neck was thicker than my bicep, and possibly even my right thigh.

"I heard this might be a crime scene."

He placed a hand out in front of his body inches away from my chest. "Where do you get your information?"

"I have my sources," I said.

Actually Ben Xander had called me when the crime scene techs were done processing the body and the area, and before the dead had been moved away. It was a cursory call, followed by a long silence on my end, but I had taken it to be anything but cursory. I stood on the other side of the crime scene tape with a blue raspberry Jolly Rancher in my mouth and a stern look on my face. Trees were behind me, and on either side of me, filled with green leaves and protruding bark, as a dog paced in the distance and a herd of mosquitoes fluttered overhead. I stood at the edge of a clearing in a secluded area where foot traffic came at a premium. The situation, however, had anything but cleared my head. I stood on my tiptoes—still several inches shorter than my counterpart—and I caught a glimpse of the body. Despite my distance, the stench pumped its way inside my nostrils and into my mouth faster than a septic tank. I bent over, doing battle with a series of dry heaves, and possibly a bout of the hiccups. The dry heaves won the first round; the hiccups came in a close second.

When I stood up, the burly cop looked at me, scrunched up his nose, and shook his head—more than once actually before the moment passed, and his eyebrows reached a state of normalcy. The image of the dead, however, stuck with me: legs splayed, naked below the waist, hands crisscrossed across her chest, and a small scar across her right cheek. One leg was bent underneath the body, while the other was splayed out at an unusual angle, much too unusual, even for someone who might have been known for her dexterity, who could have passed for a former dancer. Ben didn't tell me her name on the phone—I wondered if it was Dana, if the situation had suddenly reached an obscene level of seriousness, and if I'd play catch without the aid of a proper mitt.

I bent over at the waist again, stared at a blade of grass, and hiccupped. A white haze clouded my judgment, my legs shook, and my right hand began to flex and loosen at unforeseen intervals. I swallowed the remains of the first Jolly Rancher, pulled another from my pocket, opened the wrapper, and dropped the candy in the dirt. I pulled another one from my pocket, separated the cellophane wrapper from the sticky candy, and popped it in my mouth. My right hand completed one tremor as I finalized the action. The apple flavor helped bring me back to reality, and I lifted my head slowly. The white light ceased to exist, and calmness set in.

"Who died?" I asked. My voice sounded louder in my head.

"Are you press?"

I shook my head. "Ben...Officer Xander called me."

"What are you then?"

I shook my head to remove the sand from my brain. "I'm an accountant."

Thomas smirked. "I don't think she's going to need any help with her taxes."

I nodded, too numb to utter another word. The stars were back, brighter than ever, and filled with nearly as much life as before. Only this time my legs finally did give way. I walked toward the light not knowing where it would take me, but knowing it was a place I probably wanted to go.

~ ~ ~

The first slap jerked me away from the light; the second slap caused my eyes to flutter. "What's going on?" I asked.

"You passed out."

I opened my eyes wide, before they closed again. "Who are you?"

"Ben."

I squinted up at a man with curly brown hair and a kind face. "Oh," I said.

"What are you doing here?"

I lifted my head: It fell back down on its own. "You called me, remember?"

"I didn't actually expect you to show up."

"I had an opening in my schedule."

I was on my back, peering up at a man who hovered over me. He was taller than I was; he had the hint of light stubble on his face; and I could see the creases in his blue uniform, even though a few wrinkles started to show through.

"How long was I out?"

"Only a few minutes," he said. He rubbed his chin, his expression uneasy, and then shook his head.

"My cheek hurts."

"Sorry," he said. "The smelling salt didn't work, so I had to resort to other methods."

"You didn't try CPR, did you?"

"You were breathing steadily enough, although rather lightly, and your eyelids moved rapidly enough, indicating you were in some sort of dream—"

"So that would be no?"

"Most definitely."

"Is the body who I think it is?" I asked. "Or does this nightmare have an expiration date?"

He nodded. "Dana Wilson entered the land of the dead a few days ago. The ME still hasn't pinpointed an exact time of death. If you have any expertise in this area, you might want to speak now."

"Who killed her?"

"We didn't find a business card next to the body," Ben said, "but I have my suspicions as I'm sure you do as well."

"Oh." I lifted myself off the ground: It took a hand around my waist to complete the job.

"But we'll keep looking. You really need to trust those in a position of authority."

I thought I did rather well in the trust department. I just didn't trust men named Tommy who gave me acid reflux. "Where's Tommy Buchs?"

"I have no idea."

Having forgotten about my head, and the Jolly Rancher currently bringing a warm feeling over my body, my eyes darted across my field of vision. "He isn't going to show up, is he?"

"If he does, should I introduce you?"

I closed my eyes. "Is that your idea of a joke?"

"Maybe the start of one," he said. "You have to take the opportunities when they present themselves, otherwise a series of Lamborghinis will pass you by."

"Don't hone in on any standup comedy in the near future." I paused. "How did she die?" I wasn't sure I wanted to know, but not knowing was just as bad. I could write a book on the burden of knowledge. Numbers proved easier: They caused fewer problems.

"She was strangled with a pair of women's pantyhose, and the body was dropped here."

I stood up and wiped the last remnants of dirt off my slacks. "How do you know?"

"A set of tire tracks next to the body; she's missing one shoe—not currently in the vicinity of the body—and there are trace fibers of the nylon fabric around her neck. Plus, the stocking ripped, and she has a small piece of it clutched between two of her fingers."

"You mean the killer missed it?" I asked.

"Maybe he had other priorities."

"So now I'm looking at a homicide?" This didn't sound any better than a missing person. Either way I was out of my element and severely overmatched. If my current situation was a sparring partner, he'd most likely resemble a brick wall.

"You're definitely in over your head," Ben said.

"That's not the first time I've heard that." And I had a feeling it wouldn't be the last time either. Dana might have had a similar reaction as well, before her expiration date came due.

~ ~ ~

I walked out of the clearing of my own accord, minus the mosquitoes, my feet and mind dragging, and moving at different speeds. I'd never been hit by a bus before, but I imagined this was what it felt like. I'd never been in a car accident either, although I'd come close more than once. In the end, luck had saved me: I didn't know if it would save me this time as well.

When I reached my car, started the engine, and merged onto the blacktop, I popped in Carrie Underwood's sophomore effort: *Carnival Ride*. "Flat On The Floor" blared through the speakers, as my mind blared through a compounded effort of possibilities, the mathematical equation currently out of my realm of expertise. I had several individuals who might have wanted Dana Wilson to meet an early demise: Victor Uglow, who had avoided bankruptcy twice through the help of two corporations not based in the US; Frankie Kensington, who had lied to me on more than occasion, and I still didn't know exactly why; Jerry Duncan, who had reason to hold a grudge against Dana after being abandoned and forgotten by her; Tommy Buchs, who had investigated Dana's disappearance and had concealed rather important details about his relationship with her; Porter Reede, who I'd heard may have had a relationship with Dana, and that was why she may have been promoted to her current position; and those were only the relationships I knew about. I also heard she may have enjoyed women as well as men, but I wasn't sure how that insight would help me given the fact that I hadn't yet discovered her killer, and I couldn't accurately account for random data factors at the present time. Other than Ben, I wasn't sure the police enjoyed having me on the investigative team, especially since I'd passed out in the dirt with a Jolly Rancher stuck to my cheek. Imagining how my hair and my clothes must have looked only increased the embarrassment factor.

I concentrated on the road rather than have my head expand to the size of a ten pound sack of sweet potatoes. The road, as it turned out, took me to Dana's parent's house in a noisy neighborhood just off the main road in the heart of a bevy of activity, mostly of the little kid variety, and most of whom required adult supervision. A whiffle ball struck my windshield; I pushed the brake pedal; and a split-second later, a boy with a curly mop of red hair darted in front of my car, grabbed the ball, held it high over his head, and ran screaming—loud enough to be heard in the next county—back to his fellow partners-in-crime. I found the house I needed—with blue shutters, a pitched roof, and a bright yellow garage door—eased to the curb, exited my vehicle, and hit the clicker to lock all my doors. I hit the clicker again for emergency purposes.

I arrived at the residence of Dana's parents, pushed the doorbell, stepped back, and stared at the wooden monstrosity in front of me, a screen door separating me from my immediate competition.

The door was opened by a small woman with a small haircut, a large pair of bifocals, and a cream colored outfit that complemented her hair and the spectacles. One might even go so far as to call it fashionable. She had a kind expression and not much else behind it. A TV blared on high in the background.

"Have the police already stopped by?" I asked.

She nodded, as tears rolled down her cheeks. I reached out to touch her before I pulled my hand away, midway between the void.

"You're not one of them?" she asked.

"I'm an accountant." I told her my name. I didn't hold out my hand, and she didn't offer hers. I stood there and waited, while she used a tissue to dab her eyes.

"Then what are you doing here?"

"I work with your daughter," I said. "If I can, I'd like to help her."

Her eyes softened. Maybe because of the tears, maybe not. "Did you know her well?"

"Not well at all, really." I wasn't on a first name basis with many of the folks in the office, and I'd spent more time with Cooper the past few days than I spent with him in a month. His curiosity reached a rather excruciating level, and I had done nothing to aid its demise.

"Then why are you here?"

"Who's at the door?" a man asked. "It's not those damn Jehovah's Witnesses again, is it?" The TV didn't click off, and I didn't hear any feet shuffling, so I assumed he was more interested in the TV than what I had to say. Other than the TV and his yelling, calmness filled the air, except for a few more sporadic tears.

Sally ignored her husband.

"Because her disappearance disturbed me," I said, "and the more I started digging the more I realized this might not have been a simple crime. And that was before the body turned up. Besides, I don't think the investigation is being handled properly." I decided to skip most of the details as this would only worry her more. If she asked, I could probably get by with skimming the surface and leaving the giant iceberg beneath the cold water.

"Did you see her?" she asked. "We've been asked to identify the body, but I'm not sure I can bear to look at my daughter in a sterile room on a cold metal table with a plastic sleeping bag unzipped before me like there's some sort of prize inside."

"Yes," I said. "And then I passed out." I left out the bit about being slapped around and a Jolly Rancher sucked to half its size stuck to my right cheek.

The tears flowed faster. "Was Dana mutilated? Was there blood everywhere?"

"No," I said. "She looked peaceful like she had lain down in a field and listened for the sound of crickets." The lie, while it comforted her, upset me more than I realized. Maybe I needed to remove myself from any part of this investigation before it was too late. This woman deserved the truth, and I still wasn't sure I could give it to her. If I couldn't, I didn't know how I would live with myself.

"But you were a ways off."

I said, "I was closer than you might think."

"How did she die?"

"You weren't told the specifics?" Her head shook; the glasses danced a jig on her nose. "Do you really want to know?" She shook her head again. Then nodded. I paused, deciding how much I should reveal to a woman who had just lost her only child. "Your daughter has some irregularities in her financial records."

She closed the door and stood on the porch rubbing her arms. She had two chairs, but she made no movement to either one. "You mean the unusual payments?"

"You knew about them?" I asked.

"We knew she had some dirt on Victor Uglow, but we didn't know the specifics. Do you know the details?"

"And you approved of it?"

Sally bit her lower lip before she tugged at her blouse. "She was headstrong and fancy-free. She never listened to us, and we weren't about to change her despite our best efforts to do so. In the end, it was probably for the best." She had another tissue on standby.

I didn't think she meant her death. "Why?"

"She needed to learn the ways of the world." Her eyes, however, told a different story.

"Do you honestly believe she now has?"

"Maybe, maybe not," she said. "She had a problem committing to just one man. With guys, it's called a sex addiction; with women, it's another matter entirely. All she wanted was for someone to love her." She dabbed her tissue at her red eyes. "I couldn't provide her everything she needed, and neither could my husband. As much as he loved her, he didn't know how to handle her, and in the end, I didn't either."

"It could have been a crime of passion."

She glided toward one of the chairs and sat down; I commandeered the other one, although my legs weren't nearly as shaky as hers were. "That doesn't make it any less of a crime, now does it?"

"Just what are you suggesting?" I asked. With the door closed, the TV was less of a distraction, but that made her words more powerful. I acknowledged the wind, but I chose to ignore it.

"That my daughter deserved better than this." Her eyes grew hard, firm, and filled with life. If she had a gun in her hand, instead of a tissue, I might have jumped out of my chair.

"How do you know what fate had in store for her?"

"She was strangled, wasn't she?"

"How did you know?"

"When you mentioned the crime of passion bit. Besides, a mother always knows. Someday you might want to ask your mother about it." She paused. I heard the children playing, although I'd missed it before. "She liked to have her windpipe blocked during sex. It intensifies the orgasm." She gritted her teeth as she said this last comment, as though she hadn't approved of it, yet she felt it should be mentioned all the same.

"She told you this?"

"I might have overheard a conversation."

When she didn't elaborate further, I didn't press her on the explicit details. "Were you aware of your daughter's sexual habits?"

"You mean her penchant for male partners as well as female ones. That's not exactly a secret. Dana remained open to the end, and I didn't judge her." She rubbed her forehead with the hand not holding the tissue. "What I did do, though, was offer her unconditional acceptance with the hope that this might improve her self-esteem and her character."

I nodded, the silence nearly deafening between us.

"Do you honestly know what you're doing?"

"For this?" I asked. "I'm just making it up as I go along."

~ ~ ~

I left her sitting on the porch, her hands clasped on her knees. The sound of kids playing filled in the otherwise silent moments. I had no idea how to handle a misguided daughter, so I wasn't going to judge her. The thought of kids still startled me awake in my sleep, and I had never bothered to buy a parenting book let alone read one on accident.

I started my car and headed out the way I had come, hoping I could avoid any misguided children, although I managed to notice a few, with some being more misguided than others.

When I made it back to work—after having been out most of the afternoon—an eerie silence welcomed my return. My door was locked, even though I hadn't bothered to lock it during my rapid exit. Files had been shifted on my desk, and my garbage can had been tipped over: a trail of papers, empty cartons, cellophane wrappers, and dried fruit surrounded my desk like water under a bridge. Rather than focus on the cleanup, I decided to make a phone call before I changed my mind.

"I need to find out about Dana Wilson's female partners."

"You mean she was bi?" he asked. His high-pitched voice filled the receiver.

"You're enjoying this, aren't you?"

I heard the smile in his voice, as well as the sound of keys clicking rapidly. "I never know what research project you'll need next. I have to admit this one is near the top of my list of fantasies. If it's juicy, I'm reading the whole file, even if you try to tell me it's confidential."

"Why?"

"Guys have certain dreams that fill our otherwise dull existences," Don said, "and this would certainly be one of them. I may throw in her three-ways just for free."

"Why do I sense that your level of enjoyment has reached an optimum target?"

More keys clicked. "It probably has," he said. "This is better than PvP."

I didn't bother to ask what the term meant. He'd told me before, but I hadn't considered it a detail worth remembering. "Just make sure you keep this information to yourself. I don't want it to end up on your blog."

"I gave that up over a year ago," he said. "You really do need to get out more often."

CHAPTER SIXTEEN

Out of all the guys I've dated—and I've dated more than a few—two have ended up in the slammer, one of which I helped hand over the keys to the arresting officer, after he broke two restraining orders and tried to break my nose. When I testified against him in open court, he didn't even look in my direction: He just stared at a notepad, doodling and probably drawing dead bodies, with mine hanging from the rafters. He spent a month in jail, was released for good behavior, and he's left me alone ever since. But it doesn't mean I've ever stopped thinking about him, or his innate ability to show up at the most unexpected of moments and cause the maximum amount of carnage. When it comes to boyfriend material, he sets the bar at an all-time low, although a few others have come close, and I've had more than a few honorable mentions.

Between Porter, Jerry, Tommy, and Frankie, I couldn't decide who deserved the medal and who deserved honorable mention. When it comes to women, the surprises reach maximum intensity, and no two women act alike. But the acting had reached Broadway level, and I had more than enough information to process, much of which couldn't be eliminated, until I learned more about Dana Wilson, even though now I had to complete the task from the other side of her grave, although I hadn't lost my abilities, or my penchant for picking partners. While I had the perspective of accounting records and bits of truth mixed in with outright lies, I didn't have enough of a handle on her death to close the file without placing a series of asterisks or question marks at the end. Tommy would have enjoyed watching the circus tent unfold.

Tommy Buchs stood with his left shoulder against my door, one hand tucked inside his trousers, and the other tucked in his pocket. I didn't ask about the hand in his trousers, and he didn't offer up any explanations. He'd stopped by less than five minutes after I'd reached my desk, and so far, the sneer hadn't bothered to leave my line of sight. But he did keep the door from falling over, and his stern expression added a certain amount of harshness to the décor.

"You stepped foot on a crime scene," he said. "I could have you arrested and tossed behind bars. You're contaminating my universe." For emphasis, he even managed to lean forward and increase his firmness.

"I did no such thing," I said. "I was on the other side of the yellow tape."

He yanked the hand from his trousers (it came out clean), and rubbed his chin. "But you were there, and you even managed to pass out."

"I don't like the sight of blood," I said, "and I don't like it when you sneer at me."

"Why even bother to show up in the first place?" he asked. "Are you earning points toward a Girl Scout's badge?"

I didn't appreciate the insult: I'd never been involved in the Girl Scout's organization, although I had managed to sample their Samoas and Thin Mints on more than one occasion. I shuffled a few papers during my extended pause. "Just because you may not recognize my talents, doesn't mean everyone else feels the same way."

"You're neither a PI nor a police officer."

"I happen to have an interest in the recently deceased," I said.

"She's a colleague, and you're going to need my services whether you like it or not." And she was possibly a distant relative on my mother's side, even though this had never been confirmed nor denied. In that regard, it somewhat resembled a political position.

He scoffed and then executed a sneer. "A passing acquaintance doesn't really count for much these days. Now if she were one of your Facebook friends, we might have a legitimate case for your involvement."

I ended up with another insult right between my eyes, but I'd gotten used to the abuse. The papers in my hand helped deflect the onslaught. "You bring cruelty to a new level."

"I don't want to see you get hurt." But he certainly didn't mind hurling the insults himself and with reckless abandon.

"I'm sure that's all you're interested in," I said.

"You have no idea what I'm capable of."

I didn't know whether that was a threat or a promise. Either way, the intensity in his eyes forced me to look in the other direction. If he kept it up, I could see myself visiting the underside of a desk in my immediate future.

He pointed a finger at me, flicked it skyward, and then shoved himself out my door. I let out a breath I hadn't realized I'd been holding, the air exhalation bringing a sense of equilibrium to my universe. I shoved a blue raspberry Jolly Rancher in my mouth, savored the sweet taste, and closed my eyes to the intense burst of flavor. The sugar rush helped alleviate the insults.

I pulled out my blue yoga mat I kept beside my desk, and I did a few stretches in my cramped office, knowing I needed to take my mind off Tommy, otherwise I might lose it forever. After the stretches, I focused on the task at hand, which happened to be an overall analysis of the marketing department with the intention of cutting five percent from the budget without sacrificing any business. The task proved more difficult than I had originally anticipated, and the analysis took the rest of the afternoon. By the time I finished, I had four or five iterations completed, none of them a perfect solution, but all provided at least partial solutions, and all of which would need to be fully explained and argued. Several Jolly Rancher wrappers had congregated on the top of my desk in a pile the size of a miniature Igloo.

After providing explanations to go with my numbers, I dumped the report on Cooper's desk and darted out of the room before he could take a red pen to my project and toss it back in my face and hurl a stream of colorful insults in my direction.

~ ~ ~

Dana's brother Oliver had long, brown hair, a smudge of paint on his left cheek, more smudges on his right hand, and a slightly crooked smile. He was half a foot taller than I was, which placed him near the height of the average adult male. He lived in a studio apartment slightly smaller than my own, but his was crammed full of canvases, mostly of the landscape variety. The walls were painted the color of clay, and his living room was flanked by a cathedral ceiling. He had two plastic chairs that would have looked better on the lawn than in his living room and a sofa that might have been shot with a shotgun or tossed out a second story window.

Using his paintbrush, he motioned for me to enter. I'd avoided a conversation with him thus far, but I couldn't put it off any longer. Since he was of the artistic type, he was known more for his temper than his talent, and he and his sister weren't on speaking terms. But I decided it was better to take the plunge than to have never plunged at all. And it helped that I had called ahead and performed my part in an acceptable manner.

"We should talk about your sister," I said.

He resumed painting, as I watched, standing behind him and to his right. Brilliant, bright colors filled the white canvas. "What about her?"

"You know she's dead, right?"

He nodded. His brush stopped in mid-stroke before it resumed on a jagged path. "Are you the police?"

"No," I said, "I'm an interested colleague."

"Just how interested are you?"

"Interested enough to keep digging even if the cops close the file." The canvas popped out at me like a man with a hatchet and a ball-peen hammer. "Which officer informed you of her death?"

He ignored my question. "What if she's already caused more than enough trouble?"

"What are you suggesting? What do you know?"

He shook his head. His brush attacked the canvas with fierce intensity, colors slashing and enlivening before my eyes. "I'm just stating the obvious. Maybe it's more than you've bargained for."

I hadn't remembered taking a seat at the bargaining table, but at the age of twenty-three, I consumed enough alcohol to pass out on my living room carpet for six hours straight. I never did figure out what happened during those six hours, but I awoke fully-clothed with what I thought at the time were hairs on my tongue and my head beating louder than a base drum. "I haven't bargained for anything at the moment," I said. "But I do want to know what's really going on here. I do know your relationship with your sister was a bit strained."

"Why?"

"You haven't returned her phone calls for the last six months."

He dropped the brush on the easel. "How do you know that?"

"I have friends in unusual places."

He turned around and eyed me suspiciously. "What else do you know about Dana?"

"Her financial records are out of whack."

He grimaced. "Is that some sort of scientific expression?"

"No," I said. "But something most definitely does not add up. Your sister had more than just a few cursory problems."

"You sound more than just interested in her," Oliver said. "Are you her lover?"

"What are you talking about?"

"Dana was bisexual. You didn't bother to figure that out, did you?"

I decided not to tell him I already had my suspicions. "So her affair with Porter—"

"Was just a means to an end," he said. "She was more interested in her boss."

"You can't be serious."

He made the sign of the cross on his chest. "My sister was into the art of experimentation. What are you involved in, Sam?"

I shook my head. "Apparently I have no idea." But I had new dedication to my side project, and I hoped to figure out what happened before Tommy did.

He nodded. "You're probably right. But that's not going to stop you from digging anyway, is it?"

I studied his face for the hint of larger clues. None proved forthcoming. "Who would want to kill your sister?"

"You might want to start with the individuals who were paying her off."

"I only found one—Victor Uglow."

"You're not looking hard enough," he said.

"But there were no other anomalies in her financial records."

"Did you find indications of an unexplained raise less than two years from her employment start date with Wired Consulting?"

"Yes," I said, "but I assumed it was because she started working for Frankie Kensington. Are you telling me the raise wasn't earned?"

"That's not all it was based on." Oliver set the wet canvas aside, and he picked up another one. He set it on the easel, stared at it for several minutes, and then grabbed a brush before he went into attack mode.

I resumed my position, watching with more than just a hint of curiosity. "How much trouble is she in exactly?"

"Probably more than you realize, Sam. My sister was rather good with misfortune, but her talents failed her considerably when she tried to get out of it. She dove into the deep end of the pool without the aid of a lifejacket."

I asked, "Why do you believe this time it might be more serious?"

He handed me a typewritten note from his paint splattered pocket. A look of pure devastation was etched on his face, his eyes held a vacant, hollow gaze.

"When did you get this?"

"Two days ago."

"Have you shown it to the police?"

The brush worked with impassioned fury. "Absolutely."

I leaned in closer. "And what have they done about it?"

"Officer Buchs said he'd take it under advisement."

"But you don't believe him?"

"Why do you think I'm talking to you?" he asked. "Because I'm interested in your accounting skills?" He shook his head. "The man lied to me, but I can't prove it." He waved the brush in the air, flicking spatters of paint across the canvas. A few managed to find the cream colored wall. More, however, found their desired target.

"But I'm just an amateur."

"Amateurs have to start somewhere, don't they? So where do you plan on starting?"

"Maybe I need to go all the way back to the beginning."

"While you may be new, you certainly have a head for police work. Maybe Tommy would be willing to give you a letter of recommendation."

I didn't bother to tell him how wrong he was. "It's my attention-to-detail and my logic-oriented focus. I dream in long division."

"You also have too much time on your hands," he said.

"What are you talking about?"

His hand eased back on the throttle. "You're supposed to be at work, aren't you?"

"I'm between projects at the moment."

"I bet you are," he said.

He told me to keep the note: It asked for a million dollar ransom. The terms ended twenty-four hours after receipt, and the end result meant death.

~ ~ ~

My electric blue Corolla needed a wash, but I didn't consider the matter urgent. What I wanted to do, however, was return home and ponder this new information, most of which had caught me by surprise, and almost none of which I had seen coming despite my extensive research on the matter.

Oliver didn't live far from me, although our paths had never crossed before, or at least I didn't remember meeting him. Don Stader, however, stood out a bit too well in my mind, even though our conversations had been limited to the phone. His high-pitched voice always managed to cause a ringing in my ears.

"Well, you were right about the bisexuality part," he said. "She had a fling with a girl in college, who's now dead, by the way. And she had another one with an ex-girlfriend of Jerry's. She also managed to exchange emails with sexual undertones with her new boss, none of which were flagged by HR or the techies."

"With a last name of Duncan?"

"That's the one," he said. "The female has a last name of Kensington. What kind of twisted games have ruled this girl's life?"

"I have no idea," I said.

"But you're going to find out."

"I'm going to try," I said. "It's a bit more complicated than I first thought."

"What have you found out so far?"

"I'd rather not go into the details. If I end up in jail, I don't want you to end up in the cell beside me. I'm still not sure you could handle the pressure."

"That good, huh?"

"It might fuel a few more of your fantasies, although I'm sure your hard drive has already kicked into overdrive." I paused. "What can you tell me about Garrett Everest?"

"Is that a request or a demand?"

"It might be a little of both, why?"

"I just wanted to know what I was up against," Don said.

CHAPTER SEVENTEEN

"Why are you on TV?" she asked.

"What am I doing on TV?"

"You're on the local news channel, passed out with your eyes closed, your head toward the heavens, and you have a dazed look on your face."

If I told her the real reason for my dazed look, she'd end up passed out, and Elmer would have to revive her with his tongue. "I've become involved in some extracurricular activities."

"It's not dangerous, is it?" Felicia Dabler asked.

I paused for too long. I had a cup of yogurt and one filled with tea and the TV played low in the background with a clicking sound coming from my refrigerator and a possible dog barking incident across the hall. Life was as normal as it could be, especially without the peeper from downstairs popping out at the most inopportune moment, most of which happened when I had bags in my hand or what must have been bags under my eyes.

The rest of the workday had passed uneventfully, as I stayed in my cubicle except for carefully allotted bathroom breaks and report flybys where I turned and ran at the first available opportunity. My computer didn't hiccup once, even though it had threatened to do so for the past three days, two of which almost resorted in calls to the IT department.

"This isn't like the time you were convinced the cafeteria ladies were poisoning other students as well as yourself, is it? You aren't going to start a petition, are you?"

"I was in grade school," I said. Despite the number of years that had passed, I still hadn't been able to completely walk away from the occasion. My sister, on the other hand, had a hard time forgiving my faults, especially when it led to verbal comments strewn in her direction. One boy in particular—I think his name might have been Ned— told her she needed electric shock therapy along with her crazy-assed sister. If a teacher hadn't stepped in at that particular moment, Ned might have found himself staring up at the world from the flat of his back.

"And you managed to start quite a campaign." She paused. "Or what about the time you were convinced that Chaz Rocket had managed to sleep with every high school cheerleader twice and that the men's bathroom was filled with graffiti? Most of which had to do with cheerleaders and other assorted sluts."

A week's worth of detention set me on the path toward redemption. "I could have proven my theory," I said.

"You barely avoided suspension."

I set my yogurt aside and stuffed a Jolly Rancher in my mouth. "It was a difficult situation, and I managed to avoid the worst of it."

Elmer howled twice in quick succession, similar to a pair of hiccups. "Is that a dead body in the background?" Felicia asked.

"What channel are you watching?"

"Seven," she said. "You might want to turn it on."

"I'd prefer not to watch myself, thank you very much." The camera added ten pounds, most of which would probably end up around my middle, and I wasn't exactly known for my acting ability. I tripped over a single line in the junior high Christmas pageant, managing to end the line and my misery in a voice an octave higher than my own.

Ever since, I managed to avoid school plays with bouts of the flu, chickenpox, scarlet fever, or a sore throat when necessary.

"You still haven't answered my question." She meant the dead body.

"It might be," I said. I wasn't sure Elmer was trained in the art of CPR, or that his tongue bathing would revive a stopped heart, or that he had been given his most recent shots.

"You aren't planning to get yourself killed, are you?"

"As a matter of principle," I said, "I don't plan for these sorts of activities. I just end up in the middle with my hands thrown up in the air, and my eyes averted from the latest tragedy."

"Maybe you should find a new pastime where you aren't the center of attention."

"Contrary to popular belief, I don't enjoy the spotlight." I hated plays and parties and presentations and spelling bees with a renewed passion and vigor.

The baby cried in the background, and Elmer followed suit: His howling turned intense and forceful and nearly reached another octave. I pulled the phone away from my ear.

She said, "Maybe you should date someone. A good relationship cures all kinds of ailments. If you're not careful, you'll end up with arthritis before you're thirty-two."

"I'm not sure that would solve my problems," I said. "In fact, it might lead to more complications." I wasn't sure if I meant the arthritis or the relationship or the long list of faults best reserved for the average American male.

"You just haven't met the right person. If you made more of an effort, you might improve your results exponentially."

"I'm certainly not going to find him as long as you're the one steering the ship. You've led me into choppy waters on more than one occasion, and I still haven't managed to find dry land. My boat needs a better navigational system."

"Or you could just take over the wheel."

"I prefer to be in the background," I said. The last remnants of sugar heaven crunched in my mouth and lingered on my lips.

"Yeah right," she said. "Some of these cops are cute."

And some of them were probably married. The ones that frightened me the most were the ones not in a significant relationship. "I don't think you should get any bright ideas."

"You need a few more sparks in your life."

My bonfire could level Sherwood Forest. "Maybe you should cut back on your extracurricular activities. I'm sure Elmer could always use a little more love."

The sound of panting filled the receiver. "Your concern should extend beyond your job," she said. "Your lack of effort makes me question what you really want."

~ ~ ~

I had a cup of tea in front of me, lingering relationship questions from the previous evening, plenty of problems and few solutions, and a pile of papers on my desk that I hadn't bothered to organize. I had a stash of Jolly Ranchers stuffed in my right pocket, my hair in a chignon, a smile that appeared out of nowhere, and a special project that involved an analysis of the consulting industry with a specific focus on growth opportunities for our company in the current market. I had placed figures on three different tabs in a spreadsheet: status quo, limited growth, and maximum overdrive. I yanked figures from analyst reports, industry trends, annual reports, our historical perspective, and economic initiatives. My mind spun faster than a washing machine turned on high. I tried to limit how many times I came up for air, but I had more than enough Jolly Ranchers to sustain me for the next six hours.

My fingers pounded the numeric keypad, and I attacked my tea the way an offensive lineman might attack a BLT supreme, or a surgeon might attack an open-heart patient.

Frankie Kensington barged into my office, banged against my door, and flipped my five percent reduction report across my desk. "Do you have data to backup this garbage?"

The grape Jolly Rancher on my tongue stood at attention. "Of course," I said. "Would you like the abbreviated version or the elongated one?"

Her hands pounded my desk hard enough to rattle my mug. "Do you honestly think you can get away with this?"

"I'm not your enemy," I said.

"Your meddling has caused me nothing but headaches."

I stopped typing, my fingers poised over the keys. "Your budget has gotten bloated, and it's time we cut the excess fat."

"This isn't McDonald's," she said. "Besides, none of your analysis took into account current industry trends."

Having spent the better part of an afternoon on the report, and having checked and rechecked my figures, I held my tongue in check with a lawn rake and a piece of nylon rope. "If you turn to page four," I said, "you'll find whatever additional backup you need."

Frankie asked, "Am I supposed to cut personnel?"

Nowhere in my report did I even allude to such a drastic scenario. However, a significant decrease in the number of conferences she attended each year—disguised as essential training initiatives—would have more than accounted for the difference. Yet I feared she had completely missed the point of the exercise. I chewed thoughtfully, while she attempted to bore a hole in my forehead with her X-ray vision. Her attempt failed, while mine succeeded.

"Maybe you should speak with Cooper," I said.

"I already did, and he told me to speak with you."

Cooper had a political card in his stacked deck, and he enjoyed bringing it out at the most inopportune moments. He probably had a listening device placed in one of the ceiling tiles, or he could have just stood in the hallway with a bag of popcorn and a Diet Pepsi and a pair of headphones and a smile.

I smiled politely. "And you actually believed him?"

Frankie stormed out of my office with my report leading the way. The hairs on the back of her neck stood at attention, her face mounted with a glowing red hue.

Before I received another interruption, and was forced to deal with another colleague from the marketing department, or Cooper Strut himself, I made a bold exit from the building, citing an early lunch and client conferences for my respite. As for my destination, I chose to speak with Jerry Duncan again, since he had more to him than just surface material, and I had more than enough motive for an additional inquiry.

His truck still had the NRA sticker, and it was the color of a golden banana. Other than a missing shutter, his house seemed to be in order. I approached the foot thick steel door with trepidation, a Jolly Rancher in my mouth working overtime. He squinted at me; his close cropped hair had gotten longer, but not by much; he had day old stubble on his chin; and his eyes had dark circles under them. He wore a pair of skinny jeans low on his hips; his thumbs sticking out of his pockets.

Jerry motioned for me to come inside. His loveseat had probably experienced some love at some point in the recent past, and his sofa was an awful blue plaid. His furniture selection process had most likely not included a woman's touch, or she had been severely overruled and underestimated at every turn. "My story checked out, didn't it?"

I decided to play my own political card for obvious reasons. "I haven't been able to confirm it yet, but it certainly appears as though it does."

He stroked his chin. "I wouldn't lie to you."

I wasn't sure I believed him; I wasn't sure I disbelieved him either. "Maybe we should talk more about the circumstances surrounding Dana's disappearance."

His jaw worked the toothpick he'd shoved into his mouth. "Why?"

"She's turned up dead."

He nodded, as the toothpick kept in rhythm with his chin. "I saw it on the news. Couldn't hardly believe it myself." His eyes were cold and hard. He narrowed them. "How long ago did she die?" His voice never wavered, but it had cracks around the edges.

"The time of death is still being worked out," I said, "but they think she's been dead for at least a couple of days."

"Are you looking for my alibi?"

I shook my head. "I'm looking for answers, and I assumed you'd be as good a person as any. You cared for her, and I have a feeling she cared for you as well, despite her unusual way of highlighting the obvious."

"Don't forget the circumstances surrounding our relationship's demise," he said.

"Maybe you know more than you think you do."

He had his right ankle crossed over his left. "You think you can trust me?"

"I have to start somewhere, don't I?" I didn't tell him I had trouble avoiding the sound of the pistol, and that eventually I might lose my hearing.

"Where do you want to start?"

"Maybe we should start at the beginning," I said. "With the beginning leading to the end, we need to ensure we don't end up standing on the wrong foot."

The toothpick moved a little faster in his mouth, and he rubbed his chin again, almost as though he wasn't sure it was still there. Then his voice slid out of neutral, making its way into first gear, and he told me the circumstances surrounding the start of his relationship with Dana: where they'd met, how they'd met, and how he had jumped in over his head. "She had this animal magnetism, and I couldn't control myself when I was around her. I assumed it was the same for her other boyfriends, but I never knew for sure."

"But you were willing to make it work?" I asked.

"I knew I could, that I wanted her and nothing else. But she didn't exactly know how to stop. She had an addiction to sex. It was worse than a nicotine fix. Soon, I wasn't enough for her, and she started seeking her fulfillment elsewhere."

"You're serious—?"

"As income taxes," he said.

"But she wasn't?"

"Porter Reede charmed her in a way I couldn't. I didn't have the money, power, and influence he carried around like a pocketbook. I may have had certain attributes, but I certainly didn't have the whole package."

I said, "But you certainly kept her attention."

By the smile on his face, I didn't need to ask how. He had confidence, certainly, and a hint of something else—possibly cockiness—that lingered like too much perfume.

"You loved her," I said.

"I can't stop loving her," he said, "but I can move on from her."

"What ultimately sealed the end of your relationship?"

"You mean you don't know?"

I shook my head.

"She was carrying Porter's child."

CHAPTER EIGHTEEN

I didn't know how much more electric shock my body could take before I ended up strapped to a hospital bed drooling from the mouth. But I decided shock would not prevent me from bringing Dana Wilson's killer to justice, even though I had no previous experience with the judicial system, I hadn't yet won the lottery of jury duty, and I had plenty of questions with limited answers.

I did, however, contemplate Dana's ability to fulfill a lot of men's fantasies, and it wasn't one of the most pleasant of images. What I lacked in talent I made up for in determination, and I wasn't sure I could wait long enough for the end to justify the means. I opened my mind to a few distinct possibilities, none of which would help me sleep any easier, or help Dana's spirit leave this world any faster, or create a sense of closure for her.

I started off my morning with yoga stretches and exercises, the dragon, seal, and saddle poses being the highlight of my morning, before I took a shower, changed my clothes, and grabbed a cup of tea, as I headed out the door, rambled down the stairs, and approached my vehicle.

Before I turned the key in the ignition, my cell phone chirped, and I snatched it out of my purse. The readout screen showed restricted number. Without a doubt in my mind, I knew who was on the other end of the line.

"You sure do know how to pick 'em," he said.

"What are you talking about?"

"Garrett Everest was fired under suspect circumstances. The details presented in his personnel folder have more than a few gaps. You mind telling me what's going on?"

"I wish I knew," I said, "but I'm a little short on information as well." I didn't need to tell him I didn't even have enough gas to start my car.

"Are we talking inches or yards?" Don Stader asked.

"Most likely miles. That's why I don't do this for a living. This side project has turned into a world-class nightmare. I'm not sure I'll ever recover."

Keys clicked in rapid succession, and a grunt on the other end lingered louder than the clacking hopelessness. "He also applied for two executive positions within your organization, and he was turned down for both of them, rather vociferously in fact."

Before I could ask why, the line clicked dead in my ear. Don proved time and again to be a great hacker, but his social skills always left much to be desired.

With my errand completed, and the phone call still lingering in my ear, I set my sights on my office where refuge and more numbers awaited me. Traffic proved heavier than usual with my steady pace interrupted on two separate occasions each for a period of more than ten minutes, neither of which had to do with an actual accident on the actual roadway. With little effort on my part, my mind drifted to Dana, and before I even realized what had happened, I had reached Wired Consulting, and I managed to make it to the third floor without being stopped unnecessarily along the way, or accosted by guards taking up too much of my personal space.

Outside of my door, I had a cop waiting for me with one hand on the wall, and the other jammed inside his pocket. He was the more pleasant of the two, and he was the only one I cared to see on a regular basis, even if he did point a gun in my direction on one occasion.

I asked, "How can I help you?"

He turned toward the sound of my voice. "What did you do to piss off Tommy Buchs?"

I grimaced, and then I picked up my pace, sliding behind my desk and easing into my chair, neither of which he seemed to notice.

"When it comes to men, you really don't have much luck, do you? We're not all bad, although it certainly might appear that way at first glance."

I ushered him into my office before Norma Beemer walked through one of the walls, stood at attention, and started taking notes on a legal pad; he closed the door swiftly behind him. "What did he say about me?"

He plopped himself down on the other side of my desk, while I attacked my leather swivel chair with a vengeance. With my purse plopped on my desk, I shoved a Jolly Rancher in my mouth, and offered him one as well. Ben Xander declined with a shake of his head. The look on his face hadn't changed: It indicated more than just a passing curiosity.

"You should have told me you dated," he said.

I rubbed my forehead. "What good would it have done?" And it was only one date followed by one smack on the lips, after which I stalked away.

"He also told me he broke up with you, after you reached a new level of clinginess."

I glared at him, fire in my eyes. "And you honestly believed him?"

He shook his head. "But I was warned you had more than your share of problems. He also informed me I should stop speaking with you immediately and that Dana's case hindered on you being shown the door. He has a certain paranoia that reminds me of a schizophrenic. Do you honestly enjoy where this has led?"

"Not really," I said. "But I need to know what happened. Tommy's interest is heavily favored toward himself, and he'll use every advantage he can get, even if he has to crush a few innocent pedestrians along the way."

Ben asked, "So you only have altruistic motivations?"

Along with a rather distant relation that I planned to leave out of the press and the papers, and even the police wouldn't be able to connect unless they approached Dana's murder with a magnifying glass. "You may need to work on your naiveté, officer. I wouldn't want you to end up with your eyes wide, and the hairs on the back of your neck standing at attention."

He stood up and leaned against the chair. "What do you think happened?"

"I have no idea," I said. "I'm merely an accountant, but whoever killed her must have hated her immensely. The horrific manner in which she died isn't the sort of fairytale that helps kids sleep at night."

Ben rubbed the back of the chair. "But you do have a theory."

"She had a penchant for taking her clothes off; she had two abortions—and those are the only ones we know about—and the officer assigned to the case happens to be one of the two. I don't like those odds; I don't like Victor Uglow and Porter Reede (the other individual who had a fling with Dana) offering her a bit extra in the way of compensation. She appears to lack in intelligence, or maybe the fast track is the only track she can think about; however, she certainly uses every advantage she can get. Then we have Jerry Duncan and Frankie Kensington, who have held back more than they've offered to me. If it wasn't for Norma Beemer, my own accounting skills, and your expertise, I'm not sure where I'd be right now."

"When all the pieces of the puzzle slam into place, you know you'll have reached the end. And until that particular time, your head will continue to expand at a rapidly exceeding rate. Your actual analysis needs a bit of work, though. You can't apply numbers to murders and expect to end up with similar results."

I nodded.

"Oh, and you might want to work on how you deal with blood. If you pass out again staring up at the sky with a blank expression on your face, we might have to grab two gurneys instead of one. It wasn't exactly one of your better moments."

Before I could offer a reply, he whipped out the door faster than he had entered my world, and with nearly as much authority.

~ ~ ~

I spent the rest of the day on a slide show presentation for my special project, tweaking the numbers and letters and pie charts and pie graphs, until it looked perfect, or nearly so. Cooper liked my analysis so much he wanted charts and graphs for each of my three scenarios. He had a penchant for charts and numbers that rivaled the average accountant, even though he attempted to avoid accounting as much as possible. He claimed his undergrad was not accounting related, even though it was, delegating with an authority and complete lack of compassion. He would have delegated his liver if he decided it would increase his productivity.

My hands hovered over the keys, slamming down on them at the right moments and with what I hoped was the appropriate emphasis. Interruptions remained at a minimum, despite the various interruptions to my own thoughts. I devoured a handful of Jolly Ranchers, and dug out a few more from my bottom desk drawer when my thoughts and productivity hit a plateau somewhere around my third iteration of my presentation. The sugar rejuvenated me and filled me with impure thoughts, most of which revolved around dead bodies and dead bosses.

Before I critiqued it even further, I pulverized print, handed it to Cooper while he was on the phone, and dove out of his office before he could reel me back in like a pesky trout.

Returning to my office, I closed my door to attempt privacy, while I picked up the phone and placed it against my ear. When the male voice answered, I identified myself, and waited through an audible exhale as well as a rather prolonged silence. I took the opportunity to slam a watermelon Jolly Rancher home.

The other end of the line crackled. "Are you sure you're qualified?" he asked.

"I have a slew of qualifications."

"But none of them relate to the task at hand," Garrett Everest said. He had more than enough attitude for multiple personality disorder.

"You'd be surprised at what I'm capable of." When the situation presented itself, I even managed to pass out at crime scenes, or spray myself with pepper spray. I told myself it was only to test the side effects.

"What do you want?"

"I want to talk about your time at Wired Consulting." As a Wired Consulting employee myself, I didn't consider this to be a tremendous leap, and it certainly wasn't outside my realm of authority either.

"You know about my unlawful termination lawsuit," he said. "And you also know I relocated to Richmond. What else do you want to talk about? Do you enjoy forcing me to drudge up old memories?"

I unraveled the curlicue in my phone cord, right before it popped right back into place. I tried again with similar results. "I don't."

Another audible pause filled the other end of the line. "Then I don't have anything to say to you. For all I know, you're a company spy."

Paranoia hadn't fallen under my list of observations. But I was still relatively new to the investigative arena. "You might want to rethink that request," I said.

"Why?"

I decided to visualize my objective and then hope for the best. "Because I know you want to be reinstated." If I were in his shoes, and had a similar scandal tacked to my headboard, it's what I would have wanted.

The pause lingered long enough for me to start counting backwards from one hundred. But I had patience on my side. "Maybe I underestimated you originally. But that doesn't mean I'm going to eat out of your hand."

"You do know Dana Wilson died, don't you?"

Garrett asked, "Why should I care?"

"Because I have reason to believe you may have had a relationship with her." And based on her history, as well as his dramatic exit, she probably ended the affair, along with a few more broken hearts and missed opportunities.

Anger filled the receiver. "She helped get me fired."

I pulled the phone away, and then drew it back in. "Despite this fact, I know you still care about her, and I know you'll do whatever you can to help bring her killer to justice."

"How do you know that?" he asked. "You're just an accountant with too much time on your hands. Maybe you should be more concerned about your day job." He paused, as the silence reached a deafening level. "Are you going to finger Porter?"

"If he's guilty, I have no problem making my recommendation." What I didn't know is if I could get Tommy Buchs to listen to me for more than five minutes and keep his ego at a firm distance.

"Oh, he's guilty," Garrett said. "I'd bet my life on it."

I didn't know if this was just the jealousy talking, or if he had it on good authority. If he did, I needed to start talking to the right people. "Why do you say that?"

"You know she had an abortion while she was with him, don't you?"

I told him I did, and then I shoved another Jolly Rancher in the space between my teeth.

"Did you know he threatened her life? If she didn't go through with the abortion, that is. How's that for suspicious?"

"How do I know you're not more than a little disgruntled?" I asked. "After all, your new life isn't much better than your old one: You're not married; you don't have any prospects on the horizon; and you haven't managed to hold down a job for more than a year. Maybe you're attempting to swing the pendulum in the other direction."

"How do you know?" he asked.

I gritted my teeth. "Because I have a sixth sense for these things," I said. "I have a sixth sense for men, and I know there's more to you than what's on the surface. You have something, otherwise I wouldn't have bothered to call you, during work hours no less, and I wouldn't use my abilities to get more than just a few lines out of you." Another pregnant pause filled the vast expanse between us.

"You're persistent," he said. "I'll give you that much. As for the rest of your intelligence, that still needs to be proven. You may have an audience, but you don't have my undivided attention." He paused. "Porter Reede had more than enough motivation: You should focus your efforts in his direction. He had more than enough chances to complete the task.

"As for Dana, she was always a good planner, but she often failed when it came to execution."

Before I could ask him what he meant, I heard the familiar click in my ear.

CHAPTER NINETEEN

I closed my office door, locking it on the way out. The halls, otherwise silent, provided their own ghosts. I couldn't let the fear from Garrett's voice, or the sense of hate storm toward the battlefield. His anger filled the receiver, and it wasn't directed at Dana, despite the way their relationship ended, and who she had ended up with. His statement about failed execution had thrown me as well. She had tried to weasel her way to the top, and apparently, she'd been caught on the top rung. I shivered slightly, although I wasn't cold.

Katy Perry filled my speakers, as I headed for Poquoson, VA, a half hour north of Hampton, on Wythe Creek Road. The energetic sound and pleasant ride set my mind at ease, as much as could be expected anyway. Traffic proved light, as I navigated the highways and byways of the Hampton Roads area with a smile on my face and a song in my heart.

Green shutters and green grass welcomed me on a pleasant side street to a house much smaller than I expected. The house faced a large tree with dark green leaves. The path to the front door was laid out with large, irregular stones on a winding ascent. Navigating this sober proved enough of a challenge: I couldn't imagine trying to navigate the stones after tossing back a few. I almost tripped twice, but I managed to stay upright.

A small, buxom blonde with too much hair and too much makeup opened the front door. Her eyes were outlined in deep blue, and her lips were a shade below deep purple. Her hands were tiny, delicate, and her eyes were wide. Before I had even introduced myself, she stuck out her hand, and told me her name was Jessie. Her last name I knew was Trager.

She touched my shoulder, as she guided me inside. I told her my name, and why I was here. Her wide eyes never left my face, and her lips never parted. I didn't know if she possessed the ability to smile, or if God had not granted her this particular talent.

I asked, "Did you have a relationship with Dana Wilson?"

She shook her head.

"You might avoid the lies," I said. "The exchange of information improves when we take lies out of the equation."

"What do you know?"

"The truth," I said. "That the two of you had a relationship."

She had a cup of tea in front of her. Despite my penchant for tea, I had declined her request. I didn't know why I had, but it seemed appropriate at the time.

"But you're just a colleague," she said. "You hardly even knew her, unless what you told me is a lie. What do you want from me?"

I placed my hands on my knees. "I'd like to have a discussion."

"Are you sure that's all you're looking for? You aren't hoping to dip your hand in my sacred well, are you?"

If by sacred well, she meant more intimate matters, I decided my can of pepper spray might come in handy after all. "Maybe, maybe not. I'm not really sure what's going on. Jerry left you for Dana, and then she left Jerry for you, which doesn't really fall under your normal chain of events. From what I understand about Dana, she's not exactly an ordinary individual."

"Surely, you must have certain expectations, otherwise you wouldn't be here."

I folded my hands in my lap and offered her a somber expression. "I have certain beliefs that I can't seem to shake. Dana was killed in a rather extreme and violent manner, naked below the waist. While I'm rather new at this, that doesn't strike me as an act completed by a female."

Jessie asked, "Are you saying I'm innocent?"

"Let's just say I have certain suspicions, and you're not currently included in them," I said. My eyes drifted around the small room with boxes strewn in a haphazard fashion and sheets of tissue paper congregated in one corner. "Did you just move in?"

"No," she said. "I'm in the process of transitioning." She had hardly touched her tea, and she hadn't managed to stare at it either. *It was a prop rather than a beverage of consumption.*

"Where?" I asked.

"I'm not sure yet."

Even though her eyes never left my face, the lie wasn't lost on me. I decided to let it pass without additional thought. "Did you love Jerry?"

"I thought I did."

That was more than likely lie number two. "But now you're not sure?"

"Now I'm prone to pursuing other opportunities."

I didn't bother to add "of the female variety." Or maybe she had changed her ways yet again. She seemed more than a little lost. "Who broke it off?"

She shook her head, lifted the teacup to her lips, and took a small sip. "You already know the answer to that."

"When did you learn about Dana—?"

"And the start of her new friendship?"

I nodded.

The teacup shook in her hand: She set it down on the table. "I did-n't find out about her until later," Jessie said. "After he'd already been with her for more than a year. She didn't even have the nerve to tell me herself. She just bounced along like relationship rock climb-ing."

I didn't know why we had completely skipped Jerry, but maybe she wanted to get past that particular part of her life. In the end, she had won, as Dana left Jerry for her. Maybe that was all she had really wanted, or maybe she had a grander scheme on her agenda, besides the project that I assumed was her face every morning.

"Dana left you the way she left Jerry," I said.

She nodded. Her hand had stopped shaking. She still hadn't managed a smile, but this wasn't an appropriate occasion either. If she had been a smoker, she might have already filled the small living area and my lungs with the stench of secondhand smoke.

"Do you know who she was with at the time of her death?"

"No," she said, "I don't. And I'd prefer not to know either."

She had reached lies number three and four, and she didn't show any signs of slowing down. Her eyes, as wide as ever, appeared as delicate as crystals before me. As she spoke each lie, her voice never cracked, nor did it falter, nor did she turn away from me. I wondered how far her expertise had taken her.

"Are you glad she's dead?"

She nodded. "She ruined my life. She had fun manipulating me at my own expense, and I wasn't smart enough to realize what she had done until it was too late. I was a moth drawn to the flame, and I didn't have enough sense to pull away. You might want to rethink your approach."

Her eyes were on the verge of tearing up, but they were the tears of self-pity without the slightest hint of remorse. Her eyes had grown firmer, and the cushion beneath me poked me in a place I wasn't particularly happy about. I shifted my weight, but the cushion shifted with me.

"Are you seeing anyone now?" I asked.

She opened her mouth, closed it, and then opened it again. "Is that your business?"

"No," I said. "But I can tell you're not. Is that why you wish to leave? Are you attempting to escape bad memories?"

She sniffed. The large sound filled the otherwise quiet room. "Do you have some sort of gift? Or do you already know all the answers before you ask the questions?"

"Over the years, I've developed the ability to read people. It comes through sensitivity, as well as understanding. It's not perfect, but I do have a certain success rate with it. In situations like this, I attempt to use it to my advantage."

She considered this with both hands in her lap. "You may not want to advertise it," she said. "Not everyone would focus on the good it could provide."

"I think you deserve more than just second rate answers." I didn't need to add that I hoped she would do the same for me. As much as I might have wanted to, I certainly didn't need to restate the obvious.

The rest of the conversation proved relatively uneventful, and I left her house only slightly smarter than when I had entered it. If I kept this up, I might eventually reach both sides of the mathematical equation, but I still had a long way to go and only a short time to reach my final destination, assuming Tommy was still set on interrupting my life.

~ ~ ~

My mother answered the door with both arms held out to me, the smile on her face nothing less than genuine, her large diamond ring glinting in the light, and her long, dark hair flowing behind her. She hugged me tighter than I would have expected before she ushered me inside, and in the direction of the sitting room. She had a glass of wine that was only half-full next to her favorite chair. When she offered me one, I declined.

"You're good at taking something simple and making it complicated," she said. "You don't need so much logic in your life." She didn't have the mathematical ability I had inherited from my dad; therefore, she didn't understand the positive attributes it provided, as well as the curse that went with it.

"I like getting to the heart of the matter," I said.

Although she hadn't yet mentioned it, I assumed she had seen me on the news. She wanted to know what was going on in the world, even though she had little desire to experience it firsthand. She had never worked a day in her life. My dad, however, worked more than enough for the two of them, while she shuttled us to school, plays, soccer games, or whatever else our little hearts desired. She had lived vicariously through my sister and I, and she didn't seem to regret a moment of it. But she did like to exert authority in our lives as much as she could. She was more successful with me than she was with my sister who had a more active social life than I had ever been able to manage.

She sipped from her wineglass. "You don't need to discover the answer to everything. Some things are better off when you don't know how they work. Besides, you should be careful about where you spring into action. You might find yourself in a situation that you can't easily get out of. You're delicate, even though you like to pretend that you're not."

"How's your golf game?"

"You shouldn't try to change the subject." She leaned in closer and touched my knee. "You haven't had to use the can of pepper spray, have you?"

"No."

"But you will if you need to?" she asked. "I don't want you to end up as another statistic."

"Certainly," I said. I leaned away from her intense gaze. "But I'm more than capable of defending myself if I'm caught in the middle of a rowdy bar with large, drunken fools on either side of me."

"Why do you continue to take those self-defense classes?" she asked. "What exactly are you trying to prove? You don't need to win at everything."

But it would certainly be nice to win at something. Even though she probably didn't realize it, she had given my sister more advantages than she had given me. But I was a stronger person for digging my way out of the trenches. "I like freeing my mind of any complications."

Her lower lip retracted beneath her top one. "You aren't the least bit concerned about the consequences?"

"What consequences?" I asked. I didn't step out on the mat without being covered in pads, more than the average football player, and Dave Griffin taught us to use violence only in extreme matters. The goal wasn't to hit each other on a weekly basis. When I tried explaining this to my mother, she had stared rather hard at her wineglass, and then immediately changed the subject. A concept she despised with an unusual passion.

"Are you sure you don't overestimate your abilities?"

I shook my head.

"Are you staying for dinner?" she asked. Since my dad worked late, my parents had always eaten late as well. The concept continued even after my sister and I left the house.

"I don't think I should."

"Why?"

I didn't tell her that she wasn't exactly known for her cooking abilities, that the dinner hour involved mom grilling us, as opposed to the food, while dad appeared to look interested, even though he wasn't. The marriage lasted for reasons I couldn't explain, and even now I still couldn't quite appreciate.

I said, "I prefer some time away from home."

"Your father will be home soon."

That meant I needed to leave sooner rather than later. "I'd rather not face him right now."

"You don't think he'll approve of your actions?" she asked.

"He's more silent in his rebuttal, but ultimately, he reaches the same conclusions you do. It's a concept I'm a little too familiar with."

"He just cares about you, as do I."

"In his own way, I'm sure," I said. "He just has an interesting way of showing it most of the time." If my dad ever discussed his feelings, I'd die of a heart attack on the spot, and then I'd get run over by a bus to finish me off.

"He's a complicated man."

"I know," I said, "and I'm certainly not going to hold it against him."

"You're not exactly the easiest person in the world to deal with either. You've gotten more than a few personality traits from your father."

My back stiffened. The book case directly to my right suddenly held more interest, and I studied the shelves with an enthusiasm best reserved for chocolate and male abs. "Maybe I try a little harder than he does."

"You don't think he tries?"

"I'm not sure what he does, or doesn't do," I said. "I try not to focus on the specifics." That was a lie, and I knew it. When I could, I tried to keep the lies to a minimum. With my mother, it always proved harder than I would have liked it to. She reminded me of truth serum, only in reverse.

"You don't expect to find all the answers, do you?" She paused. "Life isn't some giant puzzle that you need to solve for yourself.

"As for your social life, you're not planning to end up on any more news shows, are you?"

"Why?" I asked. "Would you like for me to develop my new talent? Maybe I could even market my way into a fulltime talk show."

She shook her head. "You were always difficult. Your sister proved much easier than you ever did. If it wasn't for her, I might have considered putting you up for adoption."

What my mother meant was that she was much easier to shape than I was. Sometimes my sister even managed to hang on her every word. "Aren't you glad I wasn't easy?"

My mother shook her head, and then she stood up. I assumed the conversation was over.

~ ~ ~

The drive from Chesapeake, VA back through the Monitor-Merrimac Bridge-Tunnel proved much faster than the drive toward it. The familiar lights overhead guided me, and the right lane proved both comforting and disconcerting at the same time. Katy Perry aided my journey, as "Waking Up In Vegas" with the sound of slot machines—even though I had never managed to gamble—provided a level of comfort I knew I needed. While my mother had taken her small sips of alcohol, I probably should have raised my own glass, if for no other reason than to provide a sense of escape.

When I showed up at Cadence Surrender's door, I reached out my arms, and embraced my best friend with renewed purpose. I was glad she didn't comment on my shaking.

After we were seated in the living room, she smiled at me. "You haven't gotten yourself arrested yet, have you? Or have you been released for good behavior?"

"Are you taking bets?" I asked. The clink of coins in a slot machine entered my mind. And as a matter of principle, I decided I'd never bet on black.

"You know I only play craps," she said. "I like odds that are more even."

"But you haven't gone recently." The stated fact stood at attention between us.

She tilted her head slightly. "Are you offering?"

"I don't think that's a good idea," I said. The thought of winning proved a long lost concept for me. Losing, however, proved a much more readily available notion. Had I decided to go all in, I was fairly certain I'd be disappointed with the results.

"You only lost a hundred dollars the last time."

"But that was a hundred dollars I didn't have," I said. Even though it would have proved rather beneficial, I hadn't yet figured out a way to manufacture money through legal means. If I ever did, I was fairly certain I'd be satisfied with the end result, with my student loans the first to go, and credit card debt next on the list.

"You shouldn't have started playing blackjack."

"But it's such a simple game," I said. I had calculated the various odds beforehand and with each successive hand. My mathematical abilities hadn't extended to counting cards, and I didn't want to cheat my way to wealth. I didn't want tainted bills floating around in my purse, and so I'd ended up leaving the casino with fewer bills than when I'd started.

"It's supposed to be," Cadence said, "but you tried to focus on the odds, and you actually ended up outsmarting yourself, which ultimately led to more than a few wrong decisions. If you'd been more careful, you would have done just fine. Overthinking matters isn't a particularly endearing trait, just so you know."

"I still don't think it's a good idea," I said. "Besides, the closest casino is in New Kent, VA. And I don't have the desire to spend an hour on the road."

"But it's well worth the trip."

"I don't have two hours to spare, and that only includes the driving."

"It's Friday night," she said. "What could you possibly be in the middle of that would take up your whole weekend?"

"I'm not sure I should talk about it." I didn't want my best friend to end up in shock. I didn't think I could revive her with a can of pepper spray to the face.

"You were on the news," she said. Her tone was matter-of-fact and even, almost as though she were talking about the weather or her latest boyfriend.

"I wondered when you might mention it."

"You were rather hard to miss," she said, "although next time you might want to stay on your feet. The camera didn't exactly get your best side. And while I'm not entirely certain, it appeared as though you had a small bit of drool on your lower lip."

I wiped at my mouth reflexively. "You have to understand the circumstances. I wasn't in the best of situations."

She patted my hand. "Did you smoke some bad weed?"

"You know I don't believe in drugs."

"I don't believe in drugs either," she said, "but I happen to enjoy a little recreational weed from time to time." Her definition of time happened to loosen up extensively, and when she had a bit of the recreational drug in her system, it managed to loosen up even more.

I said, "You don't have the money to spend either." Her definition of saving meant she didn't have to take out an advance on her next paycheck.

She nodded her head in a self-assured manner. "I don't plan on losing."

"Even still," I said, "there's always the chance that luck could go against you. You don't want to have to swing for the fences again."

Through what could only be described as divine intervention, she had gone against her own rules, was down more than six hundred dollars, and in her last act of aggression, had dumped all of her money on a single number: eight. A blonde with a bubbly personality and not much else between her ears tossed the dice in a haphazard manner. The dice rolled quickly across the table, struck the velvet at the opposite end, and Cadence had won, recouping all of her losses in a single roll of the die.

She appeared deep in thought, as if savoring the same moment, or maybe she had another streak of luck she hadn't bothered to tell me. "I have skills," she said.

"You have no fear."

"No fear can be taught," Cadence said. "You just need to learn to trust yourself."

I didn't bother to tell her that I trusted myself just fine: It was everyone else that gave me nightmares. "I don't think I'm a particularly good candidate: The thought of losing doesn't sit well with me."

CHAPTER TWENTY

I made a right off Mercury Boulevard onto Coliseum Drive, my blinker clicking on and then off as I eased the wheel back to center. I had taillights in my mirror, a set of taillights that looked vaguely familiar, like a teacher I might have had in high school, but I wasn't sure. The car was black, nondescript, and I noticed what might have been two reflections through the glass, although I couldn't be certain of that either.

I eased through the gigantic parking lot that was split into different sections, taking the maximum speed limit of fifteen miles per hour into account. The car behind me followed suit. For the first time, I really started to question the matter, even though the apartment had more than 275 units, and I'd only met just a handful of the tenants.

I pulled into a space directly between two of the buildings—my own and the building next to mine—raced out of the car, up the stairs, and to my apartment door on the third floor. And past the unsuspecting weasel who for the moment had remained firmly grounded in his apartment on the first floor, where he belonged. Better to be overly cautious, I decided, as my instincts took over, and the first rush of adrenaline kicked in. I unlocked the door, yanked it open, and then shoved it closed behind me, panting just briefly on the other side of the door, right before I congratulated myself on my sprinting ability. Since I didn't know most of my neighbors, and I couldn't recognize them on sight—other than the weasel and one or two others—I didn't care what they thought.

I flipped on the TV for background noise and walked to my bedroom, taking my suit jacket off as I went before I dropped it on the bed. I changed into a pair of sweatpants, a baggy t-shirt, and a thin sweatshirt with a hood, wiped off the last remains of my makeup, grabbed a water bottle from the refrigerator, and had just plopped on the sofa when there was a knock on the door, loud enough to jar me out of my momentary reverie.

The sound echoed through the living room, and for all I knew, it could have probably been heard across the hall. I peered through the peephole at two men in dark suits with matching guns bulging from their suit coats, with equally long and slicked back hair, their mouths neither smiling nor frowning. My first thought was they could have passed for detectives, although I wasn't sure about this assessment; my second was I wasn't expecting company; and my third was it had only been ten minutes since the nondescript car had followed me here. I could stare at them for another twenty seconds or so, and they might go away, but if it was the same two gentlemen from the black car, they would know I was home. And if my car didn't, the sprint had probably given me away.

Unfortunately, my living room didn't afford me a clear view of the parking lot. However, I could view part of the tennis court, and I had a clear view of the basketball court, which for the most part, went underutilized.

The knocking increased in intensity and duration: I no longer had the option to stay quiet.

"Who is it?" I asked.

There was a brief pause. "It's the police," a male voice said from the other side of the door. "We need to talk with you about Dana's death."

The outfits and demeanors certainly screamed detective, but following me home without identifying who they were still led me to believe otherwise. My previous history with men didn't help matters either.

"Hold your shields up," I said. My right hand shook as I said this, and I remembered the can of pepper spray from my purse. I grabbed it, along with my car keys, while I waited for the two gentlemen to comply with my request. I didn't have a gun or baseball bat on the premises, and my knives were less than adequate in hand-to-hand combat, not that I could even use them effectively around the kitchen. The best I could hope for with the knives was to toss one at the two men and run. I decided to stick with the pepper spray.

Instead of displaying their shields, the door burst open, and the two gentlemen came through the open threshold, scanning the room as they went. Their guns were displayed in front of them, spanning my small apartment along with their eyes. I dove into the kitchen with my can of pepper spray in my hand and my keys shoved into my right pocket. I turned the can to fire mode just in case I needed it.

I popped my head up over the bar, as bullets struck the refrigerator behind me. I dove back down, took several deep breaths to try to calm myself down, as my right hand shook faster. I listened to the sound of footsteps, and the hum of the refrigerator. The rest of the apartment was filled with silence.

"We don't want to kill you," a male voice said. It was the same one that had spoken earlier. "But I wouldn't try our patience if I was you."

As for me, I had plenty of patience and plenty of juice in the can. I inched my way around the corner, and nearly bumped into a dark leather shoe. I held my breath, popped up, and sprayed the first assailant in the face. He dropped his gun, screamed, and then hit the floor, his arms and legs kicking out everywhere like a turtle standing on its shell, and he clawed at his eyes like he'd been stung by a swarm of bees. I grabbed the gun that he had kicked over toward me, and I dropped to the floor, as two more bullets struck the plaster wall where my head had been only moments ago.

"You're not playing nice," the same voice said. "Besides, the effects only last for a short period of time. You better hope I don't get to you first."

I calculated the odds in my head. If I stayed where I was, eventually the other assailant would apprehend me; the guy I had sprayed would lose the stinging eye sensation; or I could end up dead, despite the assailant's assurances to the contrary. He didn't know I had a gun, or he would have mentioned this minor detail. I did have a distinct advantage, if I used it in the proper fashion, otherwise it was useless to me. I hadn't been trained in the art of firearms, but I did have a crazy idea that just might work: I just needed to implement it without killing myself in the process. I breathed deep to steady my nerves and my errant hand, listened to the sound of fabric whisking in the living room, listened to the sound of my heart beating erratically in my chest—loud enough that I thought the neighbors might hear, or at the very least my assailant—the man on the floor continued screaming and kicking, as his hands nearly scratched out his eyes. I told myself that I may not have been a trained assassin, but that I was smarter than the two men that had been sent like harbingers of death to cause my undoing.

From behind the counter, my hand shot out, as I sprayed in the general direction of my front door. I heard the sound of whisking fabric, as I inched around the corner, popped to my feet, and sprayed shots in the direction of what I hoped was my assailant. I heard glass shatter—that might have been my TV, or it could have been my sliding glass doors—I felt a bullet whiz by my left ear, another one whiz by my right, as I emptied my clip into whatever happened to be on the opposite side of the room.

I held my breath, and yanked open my door. I dove through the empty space and slammed the door shut, as a large whoosh of air escaped me. Bullets struck the door where I would have been standing had I been fully erect. I crawled to the stairs, hopped up, and raced down the three flights toward the bottom, as more bullets rained down from above. I zigzagged toward the parking lot and the safe haven that was my electric blue Corolla.

Slamming the car into drive, I whipped out of my parking spot, ignoring the fifteen mile per hour speed limit as I punched the gas pedal. I decided I needed a hotel, and I figured Williamsburg, VA was as good a place as any to lie low for a while, or at least until I could sort out more of the mess. At least I had the weekend to consider my options, possibly obtain some new clothes, and solve the mystery of Dana's death. Or so I thought.

~ ~ ~

The entire drive to Williamsburg I played Katy Perry's *Teenage Dream* album, drove above the speed limit—with the knowledge that if I was in police custody at least I was safe—checked my rearview mirror every other second or so, and tried to control my otherwise rapid breathing. To calm myself down, I started singing along with Katy, and I really fired up my vocal chords for "California Gurls" singing as loud as I could, as my right hand tapped the steering wheel in a semi-rapid fashion. Once I toned down the tapping, I gripped the wheel tighter, hoping that might alleviate any excess energy, but it didn't offer me the desired effects.

I chose a Holiday Inn Express on Richmond Road, after the first two hotels on Bypass Road proved disappointing. I checked in, found my room on the fourth floor, and collapsed on my bed still in my sweatpants, baggy t-shirt, and thin sweatshirt.

I immediately fell asleep; I woke up three hours later. All the adrenaline had left my system, my right hand no longer had a mind of its own, and my breathing had reached some semblance of normalcy. I started pacing the room, and I did a series of yoga stretches to set my mind fully at ease. I also felt guilty about missing my yoga class. A feeling of helplessness hadn't managed to leave my side either. My attempts to shove it aside only caused it to stick around with even more assurance.

Being famous—I could only assume the news program fainting or my multitude of questions—caused my current predicament. Or maybe it was my mathematical ability which I had considerably improved upon over the years, although a math-related homicide would be a new one, even for me.

Not picking up the nondescript car until later, I had no idea how long I had been tailed, or if there were other men, or even women, out to get me. Sisterhood had been in a gradual decline, and it could have taken a nosedive straight off the nearest cliff, or parachuted out of an airplane at 9,000 feet.

Not knowing what else to do, I picked up my cell phone and called Ben Xander.

"I wondered when you might call," he said.

"Why? What's going on?"

"I left you three messages. Either you chose to ignore me—"

"Or I didn't hear them," I said. "I passed out on the bed, and I woke up less than a half hour ago. I'm reasonably convinced I can now have a coherent conversation."

"Why didn't you call me sooner?"

I didn't have a reasonable answer ready for him. "Where are you?" I asked.

"Your apartment complex has been cordoned off. You have more than a dozen shots confined to your front door, your refrigerator, and the dining room wall. I don't have to tell you that you're lucky to be alive. Your survival instincts are near textbook."

"Did you find two individuals in suits that I managed to leave behind?"

"No," he said, "but we did find a blood stain on the carpet. It'll be examined for type."

"You mean you won't be able to determine anything else?"

"Probably not."

"For all of our advances in criminology," I said, "we still have a long way to go."

"Are you okay?"

"I'm better now," I said. "I probably won't fully recover for a few more days. By the way, you owe me an autopsy report. I don't want to have to collect it in person."

"I'm not sure that's a good idea," Ben said. "I'll come and see you as soon as I can break away from this convoluted scene."

"You might want to be on the lookout for two individuals impersonating police officers."

"Is there anything else I should know?"

I didn't have a good answer for him.

CHAPTER TWENTY-ONE

For the next hour and a half, I grabbed a light snack, flipped on the TV, paced the room, attempted additional yoga poses, and tried not to think about the two men in suits with guns strapped to their hands, firing more than a dozen shots in my tiny apartment. I didn't know how my insurance company, or the management company, would feel about the redecorating opportunity. I did, however, hope I wouldn't need to seek legal action in order to ensure the return of my security deposit.

The knock at the door jarred the last thoughts from my mind. I peered through another peephole, only this time the company had been expected, and as far as I knew, I hadn't been tailed. I had certainly peered in my rearview mirror enough times to discourage followers, and I had stopped for two bathroom breaks, one of which I used as an opportunity to check out the cars behind me.

I opened the door and stood toe-to-toe with Ben Xander, although he had a few additional toes in height than I did. The look on his face was filled with concern, and I could only imagine how I looked in my sweatpants and gray sweatshirt. I hadn't bothered to comb my hair, because I didn't have a comb available, and I hadn't quite worked up enough nerve to shop for hygiene items, additional outfits, or even a pair of shoes. I had socks on my feet that were more charcoal than white, and I had what I decided was a small cut on my left heel that had bled through the sock and probably onto my driver's side floor mat. If I hadn't had the surge followed a short time later by the rapid depletion of adrenaline from my body, I might have considered scouting out an OxiClean spray bottle and a roll of paper towels.

He thrust a red gym bag into my arms, and then he eased his way into my room, keeping his eyes strictly focused on my face. "You might need this," he said. "I don't want you to show up at Target and end up being escorted from the facility by an overzealous security guard who hasn't met his monthly arrest quota."

"Do I really look that bad?"

"I take it you haven't looked in a mirror lately."

"I hadn't quite worked up the nerve," I said. "What's in the bag?"

"Toiletry items that I stole from underneath your sink, a few pairs of underwear, two bras, a couple pairs of pants, a few shirts, both long and short sleeve, a handful of socks, and a pair of running shoes."

"You went through my—"

He held up his hand and nodded.

I thanked him, and then executed a head bob, because I needed to shake loose the last of the cobwebs. I wasn't thrilled with him rooting through my underwear drawer, but I was thrilled I didn't have to make a Target run in the foreseeable future. After all, I did have other matters I needed to attend to, and the sooner those matters could be resolved the better off I would be.

I tossed the gym bag on the bed. "Did you bring the autopsy report?"

He shook his head. "But I can go over the details with you."

Ben snagged the desk chair, and I sat on the bed Indian style with my hands intertwined in my lap, and what I hoped was a solemn expression on my face. I rocked back and forth slightly, the queen size bed shifting ever so slightly beneath me.

"Can I take notes?" I asked.

He nodded, and then he handed me the complimentary pad and pen that was located on the desk. I, on the other hand, poised my pen over the pad and waited, staring at him with intelligent and slightly suspicious eyes.

"She'd been dead approximately forty-eight hours based on the decomposition of the body; the tire tracks were made by a large pickup truck, possibly a Ford F-150; she had a small piece of fabric clutched in her right hand, which was most likely torn from the killer's person—"

"Or it could have been planted," I said. I'd jotted notes as rapidly as I could, but my handwriting couldn't keep up with the words flowing out of Ben's mouth.

He nodded, his facial expression remained in the off position. "Other than the one dangling shoe, she was naked below the waist; she'd had sex within the last four hours before her death; and the stocking wrapped around her neck was her own."

"What about the fabric?" I asked.

"It was from a custom button down shirt—"

"Porter Reede probably purchases similar shirts, doesn't he?"

He smirked for the first time that evening. "Are you the investigator, or am I?"

I shrugged. "I just don't want to fall behind," I said.

Ben left before I had a chance to thank him.

~ ~ ~

I decided not to draw further attention to myself by going into work Saturday morning. I didn't need to end up with a note on my door first thing Monday morning, before I even had time to drink my second mug of tea. But I didn't want to sit back and wait for something to happen either: The last time that occurred I had two strange men show up at my door, firing before they had even bothered to ask any pertinent questions.

The night before Ben Xander told me there was a chance Porter Reede had purchased the button down tailored shirts directly from an Armani store in New York City. He said there was one cop looking into the matter, and that if it fit, it would add another piece to the puzzle. I had informed him Porter wouldn't ride in a Ford F-150 pickup, even if he had his head scrunched down in the backseat, and he was in the heartland of America. That was the only part, Ben had told me, that didn't fit with the rest of the abduction story.

But I did happen to learn a few other details, that might, or might not, help me solve the mystery of Dana's death: Oliver cared for his sister as much as I cared for mine; Dana had a loose sense of morals that I couldn't quite wrap my head around, almost as though she had acquired a level of testosterone through intravenous means; she had strong will and possibly an even stronger personality; that even though all odds pointed away from this scenario, there was a chance she could have been framed; she had friends in higher places than I did; and her sexual adventures very well could have been her final undoing, most of which had avoided YouTube or the Internet at large. Tommy Buchs had a knack for not conducting police work, and for striking just enough fear in me to believe he might have had something to do with the two sharply dressed individuals that had shown up at my door, or maybe he hired out his grunt work these days. I had also turned up another abnormality: The Wilson family came from money. If indeed the money well had not run dry, why had Dana turned to a life of blackmail? Did she believe more was a better flavor than chocolate? Or did she want to separate herself from her parents? And how had her parents fit into the equation, or had they?

The Wilson wealth pool started with a great-great-great-grandfather, a shipping magnate, who had specialized in trading between the US and Europe. He specialized in two goods more known for their differences than their similarities: textiles and steel. His great-grandson sold the business for a rather large sum, right before the price of steel went through the basement, and the Wilsons focused on inherited wealth, shunning the nouveau riche along the way, and for the most part, those less fortunate than themselves, which included about ninety-six percent of the population at large.

The money, while it wasn't nearly as plentiful as it used to be—due to a series of investments in businesses that ultimately failed—still remained plentiful and was more than enough to keep the average person, and his or her inheritors, entertained for many years to come. Oliver, Dana's brother, was worth four million dollars, the money confined to a trust, of which he took steady payments each year, with the principal invested in stocks, bonds, and mutual funds, the vast majority of which were invested in overseas companies. This left him the opportunity to pursue other means, of which he chose to confine himself to painting landscapes, many of which probably shouldn't even be displayed in an elementary school, and none of which had been sold to any reputable buyers through any reputable galleries.

~ ~ ~

I had purchased a cell phone charger should my phone run out of juice, or in a pinch, I could use the hotel phone: I wasn't entirely certain local calls were free. I had to keep my expenses within a confined range that would keep the credit card companies at bay for at least a few more days. But before I could plug my phone in, as it was currently running on life support, it rang. I didn't recognize the number, but I picked it up anyway. After I said hello, and before the voice on the other end identified himself, he plunged right in, as if he were taking a swan dive in cold water, and I was the fish at the bottom of the river.

"He wants to kill me," he said.

I had the first inclination that I might have a crank call on my hands. Not that I received these on a regular basis, but there always remained the distinct possibility. I'd left my prepared brushoff at home, but I could always improvise based on what I'd seen on TV and the movies. "That seems a bit extreme, don't you think?"

"No, I don't think it's extreme at all," he said. "My life was on the line, and running away proved to be my only viable option, and thus ensuring my survival. Now I don't know what I should I do. I thought I would be safe here..." The voice trailed off; I was met with prolonged silence and a sense of static.

I waited a beat for the caller to identify himself: He didn't. Rather than run down the short list of males that might actually call me, I decided it was better to end the charade. "Who is this?" I asked. Had I been in a more leisurely mood, I might have avoided the direct approach.

"Garrett Everest," he said. "Have you forgotten me already?"

"No," I said, "but I wasn't expecting you to call either. Aren't you in Richmond?"

"I am. And I'm not even sure I'm safe here." He paused, as static filled the airwaves once again. "His reach extends beyond mere city limits."

"You seemed reasonably sure of yourself before. What changed?"

"I received an anonymous call last night. The voice on the other end sounded garbled, and it warned me to stay away from Wired Consulting. He threatened to kill my dog."

I asked, "Do you own a dog?"

There was another pause. "No."

"But you were fired?"

"Thus, my reason to submit an application," he said.

"You didn't."

"It's not as though I had a choice. I haven't exactly discovered the perfect employment situation here, although I am still entertaining a distinct number of possibilities, most of which reach the level of impossible in a rather unfriendly and efficient manner. But the door hasn't smacked me in the face yet."

"This isn't exactly the perfect economic environment," I said.

"Indeed," he said. "And I fear that Porter Reede may have influenced the situation. If for no other reason than his own amusement. He's tossed my name into the trash along with all the leftover banana peels and orange rinds."

"How do you know it's Porter? I don't think he has enough hours in the day to sabotage every last one of your employment opportunities."

Garrett said, "The unknown caller mentioned the details of my application specifically, and I was informed that if I ever set foot on the premises, I'd end up at the bottom of the Chesapeake Bay."

"Are you sure you're not exaggerating? Maybe you've developed the ability of extensive hallucinations. Or maybe it's some sort of anonymous prank."

"Porter doesn't like to lose."

"What are you talking about?" I asked.

"I might have embezzled a bit of money on my way out the door."

I coughed. I could think of a few choice words, none of which were appropriate in mixed company. I'd lodged a sense of dread in my throat, and I wasn't quite sure how to rectify the situation. "How much?"

"Enough to set myself up in Richmond. I didn't think he'd actually miss it. I merely skimmed the money as it flowed between accounts over a two-week period."

I didn't ask more specific details: I feared I was better off not knowing. And as a forensic accountant I didn't want to negate the basic principles of my existence. If I didn't have a conscience, I would have viewed the scenario from an entirely different perspective.

"You never had a serious relationship with Dana, but you wanted one, didn't you?"

There was an audible pause on the other end of the line, long enough for me to question that the lines of communication were still open. "Why do you care?" he asked. "None of this matters now. None of it will change what happened. Either way, I'm doomed."

"Why do you say that?"

"Porter Reede has Tommy Buchs in his back pocket."

Before I could ask my next question, the line went dead. When I peered down at my cell phone, the battery light blinked at me. I didn't know if my phone had died, or if he had hung up on me. Either way, I had just crossed over the line and landed in the middle of a cornfield, possibly in the middle of Ohio and possibly after dark, and I'd left my flashlight in the car.

~ ~ ~

After I had charged my phone, eaten lunch, changed outfits,

checked out the fitness room, where I opted to pass—two guys had checked me out, neither of which was remotely interesting—and settled for yin yoga exercises instead a foot away from my bed, limbering and strengthening my joints, muscles, and mind, I forced my way into Elena Tearz's world yet again. I chose a neutral site not far from the Holiday Inn Express, but not too close either: I wanted to spot a tail if I happened to notice one in my rearview mirror. If not, I'd have a lot of paranoia on my hands for no apparent reason, and I didn't need that particular transgression on my conscience. I chose caution over practicality and living over dying.

When I arrived, she had a steaming drink in front of her, and a look of concern on her face. Her hands were folded on the table. It was small, the wood was dark, the overhead lights were muted, and the tea proved more than adequate.

She skipped right past the pleasantries, straight to the heart of the matter. "Are you in trouble?" she asked.

"Why?"

"Why are we meeting here? Besides, you don't exactly seem yourself today either. You're a little bit off-balance like your right leg is slightly longer than your left."

I didn't know how much I should say about my visitors from last night nor did I know how much I could trust Elena. Even though my instincts told me she had been more than truthful with me every step of the way, I still felt as though I could end up in a rather precarious position, and based on the weight of my pepper spray, I didn't have a lot of liquid left in the can.

I sipped from my mug, as it dangled from my fingertips. "Dana's death has been harder for me than I would have thought."

She nodded, sipped from her cup, and then stared up at me expectantly. I took a swallow, and then I took another one, hoping to dull the pain from the first one. The roof of my mouth numbed, and the caffeine slipped into my veins. Smiling, however, wasn't an option.

"What do you think of Porter Reede?" I asked.

She stared at me for a long moment: I shifted under her gaze. "Why?"

"He may have a composition similar to Teflon, but nothing seems to add up with him. He may not be guilty of murder, but I don't think he can play the innocent act to perfection either."

"What do you know?" she asked.

I gave her some of the information, but I withheld other pieces of the puzzle. Even though my instinct told me I should trust her, I just couldn't complete the task without feeling as though I had betrayed Dana, even if Elena was her best friend.

"I'm not sure I'd trust Jerry if I were you. He has the learning capacity of a socket wrench. Dana, however, told me he was good for other matters that didn't involve mathematics, literature, or social sciences."

I looked down and smiled at my cup. While I had already decreased some of the distance between the mug and myself, I brought it to my lips and took another soft sip.

"As for you, you need to be careful. I don't want to read about you on the six o'clock news with your body inside a zippered plastic bag. Dana deserves justice, but she doesn't deserve to have you killed in the process. You're more valuable alive than dead, and you can tell that to Jerry, Porter, or whoever else you may run into."

I nodded, not knowing what else to say. The murmurings continued around us, some conversations more amplified than others. A steady progress of people continued through the door, every other minute or so, and the female baristas behind the counter provided a constant stream of motion.

"This is the perfect setup," she said. "Porter has ties to Dana, and plenty of money to make a blackmailer foam at the mouth. What you need to do is see past the hazy fog and find the true essence of this heinous act. There's something missing here, and you need to find out what it is. It's more than just a simple case of whodunit and how-they-done-it. Unfortunately, you're caught in the middle of the action and so was Dana."

"I don't need a quick score," I said. "I have too much invested in the outcome already. The more I find out, the deeper the hole gets. I just hope I haven't set myself up on some suicidal mission where the only way I can survive is to change my name, relocate to Iowa, and find myself a more than adequate convent to live out the remainder of my days."

"You're probably being overly dramatic."

"Am I?" I asked.

CHAPTER TWENTY-TWO

With the potential to end up six feet under alleviated, or so I thought—the majority of my weekend spent in a hotel room with a well-built desk, a dark wood entertainment center, all the free Internet I could possibly enjoy, free breakfast every morning, and a series of yoga stretches conducted every afternoon—I spent the rest of the weekend in research mode, digging, digging, and more digging. Since I didn't have a computer, I conducted most of my digging through my confidant Don Stader in approximately fifteen minute intervals, between what I could only assume were World of Warcraft rounds, and not once did he bother to ask me where I was. Since his TV watching and World of Warcraft playing exhibited an inverse relationship, I could safely assume he hadn't seen the news—and the aftermath of my latest exploits. To round out my weekend, I conducted a couple of phone calls with Ben Xander who managed to be both charming and placating at the same time, shaking his head across the towers, and pausing only when necessary.

I drove east on I-64 only a little smarter than I was before. The radio kept me company, but it didn't really improve my mood. The traffic stalled at various intervals, and I was forced to switch lanes when a car ahead of me couldn't even keep up with the speed limit, let alone the flow of traffic.

I received two calls along the route, both went to voicemail. After watching more than my share of cell phone incidents, I'd decided driving and talking should be mutually exclusive events. Substantiating this hypothesis proved harder than I would have liked, but I had nothing if not plenty of willpower. And my social life proved more limited than it probably should have. But it wasn't like I made a concerted effort in that arena, and other than the bit of non-work-related excitement, I truly did live the life of the stereotypical accountant, except I indulged in more romantic comedies than my fellow brethren, or so I'd heard.

Both calls were from my mother—she hadn't bothered to hide her concern, or her unhappiness that I hadn't bothered to inform her of recent events—the second message more hysterical and longwinded than the first.

I had decided several years ago that my mother and a heart attack should be mutually exclusive events as well. Even if she did tend to worry more than an entire Catholic family, she ate right and exercised regularly, and there were no issues of cardiovascular disease in our gene pool, otherwise she might have seen the inside of a pine box sooner than she had planned.

Once I was safely within the confines of my apartment, having avoided the neighbors and the crime scene tape plastered on my front door, I returned her call. She picked up on the first ring, and immediately transitioned into verbal attack mode.

"Was that your apartment complex on the news?" she asked.

I paused for dramatic effect. "Yes."

"What happened?"

I paused while I shifted the phone to my left ear. Just in case the conversation proved a rather troublesome adventure, I could set it on the arm of the sofa and walk away without a scratch on me. "Why do you think I'm involved?"

"I can hear it in your tone of voice," she said. "You were never a good liar. When you were younger, you had a guilty look every time you stuck your hand in the cookie jar."

"You're already accusing me of conjuring up some sort of scheme or diabolical plot," I said. "My apartment complex has made the news before." It was ten years ago, involved a volleyball fundraising event that had taken place on-site, and the coverage had been rather minimal, but it had still made the six o'clock news. It had been a slow broadcast day, no homicides or corrupt politicians or embezzlement issues, and the former owner of our apartment complex had been a mover and shaker in the political arena, which meant he was currently serving a six-year prison sentence in a minimum security facility, of which he had served nearly two years.

"I don't think you have a diabolical bone in your body."

"But you are concerned about my well-being," I said. "And when it comes to trust, you tend to have a very short leash."

She ignored my second comment and concentrated on my first. "Of course I am."

"Because you don't think I can take care of myself."

"That's not it at all, dear," my mother said. "I care about you deeply, and I only want the best for you. I don't think ending up on the news is in your own best interest. The reporter mentioned gunshots. Were you involved in some sort of standoff?"

"Mom, you know I don't own a gun."

"But that never stopped you from firing before." One of my first dates had taken me to a gun range, despite every protest I could think of. It was an outdoor facility, and he'd handed me a .44 Magnum. I didn't brace myself properly, and I ended up on my backside staring up at a bright blue sky. If I'd struck the ground with any more velocity, I probably would have knocked myself unconscious. In the end, he hadn't garnered a second date, and if I'd had my own method of transportation, I would have walked out on him and his Ruger and his smug expression and never looked back.

"You could at least give me a little bit more credit," I said. "I'm perfectly capable of staying out of trouble on a fairly regular basis."

"You did fire a gun, didn't you?"

"Yes," I said, "but it wasn't mine."

"And you had to use the can of pepper spray, didn't you? I'll bet this time it wasn't even on yourself."

"Yes," I said, "but I had to run through it. Luckily, my eyes didn't water, and I didn't stumble out my door either." Either my body had developed a slight immunity, or I had run like the wind. Instead, though, I'd probably reached an understanding of its effects, and therefore wasn't as surprised this go round as I had been the first time.

"Maybe you should start at the beginning," my mother said. Her voice contained more than a hint of concern, but it hadn't reached the point of irrationality. Knowing my mother that would come later after the initial shock had worn off, and she had time to process the full extent of the situation, and how it might affect her next bridge club meeting.

"Are you sure your heart can take it?"

"My heart can take it just fine," she said. "I want to know that you're safe, and that you're not about to try anything as daring and as drastic as you may have in the past. You need to start thinking about a family soon."

I held my hand over my eyes and cringed. "I don't take many risks in my life."

"You take more than you realize," she said.

Despite her constant prying, I told her the details of the break-in, although I left out the part that the two suits had impersonated real detectives minus the badges, and that the guns were small caliber semi-automatic weapons. To my mother, any gun—no matter how large or small—was a death wish, and the offender should be locked away in a prison cell for the rest of his natural life. Needless to say, she wouldn't be invited to the next NRA meeting. I emphasized that I was unharmed, and I left out the part about the blood stain in my apartment that was not my own. Had I mentioned this detail, she would have only heard the word blood and jumped to the conclusion that I was irreparably harmed, hopped in her car, driven over to my apartment, and taken me to the hospital, despite no visible injuries other than a few scrapes on my elbows and knees, all of which had already been cleaned with peroxide.

"Where are you now?"

"Home," I said. "Right where I should be."

"But you were in a safe neighborhood," she said. "I don't see how this could have happened to you. What sort of trouble are you in?"

~ ~ ~

I had a Jolly Rancher in my mouth, and a rather large bald man standing in my doorway with his palm pressed firmly against the wood. He had a rather large smirk on his face, and his thumb was tucked inside his right pocket. Had I known what awaited me, I might have stayed in bed, or at least considered the option more thoroughly before making an informed decision, getting dressed, grabbing breakfast, and driving into work.

He looked about as formidable as my mother, and with a rather stern expression that she had first perfected in my youth, and only managed to increase the skill of said expression with time, patience, and two rebellious youths, one of whom was probably a bit more rebellious than the other.

"You really don't get this, do you?" he asked.

"What are you talking about?"

"This isn't some sort of game," he said. "You were nearly killed because you don't know what you're doing, and I'm not always going to be around to protect you."

First, Tommy Buchs had never protected me, and second, I had more information than he did, although he may not have been privy to the extent of my knowledge—as I had an inside source—and I hoped I could keep him firmly on his toes and out of my life. The latter proved a bit harder to pull off than I had initially anticipated. If he had been smarter, he probably would have done the same to me. "Are you threatening me?"

He shrugged. "I'm merely making a few suggestions."

I bristled, the Jolly Rancher hard on my tongue. "I don't need your help."

"Oh contraire, you need my help more than you realize. You were lucky once; I doubt very much that you'll be so lucky again."

"I don't like these games," I said.

He flexed a bicep, probably some sort of automatic response to the extent of his manhood, before he offered a smirk. "Well, these games are just getting started."

"Maybe you can figure out a way to end them in a quicker fashion," I said. "You seem more interested in prolonging your efforts than reaching any definite conclusions. Don't you think you should be a bit more concerned about the victim?" I paused; he didn't immediately jump in to fill in the void. "And you were also intimately involved with the deceased. When were you planning on mentioning that little detail?"

He snarled. "This is more than just a power play between me and you. You seem to have taken Dana's death extremely personally, and it's affecting your better judgment. I'm not sure I like the blatant accusations as well as the hidden ones."

"Have you honestly considered the possibility that her death might have been more than just an accident? There's more than just a hint of foul play. There's plenty to implicate Porter Reede, or are you blinded by your own sense of greed?" I left out the detail of the shirt fabric that was jammed into Dana's hand: It was Armani and of a similar style and cut that Porter often wore. As for the details of her sexual encounter, that remained unknown, but I still had more than a few suspects there as well. And several of them were in powerful enough positions to conduct damage control as well as extensive cover-up. And I had already tossed around more than enough accusations for one day, but I wasn't opposed to a few more. As to the extent Dana and I knew each other, I figured what Tommy didn't know wouldn't hurt him. Had he discovered our past, he probably would have found a way to use it against me in a court of law, or if he couldn't swing that particular dance, the court of public opinion came to mind.

He shook his head. "You're willing to believe any lie that will benefit you and implicate whomever you might desire."

Before I could think of a reasonably accurate reply, possibly along the lines of how I approached things mathematically instead of emotionally, he had turned and walked away, slamming the door behind him. He had not, however, rattled my incisors, the papers on my desk, or my mug of tea that was a few inches away from me.

Norma Beemer knocked and then entered my office, a look of concern on her face. She grabbed me by the arm and guided me toward the employee break room and its glass doors. Once inside, she locked the door behind her, planted me at the middle of the three tables and then sat directly across from me. Her eyes turned expressive and animated, right before she planted her elbows on the table and leaned in my general direction.

"Are you sure you want to continue with this present course of action?" she asked. Her eyes turned softer, more focused, and intently watched the expression on my face. "You may be right about Porter Reede, but there's a very good chance you could be wrong."

I had said nothing more to her about the matter before this, so I was obviously concerned about where she had gotten her information. The possibility of hidden cameras or office moles entered the equation, and provided a somewhat logical, if slightly profound, conclusion.

"I'm a more permanent fixture than the office furniture and the carpet," she said. "Nothing goes on around here without me knowing about it. You may be subtle, but you're certainly not as subtle as you think you are. Even though you haven't plastered yourself on any cameras recently, that doesn't mean your actions haven't gone unnoticed."

"You watched the news?" I asked.

She shook her head. "I don't need to. I have other informational sources. And I'm more than happy to offer a helping hand. Your encounter at the apartment complex must have caused you more problems than you realize."

"I'm over it," I said. I'd had trouble sleeping the first night, but each successive night had gotten easier and easier, until I'd pretty much forgotten about the encounter altogether. Well, maybe not, but I could hope my life might eventually reach such an outcome.

She shook her head again. "You may want to put it behind you, but this has gotten personal for you. Emotions can get in the way of logic."

I preferred not to think about such a risky proposition, but I knew she was right. "If you learn to trust your instincts more, you won't jump to the wrong conclusions. You need to make both sides of the equation equal to each other: You're not nearly as close as you think you are."

"What are you saying?"

She rubbed her left hand with her right. "There's still a bit more to the story."

"Are you going to tell me?" I asked.

"No," she said, "you're better off figuring it out for yourself. I know you're smart enough to find the solution."

~ ~ ~

I still had the ransom note and gun in my possession. The black killing machine had slipped my mind until I saw the note on my dresser, which made me remember the gun stuffed in my glove compartment. In my hasty retreat, I had tossed it on the passenger seat, only to stuff it out of sight when the opportunity presented itself in Williamsburg, outside of the Holiday Inn Express, and under the cover of darkness. I'd looked around twice, concerned I would be picked up by security cameras in the parking lot, even if the lot was only partially lighted. The better option would have been to place it in the hotel safe, and the even better option would have been to pass the gun off to Ben, but I had done neither, and I didn't quite exactly know why.

I managed to fit a much needed break into my schedule, and I managed to put Jerry Duncan at the top of my list of inquiries. I still didn't know what Dana had seen in him, but I gathered his talents didn't extend much beyond the bedroom.

I exchanged a few pleasantries with Jerry, or at least as many as he'd allow, before his look turned stern and his voice turned harsh. He had a certain surliness that hadn't been apparent before. Either he'd hidden it well, or he'd let Dana's death affect him more than I thought possible. He mentioned her fondly, as if she might spring back to life at any moment, and provide him with a nice big hug and a bottle of beer. His dark jeans and t-shirt were crumpled, but his eyes had retained a large part of their hardness, each gaze more penetrating than the last, until the giant microscope provided me with ambient light.

He had a toothpick jammed in his mouth, but it was currently in the resting position, although it threatened to give way at any moment. He motioned for me to back away, and then he joined me on what I supposed might have passed for a porch at one time. Several of the wooden boards creaked, and the furniture would have been outdated more than ten years ago. But there was a cooler handy for what I believed to be emergency purposes.

"You can't bring Dana back to life," he said.

I nodded, and my right hand bobbed in approval, before settling on my right thigh. "You knew Dana had money, didn't you?"

"Yes," he said, "but I also realized she didn't want to be some sort of charity case. She wanted to make it on her own, and she didn't always go about it in the best fashion. It didn't take her father long to disown her. She showed her independence in a sometimes unhealthy manner, but it worked rather well from my perspective." He grinned, winked, and then leered at me. "She always managed to do the exact opposite of what her father wanted her to do. He stopped reaching out to her, and she stopped trying to please him. The relationship had taken more than a slightly casual strain on both of them."

"She used sex as a weapon, didn't she?"

He nodded. "It was the only time she truly felt in control." He started to add more, but I held up my hand and shook my head.

"Even now you still love her, despite what she has become in your mind."

"It's not easy to watch someone you care about spiral out of control. She truly believed she was invincible, and that her exterior was impermeable. When you're not careful, that's the kind of thinking that can get you killed."

CHAPTER TWENTY-THREE

Back at the office, with a mug of tea on my desk, and a pile of Jolly Ranchers next to my computer keyboard, I decided I needed a few more financial revelations to make an informed decision on Dana's death. Her story had more than a few potential pitfalls and various tangents with many of them consisting of bedroom variety details.

Her parents, on the other hand, still appeared to care about her deeply, although Rick Wilson seemed a bit more restricted in his love for his daughter. Oliver cared for his sister, but he hadn't exactly been forthcoming about his trust fund, and as far as I knew, he had made no concerted effort to pay his sister's ransom. He had in fact seemed more concerned about his landscape painting that wasn't nearly as heavy on the painting end of it as it should have been. His eyes had shown remorse and concern for his sister but nothing more. Not even a hint at something deeper that might have helped prolong the relationship.

Knowing I needed the assistance of a hacker who had less than scrupulous morals, and who still harbored various fantasies of me, although he would never admit this to anyone, including himself. I dialed his number, hearing four rings in my ear before the receiver was picked up on the other end. Despite his penchant for technology, he still didn't believe in cell phones, but he did believe in every other form of technology known to man.

"Haven't you and I already talked enough?" Don Stader asked.

"I'm always in need of your valuable assistance, and you happen to have too much time on your hands."

Don was a white knight hacker who attacked various security firewalls, Internet domains, cell phones, GPS devices, etc. to look for vulnerabilities. But he had no problem sticking it to the man, as he called it, whenever he felt a company sacrificed everything else in the name of corporate greed. The list of companies on his watch list had increased exponentially over the years, and this led to anger management issues, as well as a shift in his moral compass, and possibly a group therapy session or two. Anger coupled with too much time, very little outside contact, obesity and insecurity issues, along with the ability to bottle up his emotions, meant he might very well combust one day. I was glad our relationship was limited to phone conversations, and that I had only been to his place of residence on two occasions, neither of which had ended particularly well.

"I like to stagger out my projects. I'd rather not have to deal with them all at one time. Eight hour work days are meant for the corporate bigwigs."

"Ten or eleven are probably a bit more accurate. It's not easy when you're at the top."

"What sort of information are you looking for now?" he asked.

"That of the financial variety," I said. "I need to know about three more individuals, and unfortunately, I'm not able to complete the task myself. I was only able to gather cursory information, and I don't have the time to dig deeper. Plus, you're a wizard."

He grunted, and then I felt a smirk in my ear. "That's because your access is a bit more limited than mine, although I do appreciate your effort. In the name of information gathering, you're bound to run into more than a few dead ends."

I didn't bother to correct him, since I was in ego-appeasing mode.

I had done an initial look on my own, and I had reached some rather interesting conclusions, but I wanted a second set of eyes, just in case I had missed a detail or two. What I had learned, though, could turn out to be rather revealing, and it could very well change my present course of action. I told him what I needed, and then hung up before he could ask probing questions, or begin a World of Warcraft monologue, during which I would only be able to follow a few words.

~ ~ ~

"You and I need to have a discussion about what you've been up to," Cooper Strut said.

He had summoned me into his office under the pretense that he wanted to discuss a new project with me. It turned out he wanted to discuss a bit more than mathematical formulas. As much as I wanted to walk right out of his office, my butt was glued to the black leather chair. His eyes resembled daggers punching holes in my own, and he had shed some of his boyish charm. He had a submarine in front of him, and I wasn't sure if he planned to eat it or toss it in my direction. He had on a charcoal three-piece suit, and he had placed a glass of scotch to the left of his keyboard. He had executed his hair in the traditional slicked back fashion, and his hands were currently placed on either side of the submarine.

Cooper said, "You've been rather busy lately." He held up his hand before I could interject. "You've managed to break into Dana's office twice; Grate Marketing on two separate occasions; and you're also a regular on the six o'clock news. If you're not careful, you might even receive a couple of job offers."

"Have there been complaints about my work?"

"You're doing the job I pay you to do."

"I see," I said. But I really had no clue where he planned to go with his present thought process. He had a tangent on the horizon, and he wasn't afraid to use it. I eased forward in my chair, in case I needed to bolt, or cover my head and duck.

"I don't like being blindsided by marketing department heads." He meant Frankie Kensington, who had managed to fail at every step of the political game, but she had a mouth that more than made up for her various shortcomings. She wasn't afraid to use it either. From what I'd heard, it was a rather skilled mouth.

"Was there a problem with my analysis?"

He shook his head. "In fact, it should probably be closer to ten or fifteen percent. She has excess in her budget labeled under a miscellaneous accounts umbrella that is five percent higher than any other department. However, you do need to work on your approach, if you want to keep her off my back, and in turn, you want me to stay off of yours."

"Is this some sort of reprimand?"

He shook his head again. "We'll refer to it as a fair warning. You have talent (there's no question about that), and you have more than enough potential, but you do have a problem focusing on your duties. I'd guess it's because you're being underutilized."

"Are you offering me a raise?"

"Wrong again. But if you give Wired Consulting a bad name, you'll find yourself in more than just a slightly compromising position. Despite your various talents, and your penchant for numbers, you'd find yourself out of a job." Cooper picked up his submarine and pulled off a large chunk with his teeth.

"Is that all?" I asked.

He nodded. "For now. But don't think I won't hesitate to call on you again in the future. You've got talent, but you don't always know how to use it properly."

~ ~ ~

Ben had had helped me find the tangential road that I had been driving on for the past few miles. I told him I didn't believe everything Frankie Kensington had told me, and I'd also told him about her curious exchange of emails with Dana Wilson (otherwise known as the female secretary who liked to sleep around more than most of her male counterparts, and who had managed to turn up dead on the outskirts of a wooded area on the edge of a park, and who had been found by a couple of small children who would most likely need therapy once they were old enough to realize what had happened). I was old enough to know the truth, and I still didn't know what had happened, although the fog had finally started to clear.

He had also recently commandeered the chair on the other side of my desk. I had discovered him when I returned from Cooper's office. He had this rather innate ability to show up at the most opportune of moments, and he had more than his share of smiles for me, along with the occasional condescending remark or slight suspicion painted on his face. I could probably meet my smile quota for the next month or so, if I were inclined to actually start keeping track. He had the softest hands I'd ever discovered on a man, and I had let my right hand intermingle with his for a beat longer than was necessary. It was a mistake I would have gladly made again, if he hadn't pulled his hand away, right before he eyed me suspiciously.

He had shown up with more than a few concerns, some of which had to do with me, but most of which had to do with Tommy Buchs.

"How much has my reputation been sullied?"

"He's actually told a few of his pals that you're physically impeding his investigation."

"But I haven't been around to impede his investigation," I said. "I've been in Williamsburg, and I managed to take up a weekend residency at the Holiday Inn Express."

"You didn't waste any time returning to your apartment or the office."

"If I had stayed there, I would have focused on my helplessness, and I would've let my two attackers as well as Dana Wilson's murderer win. I'm rather fond of winning to the point that I physically hate to lose. And I can't bear the thought that Tommy Buchs might figure out what happened to Dana before I do. He might have less sense than I do, but he certainly has more experience and possibly more resources."

He leaned forward. "Did you discover anything new about Frankie?"

"That's still in the works," I said. "I have my best man on it." I paused. "Would you like a Jolly Rancher?"

He shook his head. "Do you have some sort of sugar consuming disorder?"

I shuffled a few papers, rearranging a pile that was already in perfect order. "No, but I am rather fond of the grape ones."

"Did you find out anything more about the two men that accosted you?"

"No," I said. "I can only hope I won't ever see them again. I'm sure the one I shot will have more than a few reservations about showing himself at my apartment. As for the other who ended up writhing on the floor, I'm sure he won't be particularly interested in visiting me again either. If he does, I still have a quarter can of pepper spray left, and I'm fairly confident I can obtain more if necessary."

Ben looked down at his hands, and then took a gander above my head, before settling his eyes once again in my direction. "How has this sidebar affected your job?"

"Probably not as much as it should have. I was told I'm being underutilized in my current capacity, but I'm not going to experience an increase in pay." I shrugged. "It's probably safe to assume that my workload won't change either."

"Your family life?"

"I'm sure my mother lives in fear that I'll make the six o'clock news again. But I'm sure my run will stop at two." I had no idea how wrong I'd be with that particular call.

~ ~ ~

Since Don Stader hadn't bothered to call me back, I took the initiative, and he confirmed my worst fear: Frankie Kensington was dirtier than I had anticipated. She had skimmed from her miscellaneous expense fund, and she had developed a take-no-prisoners attitude. If she could have fired me, I would have already had my desk packed and sitting on the street corner in what would amount to three large brown boxes and two men in dark sunglasses and matching suits looming over said boxes with hard expressions and arms crossed in front of their chests.

Jerry Duncan and Jessie Trager had their own problems, though, and life without Dana Wilson wasn't as good as life with Dana. Jessie had received more financial assistance than Jerry, which surprised me, but it was yet another detail that I didn't plan to overlook.

Don pounded keys in the background, and he even managed to grunt on several occasions to counteract the periodic bouts of silence. My mind focused on an apple Jolly Rancher on my desk, and I shoved it in my mouth before I completely lost the extent of my thought process. I jotted a few details on my notepad, just in case I needed to reference the situation later. Convoluted happened to be the understatement of the year, and I decided therapy might be the only solution to my problem. Before I could discover Don's thoughts on the matter, he had clicked off, and I had nothing but dead air to take his place.

I placed the receiver back in its cradle, and it immediately sprang to life again. Even if he had missed a detail, Don wouldn't have bothered to call me back. My sister Felicia filled the airwaves, and her voice was filled with more than a slight hint of concern. She had instincts that only managed to cause me problems, but her heart remained in the right place, just as Elmer remained firmly attached to her side.

"You're becoming something of a local celebrity," she said.

"I can assure you it's not on purpose. I do believe my neighborhood remains safe, just in case you happened to have any ideas to the contrary."

"You've managed to get yourself in two very different situations."

"Both involved nameless individuals who had decided to do society more harm than good, so they're probably not as different as you would imagine."

Felicia said, "Have you ever considered normalcy?"

"I already have that in my day job. Besides, I need to discover new opportunities while I'm still young. I've probably managed to shave a few years off of my life, but I couldn't be happier. I feel as though my life has changed for the better, and I didn't even have to buy a new wardrobe or a new car."

"You're not with a man, are you?"

"No," I said. "I was, but I sprayed him with pepper spray. I don't think I'll be seeing him in the near future, and there's a more than good chance I shot his buddy somewhere on his person before I dove out my front door."

"Have you ever considered dating normal men?"

"Well, in my defense, these two happened to randomly show up at my door in business suits, both of which had rather large semi-automatic pistols in their possession. They claimed to be the police, but neither could back up his story with an actual shield or other identification."

"Even for you that's about as far from normal as you can get. Besides, I've never heard of stalkers who feel the need to protect themselves. Normally the victim decides that a gun might solve her problems. But that's not the case here at all. As I recall, you swore off all firearms once you ended up on your back with a .44 Magnum planted firmly on your stomach."

"True," I said. "And you'll be the first to know if I ever change my opinion. But I do have a semi-automatic weapon currently stashed in my glove compartment."

There was an audible sigh on the other end of the line followed by an elongated pause followed by some mild barking from Elmer and a hiccup or two from the baby.

"You aren't planning to grace the news with your presence again, are you?"

"I'm rather good at finding my own way," I said.

"A little too good," Felicia said. "But you do provide the evening's entertainment, and you manage to keep mom off my back, since she's constantly riding yours. I suppose I should probably thank you."

"You certainly don't need to get all soft on my account," I said.

Mild laughter filled the airwaves before more barking and hiccups.

As I hung up, the hiccups had turned into screaming which had reached a crescendo. Elmer, who had managed to add further insult to the misery, had already started barking in time with the screaming, and was probably well on his way to pursuing his usual howling.

CHAPTER TWENTY-FOUR

I decided I needed to visit Oliver Wilson and his paint splattered apartment again. After my conversation with Cooper Strut, as well as the one with Tommy Buchs, I found work to be a rather trivial concept. Numbers floated around in my head, but I didn't see any immediate solutions. The Jolly Rancher in my mouth helped, but it didn't completely alleviate matters either. The sound of my own voice rang in my head, and I closed my eyes to the verbal onslaught. When I opened them, I removed myself from my desk, discovered the front door of Wired Consulting, and staggered out into the bright sunlight without my sunglasses.

Upon arrival, I didn't remember driving to Oliver's apartment, the traffic situation, or what was playing on my stereo. I stumbled to the front door, knocked, and waited for my dramatic entrance. Several knocks later the door was yanked open. The man on the other side kept his expression neutral; the paint brush in his right hand offered a better hello than he did, welcoming me with bristles wide open. Feeling a bit misinformed and going on less sleep than usual, I skipped most of the pleasantries, exchanged a rather brief greeting, and then tried for the offensive without being too aggressive.

I said, "You should have told me you were worth four million dollars."

He ushered me inside, and then slammed the door. The paint brush didn't move, and neither did he. "Would it have done me any good?"

"It might have helped save your sister," I said.

He walked across the living room and stood at his easel with his back to me. The canvas was half-completed, and he appeared half into his current painting situation. Soft classical music played in the background, and the blinds on the windows were open. His current furniture situation, which proved rather anemic, was covered with white sheets. Since I'd been sitting most of the day, I preferred standing to the potentially paint-splattered alternative.

"My sister was dead the moment she decided to play a game of Russian roulette. She always played up to the competition, but this time she wasn't ready for the consequences."

I asked, "Did you know about your sister's relationship with Frankie Kensington?"

"Her boss?"

"Exactly," I said. My eyes bore into the back of his head right around neck level. His shoulders were broad, and his strokes were large. I tried not to focus on either matter too heavily, as I stood just off to the side.

He shook his head, dropped the brush in the slot, and turned around to face me. His eyes, though, told me there was more to Dana's story than just a simple shake of the head.

"You're not exactly being forthcoming again."

Picking up the brush, he splattered paint on the canvas in what appeared to be a haphazard fashion before he dropped the brush against the easel. His head whipped around faster than his body. "You don't exactly play fair, you know that right?"

"Absolutely," I said. "But I need to use every advantage I have. It's hard enough when you experience more than a few lies along the way. Besides, I don't exactly do this for a living. Most of the time I merely let curiosity get the best of me, and then stop my mathematical fantasies in midstream."

"It's more about concealing the truth," he said. "Her tragic death is merely another chapter in her tragic life. She lived hard, played hard, and presumably died hard. If she was nothing else, at least she was consistent."

"What are you worried about?"

He pointed at his chest. "Me. I have no concerns other than my painting. You, on the other hand, probably have more than your share of problems. You're focused only on the art of exposition, and that's not just dangerous: It could turn out to be devastating."

"How would you know that?"

"You're more on edge than you were the last time. You're wound up tighter than a trampoline, and as soon as someone drops a steel ball on your head, you're going to spring to life and annihilate whoever happens to be in your way."

"I don't like wasting my time," I said. "And I'm not fond of the art of failure."

"You're not wasting it. But you don't exactly know how to use it properly either. You're still an amateur. You can't walk right into the game and expect to be a professional. Besides, you're further along than Tommy Buchs, aren't you? Isn't that something to be proud of?"

"He's not exactly top cop material," I said. "If I merely compared myself to him, I'd have to place myself several steps ahead, and that's only focusing on intellect."

Oliver wiped his brow with the sleeve of his shirt. "He's severely lacking in a significant number of areas," he said. "But at least he tries real hard. You have to give him at least a little credit."

"No, he doesn't," I said. "He's only going to pursue this matter to the minimum extent possible. If you understood your sister, you might understand that much."

"He has ulterior motives. He's rather good at focusing his mind entirely on other matters. Since this isn't your primary duty, you should understand what it's like."

Unfortunately, I understood all of this a little too well, and I was in up to the brim of my mug with the end nothing more than an errant hallucination. "So I'm aware."

He asked, "So what else do you know besides my financial situation and my sister's bisexual fantasies?"

"Tommy knew about the ransom note, didn't he?"

He nodded, picked up his brush, and then focused his attention once again on the canvas before him. I left his broad shoulders and brush strokes behind, showing myself out.

~ ~ ~

Elena Tearz met me at the Coconut Café. She had a dark steaming liquid in front of her—presumably coffee—long, dark hair spiraling toward her shoulders, and her lips turned up, showing the first hint of a smile. She had chosen a small table near the front, to the left of the door, and she stared up at me when I walked over. I smiled, and then walked past her toward the counter, the barista staring at me with the most minimal of facial expressions.

The paneling matched the dark wood tables, a retro theme filled the walls with random memorabilia, and the wait staff wore headsets, although that seemed to be just part of the look, since I'd never seen anyone actually put one to use. Two people were in front of me staring up at the menu that could have very easily been written in another language.

Sofas and tables were fairly evenly distributed throughout the space with a few leather chairs that enhanced the overall look. A wall of mugs stood to my right in a glass case that must have spanned several decades. Some appeared more presentable than others, but all of them proved to be in excellent condition.

With my mug in hand, I returned to the table, and took the seat opposite her with my back to the door. I wasn't proud of the position, but there wasn't much I could do to fix my situation either, unless I wanted to bring to light more of my idiosyncrasies and potentially lose a confidant in the process.

"I'm glad you called," she said. "I wasn't sure if I'd hear from you again."

I nodded, sipped from my mug, and then rearranged my derriere on the hard wooden chair. "Ever since Dana turned up dead, my life has gotten tougher."

Tears formed in her eyes. "I know. It's tragic what happened to her, and I'm not proud of my involvement either."

"How were you involved?" I asked.

"I couldn't do anything to prevent her death. I feared something like this might happen to her, but there was no way I could prevent its occurrence. She's dead because I was too afraid to act on her behalf, and now I'll never be able to forgive myself."

I reached out and touched her outstretched hand. The brief contact stopped her hand from shaking, and it prevented more tears from falling. She dabbed at her eyes with a napkin, and then tried a slight smile. It failed, but I certainly appreciated the effort.

"She was such a good person, you know. She may have had a lifestyle more conducive to a male than a female, but that doesn't mean the tragedy was justified."

She rearranged several napkins, which was usually my job.

"What are you going to do?" I asked.

She dabbed at her eyes again, drying up the last remnants of what had been a full-on assault, and then sipped from her hot beverage. "I don't know," she said. "I'm rather curious about what you might find out. As much as I want to believe it was Porter, I just don't think he could have pulled it off. I've been racking my brain, but I must keep missing the obvious. Maybe I'm not as close to her as I thought I was."

"She was a complicated individual," I said. "You're not doing anything wrong. I don't completely understand it myself, but the picture is getting a bit clearer."

"You don't think it's Porter, do you?"

Rather than answer her question, I decided to pose one of my own. "Who do you think it is? You knew her better than a lot of other people in her life."

She shook her head. "I just don't know. But there is one comment that sticks out in my mind—"

"What is it?" I asked.

"Frankie threatened to kill her, if Dana ever left her. She wasn't nearly as strong on the outside as she appears. On the inside, she's a tortured mess. When it comes to self-confidence, she's severely lacking."

I finished the rest of my tea, as did she, with nary another bombshell in sight. In hindsight, though, maybe I should have posed additional questions, but I couldn't seem to circumvent the initial shock factor.

~ ~ ~

When she saw me, her mouth dropped open. She didn't slam the door, but I had the strong sensation that she wanted to. She had on a t-shirt that was one size too small, and it clung to her rather ample bosom. Her eyes and face both shone with an intensity that hadn't been present the last time I had spoken with her. She'd been more scared then: Now anger seemed to be more of a friend to her. Her lashes were dark, and it contrasted with her hair. Her skirt was a size too small as well. I focused on the total package, not just the one that had been presented before me.

She led me inside, and then she closed the door behind me. Her small hands moved the hair around on top of her head, even though a single hair wasn't out of place.

"We should probably talk," I said.

She nodded. "I thought you might come back, but I wasn't sure how quickly you would return. You want to talk about my financial situation, don't you?"

I nodded, placed my hands on my lap, and then waited for her to continue.

She wavered unexpectedly, and then she righted herself. She leaned forward. I was glad the t-shirt didn't have a scooped neck: She wasn't wearing a bra.

"I received compensation from Dana," Jessie Trager said. "But that all stopped when our relationship ended. I'm not particularly happy about the way she called it off, but there wasn't much I could do about it either. I'd gotten used to her buying me things and taking care of me, but that doesn't mean I completely relied upon her."

"Other than Dana, all of your relationships ended badly."

She nodded again. "But I still manage to get by, even though it's not easy."

I sneezed, and then I sneezed again. Not knowing what had caused the sneezing onslaught, I remained on full alert. But if I had to guess it was either copious amounts of perfume or an enemy of the feline persuasion, even though no such animal seemed present or accounted for. "You use your looks to your advantage."

"Every woman does: you, Dana, me. If you have a talent, I believe it's worth flaunting. Even if it means that other people may not appreciate it. I don't need respect to find happiness."

"I know you didn't kill Dana, but I'm fairly certain you know who did. Or at least you might have a good idea."

She swallowed hard. "Why do you say that?"

"Because you followed Dana on more than one occasion, and you even tried to get back together with her. You called her at odd hours, and I'm guessing Dana wasn't the only one to answer the phone."

"I missed her," she said. Tears rolled down her cheeks. She grabbed a tissue from the table beside her, dabbed at her eyes, and then placed the tissue on the glass table in front of her. Her lips moved, but no sound came out. Her chest heaved.

I had sunk closer to the floor than I would have liked, so I readjusted my position. "You did manage to talk to Dana, but it wasn't the conversation you had planned ahead of time."

"She hung up on me rather abruptly," she said. "But not before she mentioned the name Frankie. There was a pleasant tone to her voice when she said it. I didn't find out until later that Frankie was a woman."

"And that made the bitter taste even harder to swallow, didn't it?"

She covered her face with both hands, cried, and then hiccupped when she was through. I stuck around long enough to ensure she wouldn't do something crazy, before I left her behind.

~ ~ ~

I pulled into a Burger King parking lot a mile from Jessie's house. I wasn't feeling particularly hungry. Outside of food, I did have other matters on my mind, and those matters led me to my present situation. The parking lot was only half-full, and I pulled into a space at the far end of the lot, away from the building, and away from any other vehicles that might try to peer into my small vehicle.

I dialed Garrett Everest's number. It rang three times before it was picked up on the other end. It was almost evening, and a sleepy voice answered the phone.

Once again, I decided to skip the pleasantries. I wasn't particularly proud of it. "How do you feel about Frankie Kensington?"

"Oh, I like her even less than Porter Reede," he said. "I worked for her at one time, you know?"

I tried to keep my voice neutral. "How was she?"

"Worse than any male boss I'd ever had in my life," Garrett said. "I feared for my life every day I went into work. I never knew which of her personas would show up on any given day. She might not have had multiple personality disorder, but she certainly had a few of its symptoms."

"Why didn't you tell me you worked for her?"

"Because you never asked," he said. "I'm a private person, and I don't like volunteering information. Especially to people I've never met."

"Did she threaten your life?"

"I certainly felt the threat all the way in Richmond," he said. "She's the reason I moved here, you know? Do you have any idea what it's like to work for the wrong female boss? Every day is a struggle for survival. It got to the point that I spent more time trying to avoid her than I ever spent on my work. That's when my productivity started to suffer."

I also thought that was about the time he had come under Dana Wilson's spell, but I decided against pointing this out, afraid that I might hear a dial tone on the other end of the line. I wasn't ready to end the conversation. "I thought Porter Reede fired you."

"That's what she told me to say. She threatened to kill me from Hampton, and I believed her. I'd seen her work her magic on various employees. At one time, I might have even fallen under her spell, until I learned what she truly was. She had discovered the true art of evil, even as she attempted to show a welcoming front."

"But I thought you were under Dana's spell?"

"I was. Dana was nothing compared to that woman. She just oozed evil from her pores. Considering my options, Richmond sounded like the least of all the evils. Had I been thinking clearly, I might have been able to get her back. Focusing on Dana proved to be my ultimate demise. That bitch used it against me. She threatened me with a sexual harassment lawsuit. I told her Dana would never go for it. And then she told me the real bombshell: She already knew how to manipulate the situation and Dana to her advantage. Even though I wasn't gunning for her, Frankie played for keeps. In the end, I decided I valued my life more than an executive position."

I didn't miss the fact that he had a relationship with Frankie. That placed a new spin on an otherwise tricky situation. "You would have saved me a whole lot of time if you had bothered to tell me this information before. In fact, you were the one who told me to take a hard look at Porter Reede."

"That's because he doesn't cause half the problems that Frankie does. I can deal with Porter, but I can't deal with her."

Before I could ask a follow-up question, the phone slammed down in my ear.

~ ~ ~

Dana's parents, Sally and Rick Wilson, lived in a large home with a wooded area on one side and an equally large house on the other. A large grandfather clock stood off to one side of the living room, with an armoire next to it, and a big screen TV next to the armoire. I sat on a loveseat that was older than their combined ages, and possibly mine as well. I wasn't offered crumpets, or cookies, and I didn't plan on a group hug at the end.

Both parents were equally well-dressed in light-colored clothing and light-colored smiles. Equally trim and equally fit I guessed they both played tennis or some other recreational sport. Sally wore simple diamond earrings and a large diamond ring on the appropriate finger, while Rick wore a simple gold wedding band and a much larger gold watch.

It wasn't the first time I'd spoken with them, and their expressions leaned more toward curiosity than resentment.

"So what have you learned?" Rick asked.

"Her death wasn't a simple crime, and she appears to be a rather complicated individual. Much more complicated than I realized."

Sally sniffled. Her eyes were moist along with her lips. "Did you find out who killed her?" she asked.

I shook my head. "But I have a pretty good idea. She and Frankie had a strained relationship. Much more strained than I'd initially anticipated. Her desk was cleaned out in rapid fashion, and I've run into some resistance from some of the higher authorities at Wired Consulting. That's not what I expected either."

"But you're doing what you can?" Rick asked.

I nodded. I wasn't sure I was the best authority for the task, but I wasn't going to give up in the middle of the expedition. "Tommy Buchs appears to have ulterior motives as well."

"I never liked that man," Rick said. "He pursued Dana for her looks and her money. The man lacked substance and character. I'm not sure how he made it on the police force, and I'm even less certain of how he managed to stay."

"The department has more than a few loose ends and cannonballs."

Sally asked, "What will you do when you find her killer?"

"Turn him, or her, over to the authorities. I'm not about to make a civilian arrest. I'd prefer not to utilize my self-defense lessons again."

"You need to watch out for yourself," Rick said. "As much as I'd like to find justice for my daughter, I don't want you harmed in the crossfire."

I nodded. "Had she changed at all before her death?"

"Nothing unusual," he said, "if that's what you're asking. She was in love with a man who tried to love her back the best way he knew how, and even though she cared for him deeply, he never quite lived up to her expectations."

"Are you referring to Porter Reede?"

"I am indeed," Rick said. "He's charismatic, a multi-millionaire, with a large dimple on the right side of his face, and he had a smile that could charm the hardest heart. Not exactly the kind of man Dana could seem to let go. God knows she tried, though. She attempted to cover it up with more superficial relationships, and when those failed, she reached a new level of despair. As much as she tried to move on, her life changed for the worse."

"Didn't that create an awkward relationship, since he was the CEO?"

"What broke her heart even more was when he ended the relationship for the second time. She died soon after that, with her survival instincts moving in a backward direction."

"What about her relationship with Frankie Kensington?"

"The two of them never saw eye-to-eye, no matter what the issue. Fought as though they were at Gettysburg. Each battle increased in size, scope, and complexity, until each fight flowed together seamlessly, leaving torn bodies and wreckage in their wake."

"She didn't try to get reassigned?" I asked.

"Well, she did," Sally said. "But she was told it would take time, and before she could actually change desks, she disappeared, and then soon afterwards, she was found dead." The tears flowed, and there was nothing I could do to stop them.

"What did the police say when you told them?"

"Frankie was put under a microscope, but she came back clean, no parts dirty or otherwise tainted. We assumed Frankie had a relationship with Porter, although our suspicions were never confirmed."

"And you informed the police of your assumptions?" I asked.

"We did," Sally said. "The police found it interesting, but neither Frankie nor Porter ever admitted to a relationship, and that angle was dropped, with a giant question mark. Tommy let the thread die like the wind from a small breeze."

"What do you think?"

Sally asked, "Let me ask you a question: What causes more cat-fights among women?"

"Men," I said.

Sally nodded. "I like the way you think."

I stood up, thanked them both for their time, and walked out a little smarter than when I had walked in, although the additional knowledge only added to my confusion. The truth still seemed a ways off, but the horizon had shown the first hint of color.

CHAPTER TWENTY-FIVE

I had the wind knocked out of me, and I fell to the mat with a loud thud. I closed my eyes, and gasped for breath. My reflexes hadn't been as quick as they should have been, and I received the brunt force of the punishment. I'd stepped aside more than a half-second too slow. If the kick had caught me square, instead of at a slight angle, even the padding I wore wouldn't have provided the safety I needed.

I stared up at the harsh lights and grimaced. My sparring partner dropped down beside me, stared into my eyes, and asked if I was all right. I nodded, and then he bounced to his feet. The mat felt soft beneath me, and I felt my stomach turn over more than once. I was glad I hadn't eaten a large dinner before I set foot on the mat, otherwise my face might have shown more than just a painful and embarrassed expression.

I stood up, shook hands with the instructor, who had lost his hint of concern, and then made my way to the shower, hoping I could wash the embarrassment from my body.

The hot spray attacked my face, and I wanted to stand underneath the water forever. But I turned off the shower head, removed myself from the communal area, and dressed in front of my locker, aiming for speed, as well as efficiency.

~ ~ ~

When I left the studio, I headed away from downtown Hampton toward Mercury Boulevard. Traffic proved light this late in the evening, and I paid more attention to Katy Perry and her latest hit song than I did the pair of headlights behind me. The headlights were bright enough that I couldn't see the car nor could I see the driver behind the wheel. I peered straight ahead, singing along with Katy, despite the slight pain just above my waist. The sound of my voice set my otherwise galloping mind at ease.

I made a left onto Mercury Boulevard, heading west in the far right hand lane. Traffic proved more prominent now that I had reached one of the main drags through Hampton with its penchant for strip malls, chain restaurants, and dealerships. I managed to hit more red lights than green, or so it seemed. A new pair of headlights stood in my rearview mirror nearly as prominent as the ones before it. The driver stayed close on my tail, which seemed rather odd to me with traffic being far less than the rush hour variety. But Katy Perry, Dana's death, and the latest trivial accounting dilemma kept me from giving it too much thought. Had I known what I was in for, I might have given it further consideration.

Before I went under the overpass, I applied pressure to the brake, and made the right turn onto Coliseum Drive. I passed the Coliseum Mall, a rather inferior version of its previous self, as well as a boarded up Bennigan's where I had eaten on two previous occasions.

A pair of headlights followed close behind. I had no idea it was the same set of headlights that had been following me for more than a mile, but I did get the first inclination that something might be a bit off. It started in my belly, and it presented distinct differences from the previous kick to my abdominal region. The lingering feeling continued as I passed through several stoplights, several businesses, and watched as other cars pulled around me.

I made the left turn onto Marcella Road, and the pair of head-lights followed suit. When I turned onto Wyndham Drive, the car be-hind me inched even closer. I finally made the right turn onto Ash-leigh Drive, passed my apartment building, pulled into a space be-tween my building and the one next to it, hopped out of my car, and sashayed my way to the front door.

A familiar voice called out my name; I peered over my shoulder, discovered the face to go with the voice; I moved faster, my feet slam-ming against the pavement, as the voice behind me gave pursuit. I rushed up the stairs, as my feet pounded the concrete beneath me, as the metal railing squeaked, as the pair of footsteps increased the ef-fort of their pursuit, as the pounding in my chest increased in inten-sity. Striking the stairs on the second level, I continued to move at an expeditious pace up to the third. My lungs felt on fire, possibly more so to do with the kick than the running, but I had trouble distin-guishing between the two. I knew I needed to reach my door, struggle to put the key quickly in the lock, and then slam the door behind me before the familiar face reached me.

While I focused on the plan ahead, I missed a stair, and stumbled upward, catching myself on the top step, and pulling myself to my feet. Before I could do so, though, a hand reached out, and yanked me back down. I kicked out behind me, connecting with what I thought was a shoulder (definitely not a head). The figure behind me cried out in rage, and what I hoped was pain. I stumbled to my feet, lunged for my door, missed the lock by several inches, and then felt two hands on my shoulders. I spun around, swinging my fist out wildly as I turned, and I connected once again with a shoulder.

Frankie Kensington clawed at my eyes, her hands stretched out before her in a vicious manner, and she screamed with the full force of her lungs. I swallowed hard, attempted another punch, which was blocked by her clawing hands, and which had yet to strike my eyes—which I assumed was her intention—but she had succeeded in scratching both of my cheeks. I kicked out at her, striking her on the thigh—I had aimed for the knee—and she doubled back in what ap-peared to be pain, based on her curious facial expression.

I spun around, my key finally finding the lock, and opened the door. I stumbled inside, with my purse going in first. Before I could close the door, Frankie clawed at my back. I jammed my elbow into her stomach, and she grunted, but her hands only eased off slightly. I spun around, swinging wildly again, and once again I missed my mark. I threw out my left hand, but she blocked the punch with her longer arms, and she pushed me to the floor, slamming the door as she stepped inside.

I reached my knees before she shoved me back down. I was face down in my own living room with a psychotic menace behind me, who had most likely followed me home: her headlights being the twin pair that I had seen in my rearview mirror.

Before I could ask her what was going on, she sprayed me with my own pepper spray, depressing the button for longer than she needed to, until the rest of the contents were emptied onto my face. Not immune to the spray after all, I convulsed on the floor, my carpet scratching at my back.

Before the stinging could dissipate, she had tied me up with some rope she had either found or brought with her—I wasn't quite sure which proved to be the more accurate statement. After she tied me up, she gagged me, and then she shoved me in the backseat of my own car.

Had I contemplated the situation a bit more, I would've wondered why my neighbors had remained otherwise silent.

CHAPTER TWENTY-SIX

"Why are you doing this to me?" I asked.

I was in the middle of a large room (what might have been a warehouse or a rather large storage locker). A wooden chair was beneath me. Both the walls and the room were dark. The air was damp and cold, and my nose itched something fierce. I might have had an allergic reaction to what could have presumably been mold. Had the allergic reaction been the worst of my problems, I might not have had a slight tremor in my right hand. My hands were tied behind my back, but my mouth was no longer gagged. The room smelled like rotten bananas, stale bread, and moldy cheese. My eyes slowly adjusted to the darkness, but not to my situation. I could hear the roar of traffic in the distance, so we were either near a freeway or a large intersection. My cell phone, however, was nowhere in sight. Not that I could have used it anyway. If I had the opportunity to phone a friend, I knew just exactly whom I would call. But I hadn't been that lucky so far, so I didn't presume to have a dramatic improvement in my situation. Had this been nothing more than a test, I wouldn't have had cotton mouth, and my heart wouldn't have been racing faster than a dolphin.

"You mean you haven't already figured it out yet?" she asked.

"I figured out you're not a very nice person. When it comes to women, you've had your share of problems."

"There's more to it than that."

"I know you were involved with Porter Reede, and that you and Dana didn't exactly see eye-to-eye on most matters. But that's no reason to abduct me."

"This isn't all about you, you know. Maybe you should have thought about that before you decided to pursue Dana to the far ends of civilization."

"If you're worried about me being a flight risk," I said, "you don't need to be. I don't plan on leaving the state of Virginia for a while. I happen to like it here very much. Even though I might not have been the best accountant, I'm certainly not the worst one either."

"You don't know how to lose or how to quit," Frankie Kensington said.

"I didn't know this was some kind of test. Had I realized the full extent of the situation, I might have left this to be handled by the professionals. As it is, I'm a little lost for words."

"You have a problem with curiosity."

I tried a smile, but it executed a belly flop on the cement floor. "It's something I continue to work with on an almost daily basis. If you just give me a little more time, and the proper amount of therapy sessions, I might show you what I can really do. You might be pleasantly surprised."

"I've already seen your efforts firsthand. I'm surprised your self-defense classes didn't provide you with a bit more attitude and efficiency. While I didn't expect you to succeed, you certainly failed miserably."

"You've been following me?"

"I wanted to see just how far you'd get," she said. "You surprised me, and it wasn't in a good way. Maybe you should just stick with numbers."

I said, "I'm glad I was able to exceed your expectations."

She walked out of the room, and I worked rather furiously on the knots around my wrists. I worked my hands up and down against the back of the wooden chair. The rope dug into my flesh, tearing at the skin, but the knots began to loosen. I grimaced with each downward thrust, and the rope became slick with what I could only assume was blood. My hands and wrists felt raw, the sensation stinging, yet I kept up the motion in the hope that I could somehow escape my fate. Frankie didn't have a gun when she had come to visit me, but I wasn't sure I'd experience the same lack of firepower the next time, or the time after that. I heard what sounded like a gunshot, or it might have been a car backfiring.

I hadn't been in the large room long, and I'd remained conscious throughout the whole ordeal. She'd dragged me inside by the shoulders, as I struggled against the bindings. She was stronger than I expected (she'd taken self-defense classes at one time herself), or I hadn't prepared myself nearly as well as I should have. I had expected the fight would tilt more in my favor, but I had been severely disappointed. My side ached; my thigh was bruised; my ankle felt sprained; my eyes had finally stopped watering—I'd been sprayed with my own can of pepper spray, the last quarter of the can deposited in my eyes, causing me to thrash on the ground in a most unladylike manner; and I didn't see any direct way out, other than to continue to rub my wrists raw. The bindings had started to slacken; however, it wasn't yet enough for me to slip my hands through. The eerie silence disturbed me, causing the vibrating sensation in my right hand, which I was able to calm through a series of deep breathing exercises. Once the calmness had fully taken hold, this made the up and down motion easier to manage. By controlling the jerking, I ensured I'd have at least a few layers of skin on my right wrist.

Time passed slowly. I began to calculate the odds of getting out alive, but I stopped before I reached any definite conclusions. I didn't like the possibility of defeat, and not knowing where I was only heightened the blow to my chest. I'd never been kidnapped, and I hoped I'd never go through this again. Had I known what would have happened, I probably would have proceeded down the present course anyway, but the thought wasn't reassuring.

The ropes continued to slacken through my concerted efforts, but it wasn't yet enough to set me free. Even if I managed that, though, I'd need my cell phone with the GPS feature turned on, because I'd heard the lock click when Frankie left. Although I could make an educated guess or two where I was at (based on the length of the ride), I hadn't yet narrowed down my location to within a few hundred yards.

What aggravated me more than anything else, though, was that I had been followed, and I hadn't even known it. Assuming I somehow made it out of this alive, I'd add classes on discovering a tail to go along with my yoga exercises and self-defense classes. While I was at it, I should probably sign up for Toastmasters as well.

The steel door creaked open, and a silhouette filled the empty divide. It was the same silhouette as before, only this time there was what appeared to be a gun in her hand.

"Why don't you tell me what's really going on?" I asked.

"I don't know what you're talking about."

I worked my hands up and down in a controlled fashion, trying to hide any expression that might come across my face. The darkness helped, but I wasn't sure how much. Her hands were steady as she pointed the gun at my chest. She didn't flinch nor did she move a muscle. From what I could see of her face, it resembled a blank mask.

"Why did you kill Dana? Was it because she didn't love you back?"

She shook her head. But as to which question she had answered I wasn't sure. "I never stopped loving her," she said. "She had a vitality that I wanted for myself. A zest for living. She was the best thing that ever happened to me, and without a second thought, she threw it all away. I took her back once, and I wasn't prepared to do it again."

Her nails clicked on the cold, hard steel. She appeared to blink, as if she might have been fighting back tears. Or it might have been an adverse reaction to the stale bananas.

"Did you break it off with Porter, or did he break it off with you?" I asked. I figured the longer I could keep her talking, or at least interested in what I had to say, the more likely I could break free of the rope, and actually make it to civilization. A rather remote possibility existed that I might convince her I should be kept alive. But even I knew that was too farfetched to actually become true. Killing one more person sounded a whole lot better than prison.

"That's preposterous," Frankie said. "Nothing happened between me and that man. He's my boss; I was his employee; and I don't mix business with pleasure."

Since she had a gun in her hand, I decided not to mention that she had made a similar mistake with Dana. "I hear he has a bit of a play-boy reputation. Maybe you wanted to see how far you could take the game. After all, he is a rather handsome man, and he does have a lot of money. Some women will even take money without the looks."

She fired a shot into the ceiling. I wasn't sure if it was frustration, or to prove to me that the semi-automatic was loaded. Either way I believed her. I had the rope burns to prove the gravity of the situation. The irony, though, wasn't lost on me. First, I had been sprayed with my own pepper spray, and now I would end up dead with the same semi-automatic that had failed to cause my demise earlier. My world had ended up in a sad state of affairs. If I made it out of this alive, I definitely needed to stick with accounting.

"Where do you come up with these wild accusations?" she asked.

"Well, at least you've gone for originality," I said. "By choosing a new question, you've managed to steer me away from the obvious. You're smarter than I'll ever be."

"You're really not making much sense," Frankie said. "And it's definitely time for you to leave this world for good. I always knew you were more trouble than you're worth."

"You can do that," I said. "But I have a tracking device implanted in my shoe. If you kill me now, the authorities won't waste any time bursting through that steel door. And you'll have to explain to them how you killed me, since there's no one else around to take the blame."

She snarled, showing her white teeth in the process. The gun faltered for just an instant. "You're lying. You have no such device anywhere on your person."

"I might be," I said, "but are you sure you want to take that chance? You never did check me for bugs."

I slid my right hand through the rope, and I almost had the left one free when she leaned down, the gun near her side. I cocked my right hand, and then I drove it forward with all my might, aiming directly at her chin. I caught her at just the right angle, and her head bobbed back. The gun clattered to the floor. I dove for it (the chair was still attached to my left hand) with Frankie still sprawled on the ground. Her right leg was twisted out from her body, while her left leg was tucked underneath her.

As I pointed the gun at her immovable body (after having freed my left hand), the lights flipped on. Blue suits fanned out in all directions. I dropped the gun, and then threw my hands up in the air. Ben Xander moved to the front of the group, as he told his men to back down. He had a smirk on his face, shaking his head as he walked toward me.

Cop after cop came through the door like ants returning to an open hole. I wasn't sure how many favors Ben had called in, and I wasn't sure I wanted to know. I was glad I was safe. In the end, that was all I could ask for.

"How did you find me?" I asked.

"Cell phone. I didn't think you'd come here by choice, and when no one had heard from you—after you'd been rather prominent in the spotlight—I began to fear the worst."

"I'm glad you're a highly suspicious individual," I said.

"The gunshot certainly helped with the locating process. If she didn't have an itchy finger, we might have entered a little less enthusiastically."

"I'm just glad she didn't shoot me. If she had gotten around to it a bit sooner, you might have needed a stretcher for me as well."

For the first time, Ben looked down at the floor, right where Frankie had sprawled herself out on the cement. "Is she unconscious?"

I nodded. "I caught her on the chin relatively cleanly. Had I not put my full weight behind it, the end result might have been entirely different."

Tommy Buchs strode by Ben's side. A look of pure hatred covered his face. His eyes were as cold as black steel, and his hands were large enough to wrap themselves around my throat. Had I considered the matter more thoroughly, I might have picked up the gun again, even with all the cops around to witness the shooting. I stared him down, looking right through him and his larger-than-life persona.

I said, "I heard you've been spreading rumors about me."

"What about it?" Tommy said. "Are you going to slug me, too?"

I shook my head, and then I backed out of the scene.

CHAPTER TWENTY-SEVEN

I didn't bother trying to sleep, although that probably would have been the more appropriate thing to do. I didn't even remember returning to my apartment, although I somehow managed that one as well. The conversations that preceded it also managed to escape my memory. The last memory I had of any real significance was the gun firing into the ceiling, the conversation that ensued afterwards between me and Frankie, and then the cops bursting through the door, fanning out like the flames of a fire, and then me tossing the gun to the ground right before I tossed my hands in the air.

It was late. The microwave clock told me it was 3:00 a.m., but even if it had been midnight, I wouldn't have been able to sleep. The last threads of adrenaline had left my body hours ago, but the lingering effects seemed to remain. The sensations I felt during my time in the warehouse—fear, paranoia, dread, finality, and lost hope—continued to enter my brain at random intervals, each one staying for a brief time before the sensation disappeared, and the next one appeared. Like a hamster running on a wheel in one continuous motion, I couldn't place my thoughts in any particular order.

The fact that I had reached the end still hadn't caught up to me yet. I felt like a sprinter who was a split second behind the entire field, and no matter how hard I ran, or how hard I tried, I wasn't going to catch up to my own destiny. But I could continue to hope that I would.

Having solved the case, I didn't feel a sense of accomplishment or euphoria. Instead, I felt bruised and battered and even after two back-to-back showers, I had a level of grime on my person that no level of scrubbing could safely remove. My fluffy violet robe comforted me, along with a series of rom-coms, most of which I had seen multiple times, and at least one of which I had memorized several of the lines. But my life still lacked a certain sense of completeness and finality I had hoped to achieve. Instead, I had played a series of DVDs, none of which had fully managed to calm my nerves. Even several hours later, the last remnants of adrenaline still coursed through my veins, as my right hand still managed to do a little tango of its own. But I did feel as though I had made some important discovery about myself, much more than any series of movies could provide, as my life reached a new level of completeness.

Knowing I had a friend who didn't sleep much, who remained restless throughout the night, was somehow comforting. So I picked up the phone to call her. And I dropped to the couch before I dropped to the floor, as the last of the adrenaline left my system. Because once I was down, I had no idea how long it would take me to get back up again. And I had probably reached the end of my cop favors for the time being.

Cutting right through all the formalities, my friend addressed the heart of the problem. "Are you sure you're okay?" she asked. "You sound like you were hit by a train."

"Subtlety was never a secret worth keeping."

"If you wanted subtlety, you shouldn't have called at three-thirty in the morning."

"I didn't think you were asleep," I said.

There was a pause on the other end of the line. "I wasn't."

"I'm sorry. You're with a guy. I shouldn't have called, but I didn't know what else to do. In a world filled with water, you seemed to be the only solid, dry land."

"Are you okay?" She said it more forcefully this time. The words had brief pauses between them, like each one needed to stand on its own to truly be heard.

"I was kidnapped," I said. "I had a gun pointed at my forehead, and I believe there's a warehouse somewhere that has a piece of concrete missing from its ceiling."

Cadence Surrender took a deep breath. The jolt of silence rocked my body, and I slumped even lower against the back of the sofa. I rubbed my eyes, as the first signs of sleep took hold of me like a long lost lover.

"Do you need me to come over?"

"No, I'll be all right. It's still a bit overwhelming, and I'm sure it'll take me a few days to process it completely. I would have preferred the self-defense classes to take better care of the situation. If it hadn't been for my small hands, I'm not sure what would have happened."

"As an accountant, you sure do meet the strangest people."

I paused, staring out my sliding glass door into the dark night beyond. "I'm not sure I'll ever be just an accountant again."

"Are you having relationship issues?" she asked.

Cadence could somehow manage to turn everything back to relationships. She was like a pendulum that constantly returned to center. As for me, I wasn't sure where my center was exactly: It seemed to change with each swing of the metal weight.

"No," I said, "my problems go beyond relationship issues."

"Well, I'm not sure I can help you with your other problems right now, but I can help you find a decent man. We need to focus on one thing at a time. And girl, have I got a guy for you. He's the kind of man that can help you forget who you are for more than half an hour."

"That used to intrigue me," I said. "Now it just gives me the creeps. Besides, I'm not sure I'm ready for an emotional commitment."

"You need to loosen up, girlfriend. You're gonna have yourself wound so tight you're going to squeak when some hunk squeezes you."

"I'm not sure I need to be squeezed. Cuddling, however, is always encouraged. But not at three-fifty in the morning, otherwise he's liable to have unrealistic expectations."

"Everyone needs to be squeezed," she said.

The sound of a cupboard opening helped me realize this was more than just a dream. Despite my efforts to discourage her matchmaking abilities, I knew I would have to ask the inevitable question, otherwise she might never hang up the phone. Cadence was filled with as much stubbornness as me, and unfortunately, there wasn't much I could do about it, short of disowning her. I knew I needed her just as much as she needed me, even if she managed to set me up with the wrong men on a fairly frequent basis and forced me to eat at Cracker Barrel more often than I would like. Despite my muted protests, though, the place was growing on me, and I had to swing my arms wide as I walked by the candy portion of the store.

"So who's the guy?" I asked. "Not that I'm interested or anything, but I figure I should at least give you the courtesy of hearing you out, before I tell you you've lost your mind."

"You wouldn't know him."

That was always a bad sign. Another bad sign was when she mentioned perfect and man in the same sentence. It was a construction accident waiting to happen, possibly with an errant two-by-four. "You've told me that before, and then I did know him. And it was someone I never would have gone out with, even if I had been drunk, could no longer see my toes, and sat on the floor clutching a bottle of tequila to my chest. I think you're just covering your tracks."

"I like to cover all my bases."

I said, "You cast a pretty big shadow. And I'm wired enough that there's probably not much I could do to stop you."

"Why are you always giving me crap, girl? I'm a whole lot of woman to love. We've already gone over this. I want to cover new ground, mark my own territory, and crash my own Volkswagen. I think you and the hottie are going to hit it off just fine."

"So now he's hot?" I asked. I rubbed my eyes again, but I stopped short of pinching myself on the wrist. "Yeah, like I haven't heard that one before. I think you know way too many people. I'm going to have to start revoking your privileges. You know more white men than I do. Do you have your own groupies?"

"I run into all types," Cadence said. "I'm just looking out for your own best interests. If I don't cast the line for you once in a while, we'd both be sitting on the James River staring at nothing but blue water and dry land."

Neither one of us had ever been fishing, but I decided not to point this out to her. "I'm not even sure what those are anymore. You'll have to fill me in."

"Girl, what's gotten into you? Did the kidnapper use electroshock therapy on you? Or did the traumatic experience of sitting in a warehouse cause the inevitable brain dump?"

"No," I said, "I received the better end of that deal. I won't spend some of my better days in prison, and other than bruises, soreness, and a slight limp for a few days, I'll be more than capable of bouncing back in dramatic fashion. Before I blame anything else, I'll focus on the number of bad dates that seem to follow me better than my own shadow."

"You've got a simple problem," she said, "and your solution is pretty simple, too. You need to get laid. You need a 'throw your head back, eyes roll into the back of your head, moaning like the devil himself has taken over your body' orgasm."

"Surely you can't be serious," I said. I didn't even know such a thing was possible. Cadence, however, was known for her ability to exaggerate, so I assumed this could be another one of her tall-tales.

"Sex," she said, "is better than ecstasy. But if you're not getting the right kind, then you don't know what you're missing out on."

I wasn't planning on winning any awards for my number of sexual partners or my bedroom prowess; Cadence, however, had an entirely different agenda from my own.

"Maybe so," I said. "But I won't sleep with just anybody, despite whatever healing powers sex may possess. I want a stronger, deeper, more meaningful relationship."

There was a pause on the other end of the line. Cadence was probably trying to decide whether I was serious, or whether I truly did need electroshock therapy. I rubbed my eyes again, and yawned for the first time.

"Are you in or out?" she asked.

"On what?"

"On the date," she said. "As soon as you start letting sleep win the battle, you lose all sense of reality, or maybe you never had much to begin with. There's more to life than just a series of numbers, or an equation with letters and numbers, an equal sign, and more numbers on the other side."

I asked, "Do I have a choice?"

"Probably not," she said, "but I do like to give you the option just in case. You need to learn to relax and focus on the fun part, especially since it's all fun."

"You like to give me false hope, and then reality slaps me once across each cheek."

"I look out for your own best interests," she said. "How's the hottie on the force?"

"You have a lot of interests to look out for," I said. At this hour, I didn't want to start another conversation about Ben, because I wasn't sure I'd be able to make it all the way to the end. Besides, he did have Tommy Buchs as a partner, and that wasn't an endearing quality.

"You're on for tomorrow night at eight," she said. "Well, actually it's tonight. That is if you don't decide to haul ass toward Florida."

Even though I'd never been to the Sunshine State, I had entertained the possibility of an all-night drive in my Corolla, especially after the first stalker, who enjoyed rubbing his genitals in my presence. Unless a genie would pop out of his pants, I told him it wasn't worth the trouble.

"What if I can't make it?" I asked.

"Don't be late," Cadence said. "Men like punctuality."

On time and looking my best never quite went together. "Can I still cancel if I'm feeling less than beautiful tonight? After all, I did just go through a rather traumatic experience, and I'm not sure I feel up to punching a man across the table."

I'd never actually thrown a punch at one of my dates, just tossed the occasional glass of water, or the rare cocktail. But that didn't mean I hadn't thought about a nice, solid uppercut.

"There's no such thing as less than beautiful for you. Girl, if I had your body, I'd be having so much sex I wouldn't even wear underwear."

As I hung up the phone, I cringed. Even though I tried not to, I was actually looking forward to the date, despite my concerted protests. If nothing else, it would be a change of pace from my recent endeavors.

ABOUT THE AUTHOR

Robert aspired to be a writer before he realized how difficult the writing process was. Fortunately, he'd already fallen in love with the craft, otherwise Sam and Casey might never have seen print. Originally from West Virginia, he has lived in Virginia, Massachusetts, New Mexico, and now resides in California. To find out more about Sam or Casey, visit the author's website: www.RobertDowns.net.

When he's not writing, Robert can be found reviewing, blogging, or smiling. *Falling Immortality* and *Graceful Immortality* helped him discover his true love: hard-boiled mysteries. This is his third novel.